Chris Bunch is the author of the Sten Series, the Dragonmaster Series, the Seer King Series and many other acclaimed SF and fantasy novels. A notable journalist and bestselling writer for many years, he died in 2005.

Find out more about Chris Bunch and other Orbit authors by registering for the free monthly newsletter at www.orbitbooks.co.uk

COUNTY
LIBRARY

F/2039457

D0995496

By Chris Bunch

The Seer King Trilogy
SEER KING
DEMON KING
WARRIOR KING

THE EMPIRE STONE

CORSAIR

The Dragonmaster Trilogy
STORM OF WINGS
KNIGHTHOOD OF THE DRAGON
THE LAST BATTLE

SHADOW WARRIOR

The Star Risk Series
STAR RISK
THE SCOUNDREL WORLDS
THE DOUBLECROSS PROGRAM
THE DOG FROM HELL

By Chris Bunch and Allan Cole

The Sten Series
STEN
THE WOLF WORLDS
THE COURT OF A THOUSAND SUNS
FLEET OF THE DAMNED
REVENGE OF THE DAMNED
THE RETURN OF THE EMPEROR
VORTEX
EMPIRE'S END

STAR
RISK

CHRIS BUNCH

www.orbitbooks.co.uk

ORBIT

First published in the United States in 2002 by Roc,
Penguin Group (USA) Inc.
First published in Great Britain in 2006 by Orbit

Copyright © Chris Bunch, 2002

The moral right of the author has been asserted.

*All characters and events in this publication, other than
those clearly in the public domain, are fictitious
and any resemblance to real persons,
living or dead, is purely coincidental.*

All rights reserved.
No part of this publication may be reproduced, stored in a retrieval
system, or transmitted, in any form or by any means, without the prior
permission in writing of the publisher, nor be otherwise circulated in
any form of binding or cover other than that in which it is published
and without a similar condition, including this condition, being
imposed on the subsequent purchaser.

A CIP catalogue record for this book
is available from the British Library.

ISBN-10: 1-84149-453-4
ISBN-13: 978-1-84149-453-1

Typeset in Garamond by M Rules
Printed and bound in Great Britain by
Clays Ltd, St Ives plc

Orbit
An imprint of
Little, Brown Book Group
Brettenham House
Lancaster Place
London WC2E 7EN

A member of the Hachette Livre Group of Companies

www.littlebrown.co.uk

For
the real Michelle Reese
Marine, model, freefall artist, entrepreneur
a very good guy
and
William and Steven Courchesne,
who'll do, in a pinch

ONE

The woman was blond, tall, green eyed and beautiful. Her nearly nonexistent bathing suit, and her shade-hat looked and were expensive.

She was stretched on a poolside chaise longue, on the roof of the ultra-luxury Shelburne Hotel. The pool wound and curveted through a garden, and every bend gave the illusion of privacy.

Scattered around the rooftop were a handful of hotel guests, and their guests, enjoying the late afternoon sun. There were a few livee stars, a singer or two, a gaggle of lawyers, some managers, and five or six rich, butter-and-egg out-of-towners, being heavily charged for the privilege of gawking at, and pretending to be one of, the current crop of beautiful people.

Forty stories below, unheeded, was the moil and bustle of Trimalchio IV, its citizens busy doing . . . or being done.

Trimalchio IV was a very lucky world, in that it had no history. It was originally settled by a handful of Alliance plutocrats, who found its mild climate, islands, kilometers of beaches, and craggy mountains very much to their liking. At first, they allowed only enough riffraff in to be their servants and run the luxury shops they swarmed. Later came the restaurants, bars, hotels, and others who catered to the well-to-do. Population was very low, no more than fifty million. Surprisingly, taxes were low, mainly because the social envelope consisted of a one-way ticket to another system. It was a wonderful world, if you had money. If you didn't . . . starvation was always an option.

A security guard wandered around the fringes of the pool, feeling fat and over fifty. His gun sat heavily on his hip, although why management insisted he carry it was beyond him.

Bad things didn't happen to rich people.

He looked at the sunbathing woman, chanced a smile, and felt older as she looked through him and returned to her book. He glanced at its title, expecting to see some lurid potboiler, and saw *A Guide to N-Space Mathematics and a Theory of Their Unification.*

Way, way, way out of his league.

He went to the lift, dropped down to the lobby, and went into the security room, where a dozen vids blinked at him, showing various hotel exteriors and corridors.

The guard decided he'd spend the rest of his shift here, where he wouldn't be reminded of his age and paunch.

The primary sun moved down the horizon; the secondary, barely a flaming planetoid, had already set.

The people around the pool drifted to the lift, and to their rooms.

Yawning, the woman, M'chel Riss, checked her expensive watch, widened her eyes threatrically as if she was late for a meeting with a lover, got up, stretching her almost two-meter height, picked up her real leather bag, and strolled toward the lift. Behind her sunglasses, she was watching the scattering of monitors, waiting for when the two pickups covering the lift entrance swept away.

Then she moved, very, very fast, like a professional

athlete, behind the lift entrance, into a tiny cubbyhole between the edge of the roof and the small building.

She waited, but no alarm came.

This was her third night in the Shelburne, and she had only credits enough for one more. She was sorry she wouldn't be able to tip the room maids, but a working girl only had so many options.

She was waiting for full darkness.

Down below, streetlights flickered on, various hues intended to give the city a perpetual mardigras feeling.

Twice a lifter flew past, close enough to make Riss want to duck down. But she knew better than to move. Eight years as an Alliance Marine, and Major Riss (Retired) knew all of the tricks and traps of soldiering.

It finally got dark.

Riss opened her bag, and took out a chameleon suit, pulled it on, and ran her fingers up the sealer, turning the suit on. It took a few seconds to warm up, then, except for her hands and face, she became part of the adobe-colored wall.

Riss slid out from the cubby, and put on a pair of *kletteschues*, climbing shoes, and jumars. She sprayed a blob of climbing thread on the wall, and tucked some other items from her bag in the suit's pouches. The last item, a very natty cocktail dress, would be needed for her extraction. At least, if she was able to take the easy way out.

She unfastened straps, and the bag now became what might have been a backpack, except with little holes for feet like a child-carrier, which she pulled on.

Riss looked over the edge, and shuddered a little. No belay, no climbing partner, and she'd always disliked it when the training schedule sent her troop to the mountains.

But there weren't any options.

She clipped the jumars into the climbing thread, and eased over the edge of the building, determined not to be a dummy and look down again.

If you fall, you fall, she thought. And then a nice raspberry splotch will go nicely with those tinted streetlights.

There was a bit of a wind, and she swayed back and forth as she descended.

Counting windows, she abseiled down three stories to a small window, let out more thread and brought it back to the main line and sealed it. Now she had a loop to stand in.

She took a tiny cutting torch out of one pocket, and cut around the window plas. Unlike the other windows in this suite, security hadn't seen any necessity to rig this window for an alarm, sure that no one could ever weasel through it, especially at this height.

The torch's flame was blue, and very tiny, but to Riss it looked as if she'd set off a flare.

The plas was cut on all four sides. She shut off the torch and put it away. Riss tapped with a finger on the plas, and it fell inward. She grabbed fast, barely caught it, and eased it down until it hit . . . a washroom basin.

Good. Very good. Just like the bribed room service waiter had told her.

Riss turned in the loop, and acrobatically eased her head and shoulders through the hole.

She thought about having to go back out, having to jumar back up the thread, and didn't like the idea. If her intel was correct, she could take the easy way, and just stroll out of the suite, hand in hand with the kid.

But since when was intelligence *ever* right?

A bathroom, dimly lit by a nightlight in the next room.

M'chel pulled herself into the room, stood, waiting.

No alarms went off.

Tiny gun in hand, she paced into the room. It was bigger than her whole house, growing up, had been.

There was a little girl nine years, three months, two days old, or so the client's fiche had told her, asleep, illuminated by the nightlight. She was surrounded by animatronic toys, and, clutched to her chest, a raggedy doll that could have been her grandmother's.

Very good, very easy. Now, put on the dress, wake up the kid, and then we'll—

'Put the gun down,' a calm voice said. 'Take three steps to the side, and then stand very still. We are both pros, so nobody has to die.'

M'chel jerked, then obeyed.

A man stood from where he'd been kneeling, behind an entertainment center, then came toward her.

He was a few centimeters shorter than Riss, looked to be in his sixties, had carefully styled silver hair, a handsome, rugged face, and wore evening dress.

He also had a large Alliance-issue blaster aimed carefully at her chest.

'Very good,' he said. 'You made a little noise breaking in, which twigged me.'

'You were supposed to be at the theater . . . assuming you're one of his bodyguards,' Riss said.

'I was,' the man agreed. 'But I pride myself in never being just where I am supposed to—'

Riss had been watching his feet, and, as the man stepped on a throw rug, she dug her heel into the rug, and back-kicked.

The man yelped, stumbled, flailing to recover his balance. Before he could shoot, Riss kicked the pistol out of his hand, and snap-punched into his diaphragm, slightly pulling her punch at the last minute.

Air whooshed out of the man's lungs, and he gagged, clutching himself.

Riss took out a small tube of gas, leaned over the contorting man, and, holding her breath, sprayed him in the face. The man jerked, went down, lay still. He would be out for eight hours.

Riss, breathing hard, had the blaster ready. But there wasn't any backup.

'Who are you?' a high voice asked.

The girl was awake, sitting up in bed. She didn't appear to be the slightest bit frightened.

'Hi, Debra,' M'chel said, trying to sound calm and cheery. 'Do you want to go home to your mother? I'm working for her.'

'I figured *that* out,' the girl said complacently. 'You're not the first who's come to rescue me, you know. How are we going?'

'I'll put on a dress, and then we're going straight on out, through the suite's service entrance down the hall, and then to the lift and out, as if we were guests, bold as brass.'

'We're not going out through the window? I heard you coming down the wall outside, watched you break into my bathroom.'

M'chel realized she was going to have to brush up on her stealthy climbing techniques.

'I hope not,' she said.

'Oh. *Damn* it. That would've been *icy*.'

There was silence.

'Well?' Riss asked, ready to gas the child if necessary.

'I'm thinking about it,' the girl said. 'Mommy wasn't that nice to me the last time, you know.'

Little bitch, Riss thought.

'I guess I'll go along with you,' the girl decided. 'Daddy's been treating me like a real shit lately, not letting me go anywhere or anything.'

She got out of bed, still holding the raggedy doll.

'Okay,' she said. 'Let's get out of here before Daddy and his goons come back.'

Riss went to the bedroom door, turned the handle. She knelt, and peered down the hall at ankle height.

M'chel suppressed an obscenity.

There were two beefy men at the far end, wearing protective glasses, chatting casually. Their profession, bodyguard, was most obvious.

It would only be seconds before they missed the man with the white hair, and came looking.

Riss closed the door.

'Change two,' she whispered. 'You get to go climbing.'

'Icy!' the girl said enthusiastically.

Riss had the girl put on her slippers, put the backpack on, and indicated the leg holes. Debra, eyes wide in excitement, clambered aboard.

M'chel stood, adjusting the child's weight. Not even half as bad as an expedition pack.

She started for the window.

'Wait,' Debra hissed. 'My dolly.'

M'chel held back a growl handed the toy to Debra.

They went back into the bathroom, and M'chel hung a strand of climbing glue to the sill, sprayed out about half a meter, and glued that down.

She eased out of the pack.

'Now, I'm gonna clamber out there, and then I want you to go after me. Stand in the loop here.'

Debra nodded. M'chel eeled out the window, clung by her fingers to the far side of the sill. Debra came out backward, got her feet in the loop, and was outside. She looked down, and Riss saw her face change.

'Don't look down, dammit! And if you puke on me, your mother'll buy me a new dress.'

Debra, lips compressed, nodded.

M'chel was never quite sure how she got the backpack on again, but she did.

'Now, we're going down.'

She clipped the can of thread into one jumar, and locked the spray can's nozzle to its first detent.

Climbing thread came slowly, steadily out the can's spout, and slowly, steadily, the two went down and down and down.

Riss felt fine, other than her arm muscles were stretched a meter or so longer than they had been, and she was sure that when – when, not if – she reached concrete, she'd walk like an earth ape, knuckles brushing the ground.

She chanced looking down again, saw she was within fifty meters of the ground.

'Well,' she whispered, 'do you like this?'

'Not . . . not as much as I thought I would,' Debra managed.

'Hang on, kiddo,' she said. 'We'll have you on solid turf in a couple of minutes.'

They went on, Riss's toes sliding on the pebbly stone facing of the hotel.

Then there was something under her heels, and she was down.

She cut off the climbing thread, and, just as she started for the nearby alley, where Momma's damned lifter had better be waiting, saw the doorman bow someone out. She didn't look back, but walked a little bit faster.

The lifter was there.

Momma, a fat version of her daughter, squealed, and pawed Debra out of her backpack.

'Oh, you did it, you did it,' the woman shrilled, gathering Debra in her arms. The girl submitted limply.

'Of course, I did it,' Riss said calmly. 'I said I would, didn't I?'

'Oh, I owe you, I owe you so much,' the woman burbled. 'I'll be cutting you a check in the morning, and believe me, there'll be a sizeable bonus to it.

'You can trust me on that.'

Riss started worrying.

TWO

Two weeks later, M'chel Riss sat in a canalside café, considering the croissant and herb tea on the small table in front of her. That would be both breakfast and mid-meal.

She tried to stay cheerful, but it looked as if the man who'd been so enthusiastic on the vid about hiring her wasn't going to materialize.

So much for the old 'go almost anywhere, do almost anything' personal ads.

What came next?

She had less than no ideas for the future, so she reconsidered the past.

Would it have been a total pain to have stayed in the Marines and taken the assignment that dickhead colonel arranged for her, merely because she wouldn't be his 'assistant' on a 'inspection trip' to a certain gambling planet?

Yes, it would've. She'd called up the fiche for whatever satellite of whatever frozen giant she was supposed to be the garrison CO of.

It was whatever is outback of the outback.

Or, come to think about it, should she have packed the old negligee and gone along with the colonel? He wasn't the worst-looking man she'd gone to bed with.

Her stomach roiled. She'd never yet had sex with

anyone when it wasn't her idea, and she'd rather starve than change that.

Speaking of starving, her stomach reminded her. You're a big healthy girl, with a big healthy appetite. So what's this roll and tea business?

Don't think about how few credits are in the old hidden pouch under your slacks. Or what'll be for dinner at that warehouse district diner, which served a meat none of the reluctant poverty row customers had been able to identify.

Not that anyone tried hard.

Or let's not think about sneaking back into that lousy little room in the lousy little hotel hoping the manager wasn't on duty, and what lie she might come up with to keep a cot under her for one more night if he was.

M'chel ruffled her tawny hair. Come on, brain. You've never given up before.

I've never been this hungry before came back at her.

There was a newsscreen on the next table, and she was thinking about going to the ads, and seeing if Trimalchio was hiring women in other categories than highly technical or highly available.

At the moment, waitressing looked pretty good, if anybody would consider hiring a waitress with no better experience than opening ration paks.

Then, coming out of the café onto the patio was a man she recognized, and who she hoped didn't recognize her.

He was Fal'at's bodyguard, whom she'd knocked sprawling and then gassed two weeks ago.

The man saw her, smiled brightly, and started over.

Riss's hand slid down into her boot top, and the tiny pistol was in her hand, held under the table.

The man saw the movement, held up both hands, palm out, and waited.

M'chel thought, couldn't see any problem, since she had the ready gun and he didn't, nodded.

The man came to the table, still keeping his hands motionless, bowed.

'I am Friedrich von Baldur,' he said. 'At your service, Miss . . . ?'

Riss gave him her name.

'May I join you?'

'Why not?'

Baldur sat down.

'This is a much nicer milieu than the other evening.'

Riss managed a smile as a waitress came out with a heavy tray. She saw Baldur, brought the tray over and set it down.

M'chel tried not to look at the tray as Baldur paid. There was a jug of caff, toasted breads, buttery and steaming, an omelet, sausages, and cheeses.

Baldur noticed her expression, misread it.

'I know,' he said. 'I am a slave to my stomach. At least I do not put on weight easily. But I should eat more like you.'

M'chel tried, without success, to keep a deadpan expression.

Baldur caught the flicker.

'Ah,' he said, 'I *had* heard that the former Mrs. Fal'at is reluctant to meet her obligations. My sympathies.

'I, too, am at liberty, although at least I was paid before being punted onto the welfare rolls.

'Paid well, with the correct amount for severance,' he said thoughtfully, and motioned to another waitress.

'Could we see a menu? My friend here is hungry.'

'No,' M'chel protested. 'I can't . . .'

But her mouth was filling with saliva.

'Yes,' Baldur said firmly. 'You can. And the only debt

you will owe is to do the same for some other soldier who has fallen on hard times.'

M'chel knew she should protest, couldn't. She ordered baked eggs, juice, multiseeded toast, unbuttered, and fruit.

'Good,' Baldur approved. 'Starving to death is most terrible.'

'How did you know I was a soldier?'

'My dear Miss Riss, very few people end up in our chosen line of work without some form of military training. And none of the amateurs would dare that entrance from the roof that you made.'

'Thanks, I guess.'

'If you do not mind,' Baldur said. 'My toast grows chill.'

She nodded, and he began eating. A few moments later, Riss's order arrived, and the world vanished as she gorged, wanting to gobble with both hands, but managing to eat in a civilized manner, even if all her plates were bare in a few minutes.

'Might I inquire about your current employment?' Baldur said, who'd finished minutes earlier, and was watching her, a small smile on his face.

Riss thought of lying, thought why bother?

'Since that bitch didn't come through with the money for rescuing her crumb-snatcher, I'm looking hard. I was supposed to meet some bastard here about a courier job, but he's a no-show.'

'Just as well,' Baldur said. 'All too many of those courier contracts mean you are carrying stolen objects. Or else drugs.

'Not that I object to either, but I distinctly dislike being the patsy in the middle who is caught with the loot, and will have to do the time, since there is no one he can sell out to save his own hide.

'What a *dirty* trade we have chosen.'

'Maybe,' Riss said. 'But there's worse.'

'True. True. There is always worse. Might I inquire as to your background?'

M'chel gave a brief, succinct resumé of her career.

'Most impressive,' Baldur said. 'I especially like your time in Intelligence, and the three Expeditionary Force landings.

'You *have* seen the elephant.'

'Since we're giving out bios?' Riss asked, waiting.

'There is little to mine,' Baldur said. 'I retired as a Colonel in the Alliance Navy after twenty-five, some four or five years ago, when I realized my career was not advancing as I wished.

'I am qualified on most spacecraft, have had the usual number of investitures and excursions.

'I also, although the way you caught me by surprise the other night would seemingly disprove my claim, have dabbled in some of the martial arts.'

'Well,' M'chel said, starting to rise, 'I can't thank you enough for the meal.' She smiled wryly. 'Now, I've got to be out and about, and find a way to pay for my lodgings.'

'Actually, that was why I came over,' Baldur said. 'I am, as you shall no doubt learn, a creature of rapid decisions.

'How would you like a job?'

'Doing what?'

'As a partner . . . on a trial basis, of course . . . with my firm. Star Risk, Ltd.. I have a decided need of skilled operatives.'

Riss gaped, sat back down, realized her jaw was dangling, and stared at von Baldur, speechless.

'Perhaps we should adjourn to my offices, and you shall understand my situation more clearly.'

*

The building was ultramodern, in the current style dubbed 'Unsupported Freeform.' Polished steel beams jutted up, zigged at impossible angles that could never buttress or support the alloy structures scattered among them. Riss had once read an article on the style, knew that antigrav generators, each hopefully with emergency backup power, actually kept the fifty-story building from toppling.

The lifts were clear platforms that seemed to hang from spidery cables. Again, hidden antigravs did the work.

Baldur bowed Riss out of the lift on the forty-third floor.

Directly opposite were tall double doors, of what appeared to be real wood, with small, discreet lettering: STAR RISK, LTD.

'Actually, there is no such thing as a "limited liability corporation" anymore,' Baldur explained. 'But Trimalchio does not much care what you call yourself, so long as your taxes are kept up to date.

'And I always thought "Limited" sounded most elegant.'

'A question,' M'chel said. 'What's the significance of "Star Risk"? I mean, it's sexy and all, but does it have any intrinsic meaning?'

'As you said,' Baldur said, 'it *is* a sensual name.'

He touched his finger to the print-lock, and the doors opened.

'Actually, not wood, but fireproof metal under the veneer,' he went on. 'Also guaranteed to stand up to at least two direct blaster hits.'

He entered, coughed apologetically.

M'chel followed, looked around, and started laughing.

'Now,' she eventually managed, 'now I see why I've been offered a partnership.'

The offices had expensive carpeting and more expensive vertical shutters.

And nothing else. No desks, no vids, no computers, no files, no employees.

'You spent all of Mr. Fal'at's payoff renting this?' she gurgled.

'Actually, no,' Baldur said. 'The architect, also the owner of the building who incidentally has the penthouse suite, owes me a considerable favor. Also, this style of architecture seems to make prospective tenants a little nervous.

'He discharged his obligation by giving me this suite on a year lease.

'Now I am required to make it work.'

'Um, could I ask on what basis you thought Star Risk would be a go?' M'chel asked.

'Certainly. These are times, as someone or other once said, that try men's bank accounts. The Alliance can hardly be considered a strong government, and there are many, many people who think that right grows from the barrel of a gun. Or from a very entrepreneurial law firm. Or from a malleable legislator.

'Not that I am particularly shocked by that proposition.

'But in times that are close to lawless, men will seek out their own law.'

'Star Risk, Ltd.?' M'chel asked.

'Yes,' Baldur said. 'Or, since a true mercenary judges not, Star Risk is there to assist those who are acquisitive.

'Assuming,' he added hastily, 'they can pay for our services. Pay handsomely.'

'I don't know if I like the idea of working for the bad guys.'

'That is why I use a sliding scale of payments, depending on our involvement or feeling, if any, in a particular cause.'

'Credits cancel morality?' Riss suggested.

'Well, I would not put it *quite* so bluntly,' Baldur said. 'But a hefty bank balance makes it much easier to look in the mirror each morning.'

'So what happened? I don't see a long line of clients, wearing either black or white hats, streaming in the door.'

'I may have made some minor miscalculations,' Baldur admitted. 'Have you ever heard of Cerberus Systems?'

'No,' Riss said. 'Wait. Yes. I saw something on a vid a few months ago. They're a private security service, right?'

'That, and everything else,' Baldur said sadly. 'They'll do anything from espionage to counter-espionage to union security to strikebreaking to investigative work to military advisory work to collapsing currencies to riot incitement to . . . and this is only a bit more than a rumor, directed violence beyond any law's forgiveness.'

'How far will they take *that*?' Riss asked.

'The only limits are what you can pay for, the story goes. Murder is supposedly called "End Certification" by them. But that is neither here nor there, other than I generally discourage assassination. It has a nasty, nasty way of being found out, and the act blowing back on you, the poor operative, rather than the villain who hired you for the dastardly deed.

'Cerberus is also very, very active in dealing with competitors. They'll pass out false rumors, put their operatives in the way of a competitor finishing the mission they were hired for, even if they themselves have no interests in that area.

'Cerberus is one problem. Another is that I am not the only one who has considered a mercenary career. It seems that every half-witted knuckle-dragger who can afford a blaster and a license to carry it are suddenly Emergency Situation Specialists.'

M'chel looked down at the carpet.

'I am sorry, my dear,' Baldur said. 'I was not referring to you.'

'No,' M'chel said. 'Don't apologize. Even though I think I've got talents and skills beyond ruining my manicure on the pavement.

'In fact, I've got a question. When I was in the Marines, one thing I specialized in was Target Analysis.

'Let me,' Riss said, unconsciously taking on the tones of an instructor, 'ask about this Cerberus Systems.

'I really don't care about how ruthless they are. Are they any good?'

'They are,' Baldur said reluctantly. 'They are big, so they can put a lot of operatives, equipment, resources into any operation they undertake.

'They pay well and they actively recruit. I am surprised, quite frankly, that they did not attempt to add you to their organization.

'Overall, they operate on the basic premise that any person is corruptible in one or another way, and all that matters is the size of the bribe.

'Which, in our chosen field, is not altogether an erroneous way to think.'

'Fine,' Riss said. 'What are their weaknesses?'

Baldur considered. 'They are slow to move, like any colossus. And once they move in any direction, it is hard for them to change direction. Also, once they decide on a given course, they are reluctant to accept input that might suggest their original examination of the situation was faulty.

'They are bureaucratic, naturally. The longer you are in their employ, the greater respect you are given, and the less likely you are to be terminated without making a series of extreme errors.

'I personally think their board of directors is hide-bound, prone to doing business as they did last week and last year, and that they apply the same tactics to Situation B merely because it appears to resemble Situation A, where those tactics worked very well.

'So now you see the reality of my situation. Do you think you might be of service?'

'I don't know,' M'chel said. 'I don't think I could make it any worse.'

'Good. Excellent in fact. It gets most lonely, beating your head against brick walls each day.'

Baldur walked to one door, pushed it open. 'You mentioned that you were having a bit of problem with your digs. This shall be your office.'

He went to another door, and opened it. Inside was a camp cot, a clothes rack, a small refrigerator, and a convection oven.

'This is *my* office. So you can see that I understand your difficulty.'

Riss hesitated.

'There is a lock on the door,' Baldur said hastily. 'And you can perform your ablutions in either of the suite's two bathrooms. There is a salvage store two blocks away that can provide you with a cot and whatever other necessities you desire.

'You do not have to worry. I have never screwed one of my partners.

'At least,' he said thoughtfully, 'not in that particular sense of the word.'

M'chel thought about things. She certainly didn't trust Friedrich von Baldur at all.

But on the other hand, there was that mystery meat, a flea-bitten single room, a glowering hotel manager, and another goddamned sugared bun for the next two meals staring at her.

'Since I can't see that I've got anything to lose,' she said, holding out her hand, 'we have a deal.'

'For six months,' Baldur said.

'For six months,' Riss echoed, and Baldur touched her palm with his.

THREE

Dmitri Herndon was a happy man. A sweaty, tired happy man.

He pushed the ore-carrier ahead of him, toward the welcome gleam of his ship's floodlights.

There was enough high-grade in the carrier to pay off his bill with Transkootenay, grubstake himself for another lonely six weeks in this desolate belt, and some to send home to his sister on Lorraine VII. And the hold of his shabby, converted yacht was about half-full of other saleable metals.

Better still, he thought . . . hoped, rather . . . that he had seen trace enough to think there could be a diamond 'pipe' here on this rotten planetoid, which would make him slightly richer than the revered Joseph Smith.

If this belt was indeed part of an exploded planet, God hadn't blown it up nearly enough, Herndon thought sourly, looking out into hard blackness, and thousands of spinning dots, not stars, dimly lit by the system's dying sun.

But then, if God hadn't blasted it, there wouldn't be any miners in the system, wouldn't be any fissionable ore in Herndon's carrier and ship, and Herndon himself might still be back teaching basic chemistry on Lorraine.

He often thought of the image people had of deep-

F/2039457

COUNTY
LIBRARY

space miners – brawny, bearded, quick to brawl, profane.

Herndon may have had the beard, but little else. In fact, he'd grown it to not look entirely like the image of a professor, which stereotype he *did* resemble.

He'd quit teaching, dreaming of riches, and followed the rush into this system. It'd been six months of the hardest, most dangerous work he could have imagined. If he wasn't carefully placing and blowing charges, ever aware of the likelihood he'd blow himself to flinders as a self-taught powder monkey, he was breaking big rocks into little rocks with a powered drill, then checking them with his belt analyzer. Not to mention keeping himself somewhat fed, and his ship from expiring in a smolder of circuitry.

He considered what he'd do if there *were* diamonds on this stupid rock.

Real riches.

He'd put his ship in the shop, have its rotten, hiccuping secondary drive rebuilt, first.

No. He'd just find some other duckling, fresh into the Foley System, and convince him the bucket was just what he needed to go mining. Just as another miner had trapped Herndon.

Then he'd buy another ship, and . . .

No. He'd buy out his contract, and, if there were enough money, just retire. No benders, no jags, just a chance to go somewhere quiet, somewhere with a big computer, and he'd spend the rest of his life happily researching the break between alchemy and real chemistry.

Maybe a planet with a big library, a big computer, and some nightlife. Professors didn't *have* to be reclusive, especially not rich professors.

Something like Trimalchio IV, which he'd seen on the vids, heard stories about its decadence, never visited.

His mind drifted, though he never lost his balance,

bounding in ten-meter leaps toward the ship. Showgirls. Tall showgirls. Tall, blond showgirls. Or maybe brunettes. Smiling, barely clad, to be wooed with a handful of diamonds into impossible lusts.

At least he'd had brains enough to register a claim on this jagged piece of stone as soon as he'd brought in the first load of ore, so he had all the time in the world to pick its bones, dreaming all the while of wealth.

He slid open the cover of his ship's exterior control panel, touched a sensor.

The cargo hatch slid open. He pushed the carrier inside and dumped the ore into a expandable hold.

He closed the hatch from the inside, and went into the hold's airlock, cycled it.

The inner lock door opened, and Herndon unsealed his faceplate, winced, as always at the, well, reek. A few hours on the dry, recycled suit atmosphere, and he'd forget just how bad the cabin smelled, a mixture of bad cooking, and human odors.

He decided he could allow himself one slivovitz, no more, after he checked to make sure the ship hadn't developed any more mechanical surprises.

Sitting, very much at ease in one of the control room's two acceleration chairs, was a large man, beard trimmed like a dandy.

He lifted the blaster in his lap, pointed it at Herndon.

'I coulda just grabbed the ship, and left you to breathe space, y' know. But I'm a kindly man.'

Herndon had heard of highgraders, had friends who'd been robbed.

He'd determined this wouldn't happen to him, and had bought a pistol when he'd last resupplied, clipped it under the chart table.

He put a smile on his face, lifted his hands, then dove, twisting, for the table, two meters distant.

He never made it.

The bearded man cursed, shot him twice in the side. Herndon crashed into the table, headfirst.

'Goddamit, you didn't have to go and make me do *that*,' the bearded man complained, wrinkling his nose at the stink of burnt flesh.

Dmitri Herndon lay perfectly still, made no answer.

FOUR

'How about this?' Friedrich von Baldur asked, peering at the screen of the archaic computer he'd managed to acquire somewhere. Also scrounged were the two camp chairs and table set up in the office lobby. At least they'd found the money to have a vid installed in Baldur's office/bedroom.

'"COVERT ADVISORS needed. Growing, progressive system, troubled with internal and external troublemakers, urgently needs specialists to organize, lead its special operations. Lehigh is a—"'

'Forget that,' M'chel Riss interrupted. 'Lehigh's been looking for advisors for years. What they want is someone to organize their death squads for them.'

'As long as I am not the one murdering the widows and orphans,' Baldur said, 'I have little trouble sleeping at night.'

'I do,' Riss said. 'But that's not the point. They came to the Alliance Marines, with the approval of the Alliance, when I was still aboard, wanting advisors, promising they'd join the Alliance as soon as their government stabilized. We sent out a survey team, and a friend of mine was on it. She came back shaking her head, saying there's at least six factions, all playing against the middle, and nobody necessarily knows who's really on whose side.

'First they try to subvert you; then, if you don't subvert, you're on the kill list.'

'As you said, forget that,' Baldur said. 'Pity. They even claim to offer a health fund, and I would like to get a varicose vein or two removed.'

'Keep looking,' Riss advised. 'Somebody out there's got to be an honest sort needing thugs. Or,' she added, thinking of just how low Star Risk's resources were, 'semihonest will fly at this point.'

The door opened, and a woman came in. Both Baldur and Riss looked at her, and blinked.

M'chel Riss had, as all beautiful women do and deny, realized at a very young age that she was beautiful.

But this woman was beyond beautiful.

She was about four centimeters shorter than Riss, had gently curling dark hair with golden tints, around a face that could have launched a thousand starships, blue eyes, and a perfect figure.

Riss thought about hating her.

'Welcome to Star Risk,' Baldur said, and introduced them. 'Forgive our lack of amenities, but the press of events—'

'I'm Jasmine King,' the woman said, and Riss thought even her damned voice was perfect. 'And I'm well aware of your financial precariousness.'

'Oh,' Baldur said.

'I'm interested in applying for a job,' King said.

'Uh, forgive my slowness,' M'chel said. 'But if you know how broke we are, you've got to be aware your paycheck would most likely bounce. I assume you work for high credits.'

'True,' King said. 'But I have a personal reason for wanting to work for you.'

'In what capacity, if I may inquire?' Baldur asked.

'Office manager and research specialist,' King said.

'We certainly don't have much of an office to manage,' Riss said. 'But we hope to. And what's this personal reason, if I may inquire?'

'Until yesterday, I was the head of Cerberus Systems' research department.'

Both Riss and Baldur reacted in surprise and some degree of suspicion.

'You'll forgive my skepticism,' Baldur said. 'But Cerberus has the reputation of being tough in their practices, willing to do just about anything to keep prospective competitors from competing.'

'That's correct,' King added. 'Up to and including false lawsuits or bombs over the transom.'

'I think what Freddie's trying to say,' Riss said, 'is how do we know you're not a spy . . . or a wrecker?'

'You don't,' King said. 'But why don't one of you check my resumé with them? Don't claim to be anything in the way of a security service.

'Maybe a library.' She opened a small purse, took out a fiche.

'Here is a copy of my personnel record I stole before leaving. Check what the head of Human Resources at Cerberus has to say against it. Their vid address, here on Trimalchio, is—'

'I shall look it up,' Baldur said.

'Good,' King said. 'It's too easy for someone to give a false number, and have a henchman at the other end feed you exactly what that person wants to be said.'

Baldur looked at her carefully. 'You *have* worked for Cerberus.'

King smiled placidly. Baldur, intrigued, started for his office and the vid.

'Wait,' M'chel said. 'One question you didn't answer.

If you work for top credits, how do you expect to get paid by us?'

'I can defer my salary until the credits are there,' King said. 'I have sufficient resources for a year or more.' She smiled slightly. 'Don't think I'm an altruist. When the time is ripe, you'll think your accounts have been struck by a tornado.'

M'chel grinned.

'Go ahead and check her,' she said. 'Now I'm getting curious, too.'

Baldur went into his office, closed the door.

M'chel and Jasmine looked at each other. For some reason, Riss didn't find the silence uncomfortable.

'A researcher? In what field?'

'Anything that seems important to my employer.'

'Do you think you're an expert at anything?'

'Oh, I could say, "Riss, M'chel." Or "von Baldur, Friedrich."'

King reeled off the high points of Riss's service record.

'Great gods!' Riss said. 'I don't know if I like anybody knowing some of that. Let alone how you managed to find things out. I thought military records were sealed from the general public. Or is Cerberus that much in bed with the Alliance?'

'Not at all,' King said. 'I discovered all that on my own when I decided I'd like to work for you.'

'You're that good?'

'I'm that good,' King said, not bragging, but stating a fact. 'And that quick, too. I have a lot of interesting friends in interesting places who don't mind telling me things.'

Riss took a minute to recover, then: 'There's other security firms . . . mercenary companies. Why us?'

King smiled. 'I want to be in at the beginning of things. There's always more excitement at the start of an affair than in its middle.'

'True,' Riss said. 'What about my partner?'

'Baldur, Friedrich von Baldur. Real name, Mital Rafenger. Claims to be in his fifties, actual age sixty-two E-years. Born—'

'Skip ahead to the service record,' Riss said, holding back laughter. Mital Rafenger, indeed.

'Claims to be a retired admiral, Alliance Navy, with twenty-five years service. Actually, was a Warrant Officer, Fourth Grade, fourteen years of service. Retired and I quote, "for the good of the service." Unverified information suggests Baldur left the military shortly ahead of a court-martial on charges of misappropriation of government property, alteration of government records, suborning government officials.'

'That figures,' Riss said. 'What about his talents?'

'Claims to be familiar with most Alliance and civilian standard spacecraft. That is true. Claims to have martial arts skills. That is—'

'Also true,' Riss said. She'd sparred with Baldur, and, in spite of his age, the man could beat her two out of three times.

'Never married, no known children, no fixed address. Do you want further details?' King asked.

'I don't think they'll be needed.'

Baldur came out of his office.

'Mercy, but the plot does thicken. You were right, Miss King. The Resources Director at Cerberus says you only worked there two years, as opposed to the eight years on your record, that you were never more than a minor clerk, that you were discharged for laziness and inability to perform.'

'Makes me wonder about all of those glowing letters of commendation in the file.'

'They are trying to keep me from finding any work at

all,' Jasmine said, trying to keep her voice even. 'They want me to crawl back to them.'

'I can see why you want to break it off with them now,' M'chel said. 'But what started, if you'll forgive the vulgarity, the pissing match?'

'They informed me that they were no longer willing to pay me, and that I was the property of Cerberus Systems,' King said.

'Property!' Riss said. 'Now they're slavers, as well?'

'No,' King said. 'They claim that I'm a robot.'

Riss kept from jumping.

'Nobody that I know of can build a robot that's as much people as you look!'

'That's what I told them,' King said. 'But they refused to believe me. One of their vice presidents said he thought I was of alien construct, meant to infiltrate human society.

'I'm afraid I started crying,' King said. 'I should have cursed him, or hit him, or something.'

Blinking rapidly, she looked out a window, breathing deeply. She found control.

'What about your medical records?' Riss asked. 'Couldn't they just check them?'

'That . . . and other things . . .' King said, a bit primly, 'are things I take care of myself, and don't give out to anyone, least of all my employers. I'm a firm believer in privacy.'

'I'd think . . . Cerberus being what I've heard it is,' Riss said, 'they could've set up a hidden X ray or something.'

'For some reason I can't fathom,' King said, 'X rays don't seem to work on me. I guess it's a peculiarity of the world I come from, or something.'

'There goes our health plan,' M'chel murmured. 'Assuming we can ever afford one.'

'I think this whole subject is absurd,' Baldur said.

'But . . . I do not mean to be rude, *are* you a robot?'

King looked at him, a touch haughtily.

'Now, if I was, and willing to lie about it to Cerberus, wouldn't I be willing to lie to you as well?'

'Conceded,' Baldur said. 'M'chel if you'd step into my office for a moment?'

Riss followed him.

'Well?'

'I don't give a damn if she's a 'bot from Planet Octopus, with a pocket nuke in her purse and evil intent,' Riss said. 'She surely knows her stuff.'

'And we could well use a good . . . I think the term used to be "gumshoe," couldn't we?'

'We could. So let's not keep the poor woman waiting,' Riss said, and they went back out.

'Welcome to Star Risk, Ltd.,' Riss said.

Jasmine King grinned, and then it appeared as if she was about to cry again.

That settled matters for Riss.

Robots couldn't cry.

Could they?

Riss was making a list up of old Marine colleagues, intending, forlornly, to drop them a line and ask if they knew of any free-lance militarying, when both doors opened, and a being entered.

He needed both doors, for he was very large.

M'chel guessed his height at two and a half meters, width at a meter, weight at maybe four hundred kilos-plus. He was covered with long, silky fur, had long, delicate fingers, six to a hand, plus thumb. He was pro-portioned like a man, not an ape, and had a humanoid number of arms and legs.

His face was like that of a thoughtful Earth lemur, but in proportion to his size.

He wore sandals, a pouched belt, and, most incongruously, a black-and-white tam.

She blinked, and managed, 'Good morning, sir.'

'Good morning,' the being said, in an attractive, accentless bass. 'I am Amanandrah Grookonomonslf. I seek Jasmine King.'

'I'll see if she's here,' Riss said, having no idea what business this heavy equipment hauler wanted.

Jasmine burst into the room, squealed 'Grok!' and flung herself into his arms.

'You are as pretty and ageless as ever,' the being said gravely.

'And you are a gentlebeing as always,' Jasmine returned, coming out of his arms. 'M'chel, this is Grok. You do not have to use his full name, not ever.'

'Especially since the Basic version of my name is not that close to being correct,' the monster said.

'Delighted,' M'chel said, very grateful that the Marines had sent her on more than a few missions to alien cultures, so she was used to nonhumanoids.

'I got your message,' Grok said to Jasmine, 'and am only too delighted to offer my assistance.'

'You're not a client,' M'chel said.

'I detect disappointment,' Grok said. 'No. I am no more than an ex-service person, currently looking for a bit of excitement.'

'Grok was in the Alliance Army for about eight years,' Jasmine explained. 'He is a specialist in communications, SigInt, surveillance, and other specialties. He left the service because . . . you tell them.'

'I suppose I should be ashamed of my tastes,' Grok rumbled. 'But every now and then I like a good dustup, as I think you call it.

'My own worlds generally prefer the calm of philosophy, although I maintain philosophy without action is like, forgive me, masturbation without a climax.'

'You don't offend,' M'chel said, grinning. 'If I were educated, I might agree with you.'

'I met Grok when he was hired as a contract agent for Cerberus,' Jasmine said. 'The experience was not a good one for him.'

'You speak in understatement. Cerberus not only is a very slow-paying employer, but if matters become serious, as they did in my particular case, they're quite willing to disavow their employees.

'I might do that myself, being a professional. But I would not lie to my agents in the beginning and tell them I am behind them one hundred percent.'

'Cerberus is *always* behind their agents,' Jasmine said. 'Far, far behind, or else ready to give them a push.'

'Now, Jasmine. Learn to put bitterness behind you,' Grok said. 'Revenge is a dish best eaten cold.'

'Sorry.'

'At the moment,' Riss said, 'we unfortunately don't have any open assignments.'

'So I was advised. But Jasmine also told me that you might be open to investors.'

'Oh?' M'chel was very casual, considering how little money a soldier would be likely to save. 'The company head, Mr. von Baldur, is out at the moment, and you'd have to discuss the matter with him.

'But I'm a partner as well. Might I inquire as to the amount you might be interested in investing?'

'Perhaps . . . half a million credits.'

Again, M'chel swore at her inability to keep a deadpan face.

'That's a considerable amount,' she managed.

'I am aware of that,' Grok said. 'And I also expect I should offer an explanation.

'In addition to my other skills, I consider myself good at what you humans call a game of chance.

'Quite good, indeed,' he said thoughtfully.

'Half a million,' Riss said, in a bit of a daze.

'Just so,' Grok said.

'I think Mr. Baldur would be very, very interested in you joining us,' M'chel said.

Grok made a noise that Riss took as approval and happiness. Or something like those feelings.

'Now are our immediate financial woes out of the way?' Jasmine said, grinning.

'I should think so.'

'Now,' King said briskly, 'all we need is a job.'

FIVE

The man eased open the door stenciled: TRANSKOOTENAY
MINING. AUTHORIZED PERSONNEL ONLY. He propped the
door open, and eased an antigravity ore carrier, about the
size of a wheelbarrow, through.

The ore processing plant was almost wholly automated. The few people Transkootenay needed to run it
worked only a 'day' shift, since not enough ore was
coming in to the asteroid outstation to warrant an
around-the-clock crew.

There was no ore on the belt, but the machinery
hummed in quiet readiness.

The man floated the carrier to the loading bay, and
dumped the carrier's cargo, a single boulder, in.

He muttered at all the extra work he'd gone to, cam-
ouflaging the charges inside the boulder, acquiring a
genuine mining ship to reach the plant looking innocent,
disguising himself in a miner's suit, even providing himself with false ID.

None of which was necessary. Transkootenay's security
was nonexistent.

He decided they were, in the old phrase, too dumb to
live.

That made him grin.

The way things were going out here, they wouldn't for very much longer.

Tough for them.

The man took a small box from his belt, went into the small operating room.

He positioned the box over a large, red switch, and turned the timer on.

Being a careful sort, he took out a plas sheet, and, even though he'd memorized his instructions, went through the checklist as he brought the processing plant up to ready state.

Then he started the timer, went out of the room, and the plant.

There was a watchman at the entrance to the field, snoring in his booth. But there were no fences around the prefab building, nor around the two barracks, one hundred meters distant.

The man threaded his way to his stolen ship, boarded, and lifted away on antigravs. One hundred meters clear of the rocky field, he went to secondary drive, watching the planetoid dwindle in his screen.

Forty-five minutes later, the timer clicked to zero, and the processor hummed into life.

The watchman woke with a jerk, feeling the vibration in his hut.

He sealed his suit, and cycled the hut's lock, awkwardly loading his blaster, as the processing plant fed the 'boulder' into the crusher, which sized the rock, and hammers came down to break the boulder into chunks.

The first crash was buried under the slam of the explosives in the boulder, as they, fused with a pressure-sensitive device, went off.

The explosion could be seen fifty kilometers in space, as the processing plant fused, melted, tore itself apart.

The watchman, surprisingly, had been alert enough to

go flat when the plant blew up, and survived, although he had nothing at all to report to Transkootenay system officials when they arrived from Sheol half a ship-day later.

STAR RISK

SIX

Former Alliance Army Captain Chas Goodnight slid easily from his hiding place, stretched, looked around the museum.

He could piss better security than it had, he thought.

Goodnight was tall, almost two hundred centimeters, slender. He had sandy hair, a square jaw, an honest face, and an easy smile. One of his lawyers had, fairly correctly, said that Goodnight was a textbook example of a sociopath.

He wore expensive civilian clothing that just happened to be dark hued, shoes that just happened to have soft soles.

Nobody'd seen him, just at closing, duck into the convenient exhibit of a mock spaceship lock, past the half a dozen bewildered-looking men, women, and children, wearing tattered shipsuits. The exhibit was labeled MAN'S FIRST ARRIVAL ON TORMAL.

Since the colonists weren't crouched behind crew-served weapons, or waving hand-helds, he figured it was a phony.

Anyone this naïve . . . or innocent . . . didn't deserve to have that lovely case marked OUR FIRST FAMILY'S GEMS.

Especially since the jewels appeared to be most real.

Nobody did that.

Not anymore.

You sent your crown jewels to Earth or another techno world, had copies made, and stuck the originals in a vault somewhere.

Or, if you thought like Goodnight, you quietly sold them to Tiffany's and pocketed the profits.

It was quiet, dark, and deserted.

And time to go to work.

Goodnight pressed a slight bulge at the angle of his right jaw, and transitioned.

His reflex time went up by three hundred percent, his eyesight expanded into the infrared, his hearing became more sensitive than any feline's, and the radar antenna implanted behind the skin of his forehead came alive.

He scanned the big exhibit hall.

Nothing and no one.

Good. He turned his sensors off.

He had about another nineteen minutes left on his battery charge.

Goodnight shouldered a small daypack, moved forward, walking toe-and-heel as he'd been taught, and practiced on a hundred covert missions for the Alliance before he 'woke up' – his phrase – about who was the patsy and who was making the profit on his oh-so-elaborate and painful surgery, the so-called 'besterization.'

After that realization, he'd had a wonderful two years as a cat burglar, until he got caught. He'd been stealing an Alliance ambassador's jewel chest, while she and her husband oversaw a grand masked ball downstairs in the mansion, and two thugs with badges came out of nowhere.

At the court-martial, his defense counsel, who he thought was lovely, even if she wouldn't bed him, but was also slightly thicker than dirt, asked him, 'How *could* you?'

'She had the best jewels on the post,' he answered reasonably.

'But . . . an ambassador!'

'She . . . or maybe her husband . . . could afford it,' he pointed out. 'Besides, she was probably insured.'

The woman looked sadly at the man. Just under two meters, sandy hair, brown eyes, an easy smile. She thought him as good looking as any livee star.

But hopeless. Beyond morality.

She accused him of that, and he got indignant, saying he'd never killed anybody while stealing, at least not yet, and the only people he had killed were at Alliance orders.

That didn't seem to improve her attitude, or the quality of her defense.

She argued that Goodnight had a perfect combat record. Combat, and in other classified areas the court-martial board refused to hear in an open courtroom.

It didn't matter.

Goodnight was given the choice, after the guilty verdict: Ten years on a penal planet, which meant no survival, especially since he doubted they'd let him take any spare bester charges.

Or . . .

Or cooperate.

Goodnight sang like an Earth nightingale, giving away his fences, where he'd stashed the money he'd made, and what his future scores were to be.

He didn't reveal his accomplices, because he never had any, always having known, since the crèche, when it was him and his brother against the universe, a man travels quicker when he picks his own company.

Besides, he was never sure what the word 'friendship' meant to other people. It meant one thing to him, the same to his little brother, Reg, but who knew what definitions others used? He'd had a pretty good idea what that meant to the others in his Special Operations Detachment, which is why he'd never considered stealing anything from them.

But outsiders?

He chose not to find out the hard way if they could be trusted.

They gave him two years in a planetary prison.

He was out and gone in a month, went to ground, then made two big scores which covered his new ID and passage offplanet in two more.

Goodnight began to enjoy himself then, moving from world to world, system to system, seldom hitting more than once on a planet, well on his way before anyone thought to raise the hue and cry.

He was generally very careful to investigate a target world's laws, making sure none of them had barbaric penalties for a simple, harmless thief, merely making his way through a hostile universe.

And now he was on Tormal, making as big a score, perhaps bigger, if his handy-dandy pocket analyzer had told the truth about those jewels, than he'd ever made before.

This was necessarily to be a fast in-and-out. He'd heard of these jewels and done his research on another world. He arrived on Tormal as a tourist, cased the museum on his second day, and this was his third. On the morrow, he'd be gone. That was the safest way to operate on a sparsely settled world, where strangers were always noted.

Perhaps he ought to, after he cashed in the geetus, find some nice tropical world, somewhere like Trimalchio IV, which he'd seen on the vids, but never visited, lay back for a while, relax, and enjoy his million-plus hidden in an impenetrable bank account on a world he didn't even name in his thoughts.

Perhaps.

Maybe after one or two more jobs.

In the meantime . . . he slithered on, never missing a step, or making a sound.

Twice more he checked his radar, his IR.

Slick and clean.

He came to the huge doors that opened into the PLANETARY TREASURES room, went past them, to the small door inconspicuously labeled STAFF.

The big doors, and this small one, were alarmed.

It took only a few seconds for him to wire around the sensors on the staff door, so that he could have blown it open and nothing would have gonged.

Goodnight was about to pick the lock, when he decided to make another check.

He felt prickly, as if he was being watched. That was one of his own senses, field trained, not one provided by Alliance neurosurgeons.

Nothing.

He took out a springload and a small pick, bent over the lock, then caught himself.

Cute.

Most cute.

The lock had a built-in alarm, one which an official key's tiny transmitter would keep from setting off.

Goodnight opened his belt pouch, brought out a small tube, a bit fatter and longer than a pen. He turned it on, held its end against the keyhole, watched its light blink green, green, then flash red. The light held red, then went green. The 'pen' had found the alarm's frequency and blanked it.

Picking the lock itself was very easy.

Goodnight opened the door, but didn't enter the room, lit only with two lights at either end.

He'd seen the floor-alarm pickups during the day,

sneered at them. He didn't plan on getting to the jewels by walking.

Goodnight touched his jaw switch, transitioned, checked the room. Nothing.

He braced, jumped for a long display case three meters away.

He cat-walked along its edge, feeling the metal bend under his weight, recover.

Another leap, another case.

Five meters out from the wall was his target case.

Goodnight wasn't looking at it, but at a very solid light fixture overhead.

He took a roll of very light climbing rope from his pack. Its end was stickied, for three meters, and with a light weight.

He whirled it slowly, then faster, then cast it upward. It coiled around the fixture, almost fell free, his heart almost stopping, then wrapped tightly around the fixture.

He tugged, and the fixture held firm.

Goodnight reached up as high as he could, moving quickly, feeling his battery charge running and swung out, kicking hard, into emptiness, then swinging back high, and the case was under him, almost at the apex. He let the rope slide through his fingers, landed a little harder than he would have wanted on the case.

But the heavy plas didn't break, and he was crouched atop the case. He took a tiny flash from a pocket, and shone down.

The one worry he'd had – that they moved the jewels into a vault at night – vanished.

They gleamed up at him, a friendly gleam, wanting to be in his possession, luring him.

Chas Goodnight grinned happily, put away the flash, and took out a small laser cutter, and made his first cut, along the far side of the case top.

He never heard the panel slide open just below the ceiling. The inefficiently human guard, one of four covering the jewels, guards changed every hour on the hour, leaned out, aimed, and fired a tranquilizer dart into Chas Goodnight's side.

He thudded to the floor, and then the floor alarms went off and lights flared.

SEVEN

M'chel Riss was getting tired of solitaire when her intercom buzzed.

'Yes?' she said in her most cultivated executive manner, although it was probably just Jasmine saying she was calling down the lunch order to the sandwich shop in the basement.

'Work,' King's lovely whisper came.

Without waiting for more details, M'chel boiled out of her office. Her other two partners were moving very fast in the same direction.

Their suite was now decorated in the currently popular eclectic style, with old-time prints interspersed with moving wall sculptures, the furniture made of steel, wood, and leather padding.

But Star Risk still didn't have a job.

Unless . . .

'You got?' Riss asked, as she came into the reception area, where Jasmine sat behind three computer screens, a fourth coming to life.

'I hope,' Baldur said sedately, 'something that will finally justify our faiths in ourselves.'

'Maybe,' Jasmine said.

'When you're out almost half a million credits,' Grok

growled, 'even "maybe" sounds pretty good. Give, woman.'

'Perhaps none of you have heard of Transkootenay Mining?' Jasmine said. 'A second-tier mineral exploitation company, stocks closely held. It's not as big as, say Trayem Mining, but it's hardly in danger of going bankrupt.

'Transkootenay is known as a company that moves very fast. It also hires ambitious young women and men, pays them very well, and promotes them quickly. The other side is that they are very reluctant to forgive a mistake, and so their various departments at times resemble warring kingdoms.

'Transkootenay specializes in being first to open a previously unworked area, which it's been quite successful at.

'Recently . . . about three E-years ago . . . it began exploration in the Foley System.'

'Which is where?' M'chel asked. Jasmine spun a screen around. Riss studied it.

'I think I know where it might be. Nowhere close to us.'

'Nowhere close,' Jasmine agreed. 'There are six worlds, three habitable. One, Welf, is barely habitable, close to the sun. The second, Glace, fairly earthlike, has the most people, only about a hundred million. The next world out, fairly desertlike Mfir, is where Transkootenay has its headquarters, in the charmingly named city of Sheol.

'The problem the system has is being fairly rich in resources, but without the capital to exploit them, and without a serious population base for miners and support personnel.

'One of these resources is two exploded planets, forming an extensive asteroid belt.

'Which is where Transkootenay came in, licensing the

rights to exploit the asteroids from the System Government.

'Transkootenay was doing fine until about a year ago.'

'Go back one,' Grok said. '*Two* exploded planets? That's unusual.'

'Theories vary as to what happened,' Jasmine said. 'From encounters with a massive meteor shower to unknown causes to the Ancients.'

'Pfoh,' Baldur sneered. 'There are . . . were . . . no Ancients.'

'My system's legends say otherwise,' Grok said calmly. 'Far before Man expanded into the universe, far before even we were capable of interplanetary travel. Some suggest the old tale of the Firebringers is actually a First Encounter by these beings.

'Besides, how do you account for so many cultures having tales of these Ancients?'

'With never a description,' Baldur said. 'A lot of worlds also think there's a god, so what of that?'

'This isn't getting us anywhere,' M'chel said. Jasmine nodded her thanks.

'As I was saying,' King said, 'Transkootenay has pulled gold, platinum, and fissionable ores out. These ores are the first and biggest profit maker. Recently, diamonds have been discovered, which sparked a secondary minor rush into the system.

'Transkootenay works the system in the usual fashion – they hire contract miners, provide bases with suitably priced supplies and recreational facilities, and processing facilities, and pay royalties four times a year to Foley's SysGov.

'About an Earth-year past, they started having trouble with robberies. Mining ships were seized, looted, and about twenty miners, who evidently objected to the process, were murdered.

'The situation escalated recently. One of their robot processing plants was blown up, and three of their security ships have been ambushed. No survivors.'

'Py-rates,' Friedrich said sarcastically. 'With wooden legs, parrots, and big, sharp prybars, which they wield as they sing pirate songs.'

'Pirates cannot exist in today's economic conditions,' Grok said.

'We could debate that,' Baldur said. 'Go on, Jasmine. Who's doing the dirty work?'

'That's the unusual thing,' King said. 'No clues, no drunken boasting, none of the reported items have shown up anywhere.

'And none of the various attempts by Transkootenay Security have found anything, although their files suggest an entire navy could be easily hidden among the asteroids.'

'So where might we come in?' Baldur asked.

'Transkootenay has always kept its problems inhouse,' King went on. 'But this new situation has them baffled.

'Also, their executive in the Foley System is very much on the spot. He must either solve the problem, or else SysGov will cancel the mining agreement, forcing Transkootenay to withdraw. That, of course, would mean the end of that system exec's career.

'So they're looking for an outside service to take over, provide security and find out where these raiders are, how many of them there are, and take appropriate measures.'

'They haven't gone to the military?' Grok asked.

'They did. The Alliance sent a destroyer squadron through on a one-week sweep, found nothing.'

'Typical,' Riss murmured.

'So now Transkootenay is looking for a savior,' Baldur said, rubbing his hands together and smiling a rather capitalistic smile.

'Indeed,' Jasmine said. 'In fact, they've asked Cerberus Systems to put together a proposal. A study team has been established, and is evaluating the situation.'

'Shit,' Riss said. 'That keeps us right on out.'

'Not necessarily,' Jasmine said. 'At least, not if there's an appropriately bold response, made immediately.'

'What?' Riss said. 'We're supposed to come up with a quicker, trickier way to go than Cerberus has come up with?'

'Oh no,' Jasmine said. 'Cerberus does incredible presentations. Not to mention that if one of us went to the Foley System, and word got out why we were there, it isn't inconceivable harm could come.'

'But you have an idea,' Riss persisted.

'No,' Jasmine corrected. 'I have more interesting facts.

'The head of Transkootenay Mining's division in the Foley System, in Mfir's Sheol, is a Reg Goodnight. A very well-respected, high-ranking executive. Admired for his youth and ability, if treated a bit warily for his, shall we say, tactical abilities in the field of corporate infighting. Also, as I said before, with his career very much on the line.'

'So?' Baldur asked.

'Mr. Goodnight has an older brother, a certain Chas Goodnight,' King went on. 'Formerly a member of the Alliance Army, ranking Captain, assigned to a Special Operations Detachment.'

'A bester?' Baldur asked.

'Yes.' King said.

Grok looked puzzled, and Baldur explained the nature of these surgically modified commandos.

'Interesting,' the being murmured. 'A formidable operative.'

'There is, of course,' Baldur said, 'a limitation.'

'Is there not always?' Grok asked.

'The bester operates not just on his natural energy, but on a tiny battery that is hidden under his coccyx . . . base of his spine. He has from twenty to thirty minutes before the battery runs dry. But he cannot just slide in a new battery,' Baldur said, 'since he will have burned up his reserves. He needs to refuel, which means consume calories like he is a raging fire. Once fed, and rested, he can replace the battery, and go again. He can maintain this cycle for no longer than three, perhaps four days, then needs an extended rest.

'I am sorry, Jasmine, to have interrupted. Go on with your briefing.'

'The two were orphans, I've learned. Grew up in a crèche. The older brother, Reg's idol, went into the military, used his money to pay for his brother's education, which was of the best, and hence expensive,' King said.

'Possibly making those expenses on a soldier's pay made Captain Goodnight go spectacularly bad. He used his talents to become a burglar, a jewel thief, quite a good one, in fact. He was caught, court-martialed, thrown out of the service, and sent to prison.

'He escaped, and set about a string of robberies, very cleverly put together, very skillfully done.

'Goodnight has never been caught again.

'Until three weeks ago.

'He decided to steal some fabulous jewels on a backwater planet named Tormal. Unfortunately, he was caught.

'Even more unfortunately, it seems that Captain Goodnight didn't do his homework adequately. He generally hit targets that were easy and, just as important, on worlds where his punishment would be fairly light.

'Not so on Tormal, which has some fairly barbaric laws.

'They've quickly condemned him to death, which will

be by slow strangulation.

'He now languishes, all appeals denied, in his death cell, to be killed within the month.'

'I think I see where this is going,' Riss said.

'As do I,' Grok said.

Jasmine smiled.

'I love working for people who are intelligent. It would seem to me that all you would have to do to win Reg's, and hence Transkootenay's, undying love and gratitude, would be to break Chas Goodnight out of prison.'

'Lovely,' Baldur muttered.

'Plus,' Riss said, 'you notice how it's suddenly become "you" instead of "us?"'

EIGHT

Tormal may or may not have been colonized peaceably, but at one time in its past it must have had some formidable enemies.

The great fortress, now Tormal's maximum-security prison, sat atop a mountain crest like a great spider.

Friedrich von Baldur looked at it dubiously as their hired lifter approached.

'Guess we can give up the tunnel idea,' he said.

'Sssh,' Jasmine King said as the com crackled on.

'Unknown aircraft, this is Tormal Citadel,' an obviously synthed voice said. 'You are entering a forbidden zone. Identify yourself. Over.'

Baldur scrabbled for, found a microphone, keyed it.

'Tormal Citadel this is lifter, uh . . .' He saw the vehicle ID on the dash, read it back. 'Two passengers, from Alliance Prisoners Aid, cleared by the Alliance Consulate and Tormal Corrections Authority.'

There was a pause, and Baldur busied himself with a camera as they closed on the fortress.

'This is Tormal Citadel. Landing approved. Your controls are now under our direction. Do not attempt to make corrections, for fear of being fired on by automatic devices, now tracking your ship. Clear.'

'Very good,' Baldur said with satisfaction. 'Did you notice, not one single real person talked to us?'

He smiled sharkishly.

Jasmine looked bewildered.

'Condemned Row . . .' the speaker blared. 'Prisoner Goodnight, Chas. You have visitors. Cell door coming open.'

And the door to Goodnight's cell slid open. A small, wheeled robot buzzed down the aisle, stopped at his cell. A green light atop it began blinking.

'Who's visiting me?' Goodnight wanted to know, but the robot just blinked.

'I'll be dipped,' he said, and bounded out.

The other prisoners on Death Row came to their cell doors, which appeared to be unbarred glass, with an opening along the top.

'Guess the real truth is coming out, boys, on just how bleedin' innocent I am,' Goodnight said as he followed the robot.

'Prob'ly gonna geek you early,' someone came back.

There were boos, some cheers, a lot of grins. Goodnight had taken care to make himself popular since he'd been condemned to death. No one who's ever been in jail makes enemies out of his fellow cons without good cause.

The robot took him to a lift, and he dropped calamitously downward. Prisons don't much care about whether or not inmates' stomachs get unsettled.

Death Row was on the top level of the fortress, and the prison's entrance/exit was on the ground floor.

He was escorted by the robot into a room with a plas wall down its middle. On either side of the wall were tables and chairs. A microphone and pass-through were in the middle.

Set unobtrusively in two walls, high up, were two monitors.

On the far side of the wall was a silver-haired man who could have been a diplomat, and the most beautiful woman Goodnight had ever seen.

Goodnight looked at them, and hid his disappointment. He didn't know who he would have wanted to see – maybe his brother? No. What would Chas have to say, other than confess failure to Reg? That'd be hard, since Reg had always looked up to him, he thought, even if the two were always competing.

'I don't know you,' he said cheerily, sitting down.

'Hasford Klinger,' the man said. 'Of the Alliance Prisoners Aid. And this is my assistant, Choly Wells.'

'I've never heard of your organization, sir,' Goodnight said. 'And the one time I was regrettably incarcerated, no one came to see about my welfare.'

'The Alliance, sir,' Baldur said, 'is constantly growing, changing to meet the needs of its citizenry. We like to think we represent a kindlier, gentler part of the great galactic civilization.'

Goodnight decided that Klinger was certainly what he claimed to be. No one but a bureaucrat working for some Warm & Cuddly Organization could make a speech like that without vomiting.

'I'm surprised to see you, in any event,' Goodnight said. 'Are you bringing fruits and candies, perhaps? Or flowers?'

He looked at 'Choly Wells,' thought wistfully of conjugal visitation privileges, shut off that train of thought. Miss Wells, if she was available, would certainly not be interested in a bearded, scruffy man about to get his neck squeezed.

'We are not in the business of providing small comforts, sir,' Baldur said.

'No,' King added, 'we ensure that a prisoner who is not a member of a planetary society is given all the rights of a native, and that no discrimination is made against him.'

She opened a briefcase, took out a thick document.

'This is the first item we'd like you to read and if you can agree with the statements made, you initial each page. There are three copies.'

She passed the document to Baldur, who flipped through it.

'Yes, this is the standard form,' he said. 'I'd appreciate you signing where marked, and initialing all other pages.'

Goodnight started to lose his temper.

'I came down here, out of a perfectly good erotic fantasy, so that you can be sure I'm going to be killed in an ethical manner?'

'Now, Mr. Goodnight, I know you're under great strain,' Baldur said. 'But our having this document conceivably can open other doors.'

'Such as appeals to the government for clemency, off-worlders who might wish to protest the circumstances of your sentencing, possibly even stays of execution,' King added.

Goodnight stared to stomp out.

But he saw the tiny sideways movement of Baldur's head.

'All right.' What did he have to lose, and besides, this'd make a good story for the other doomed ones.

He went to the pass-through.

Baldur opened the cover, put in the document, took an ornate, metal-worked pen from his pocket and set it on top of the ream of paper, just as King was seized with a spasm of coughing.

Both men turned to her, concerned.

'Are you all right?' Goodnight asked.

'Just . . . just a bit of an allergy,' she managed. 'I'm not used to Tormal's air yet.'

Baldur patted her, while Goodnight wanted to take her in his arms and comfort her.

Baldur waited for the pass-through to cycle, but nothing happened.

He swiveled, looked up at one of the eyes.

'Well?'

There was a click, and the pass-through carried its cargo through to Goodnight's side.

Goodnight started to pick up the document, but, as his hand moved underneath it, he felt something. Something that felt most familiar, something that definitely shouldn't be there, absolutely shouldn't be provided by a Prisoners Aid representative, unless said representative was working to the extreme limits of his job description.

Two fingers curled the bester battery into his palm, and he picked up the pen atop the document.

Taking it out, he slipped and dropped the sheaf of papers.

By the time he scrabbled them up, the battery was safely tucked in a turned-up cuff of his prison coverall.

'Well,' he said, voice suddenly oozing friendship, as he began signing and initialing pages, 'I'm sorry if I was less than polite when you came in. I sincerely hope that this won't be the first of your visits.'

'As do we,' King said, taking out another form. 'Next we have some questions I hope you won't mind answering. First, is your cell comfortably located?'

Her last word was slightly emphasized, and Goodnight caught it.

'Yes, yes it is. It's right up under the roof, on the eastern side, so it gets the benefit of sunlight.'

'That close to the roof, are you bothered at night by the guards' movements?'

'No, that's no problem,' Goodnight said. 'Everything's automated, so except for the whir of machinery, that's not bothersome.'

'Are there others in the Condemned section?'

A buzzer went off, and a metallic voice said, 'That is not a permitted question.'

'Oh,' Jasmine said, 'I'm sorry. Let me move to the next one. Are you fed in your cell, or are you permitted to associate with others?'

'The ten of us on Death Row eat together,' Goodnight said. 'There's a small rec room we're permitted to use during the day, and that's where we get meals, which come up from the kitchen on—'

The buzzer went off, somewhat belatedly. 'That is not a permitted answer. Any repetition of these breaches, and your visitors will be required to leave.'

'Which we would not want,' Baldur said. 'Since we prefer to make our visits when it's convenient for Prisoners Aid, as well as this Institute.'

King turned a page.

'What is your diet, and are you happy with it?'

The four listened as Goodnight's answer played back from the recorder that had masqueraded as Baldur's ornate pen.

'It isn't bad,' the voice said. 'There's enough of it. Most of it's pretty starchy, so I'm putting on weight. I work out when I can, and—'

'Very good,' Riss approved. 'Do you think we have enough?'

'We do with what Jasmine has, I think.'

King obediently swiveled a computer screen. 'I just happened to find this in Government Historical

Publications. It's a floor plan of that fortress, back when it was a fortress.'

Riss studied it, nodded.

'We can do something with that,' she said. 'Assuming our pet idiot won't shove his battery up his heinie and run amok before we bust down the doors with the rescue squad.'

'I found it very interesting, not to say comforting,' Baldur said, 'that the security system, particularly those four gun turrets on the roof, is almost completely automated.'

'I do not understand,' Grok said. 'Robots do not take naps, or show up with hangovers.'

'True,' Baldur said. 'But all they can do is what they are told to. Surprise them a little, and it takes a while for them to either flip to another program, or else whine for a human supervisor. A good example is their rather bird-brained Landing Control System.'

'Ah,' Grok said. 'Of course.'

'Which brings us to you, my fine-feathered electronics specialist. I think we shall need some surprises, which I shall suggest, and I am sure you'll have even more sophisticated alternatives,' Baldur said. 'And we shall need them rather rapidly, since sooner or later somebody at the dozy Consulate is going to route our credentials on up, and find out there doesn't seem to be anything called the Prisoners Aid Society.'

'I've managed to round up some surprises of my own,' Riss said. 'While you two were out playing pious pilgrims of the cosmos, I was lurking around some barrooms.

'Do you know, no matter how tough a system's security is, how careful their gun laws are, if you have money and a day, you can always acquire whatever artillery you need? Although, I'd still rather bring my own machine gun to the dance.'

'Unless the provider is doubling for the government,' Baldur agreed.

'A little care,' Riss said, 'generally keeps you from being trapped.'

'I didn't know the Marines taught you how to buy illegal arms,' Jasmine said.

'They don't,' Riss said. 'But some of us keep our ears open when we're covert, and learn from others.

'I've found a man who is absolutely in love with money, says he can get anything.

'With what you've got, I know what I need.

'So the day after tomorrow might be a good time to go operational.'

'How,' Baldur persisted, 'will you keep this contact from selling you out, after he's made the last delivery? It is unfortunately common for a criminal sort to be dishonest, selling the customer what he wants, and then set him up for a fall once payment has been made. The illegal materials go back to the criminal for sale to another sucker, and he also gets points with the law for helping them.

'The only one who loses is the poor buyer.'

'Right,' Riss said. 'And I don't trust this little bastard any more than I can throw him.

'So what I'll do, when I make the final pickup,' M'chel said, 'is put in for the biggest buy of all. I'll give him half . . . sorry, Grok, for thinking so freely about your money, like you were the government or something. I'll only pass across say twenty-five C in front for something that'll be sure to have every lawman in the system wetting his little panties. Delivery to be made, oh, two days after we're either gone or in a cell next to Goodnight.'

'What'll that be?' a fascinated Jasmine asked.

'Oh, I don't know. Perhaps a pocket nuke, and

instructions to the statehouse or whatever they call it around here,' M'chel said carelessly.

'*Gad*,' Baldur said in mock shock. 'I have been nurturing a viper at my bosom!'

NINE

'At least we have something I can fly,' Jasmine King said, checking the controls of the luxury lim they'd rented.

M'chel Riss noted her voice was a little shaky.

Riss made sure her own voice was calm, reassuring.

'We just want you to be happy.'

Jasmine managed a smile. 'Sorry . . . but this is the closest I've been to the action so far.'

'See the advantage of working for a small company?' Riss said, grinning. 'Before too long, you'll be over-throwing whole governments with a smile on your lips and a song in your heart.'

While M'chel spoke, she was sliding blaster charges into bandoleers, and laying them out beside the weaponry she'd assembled.

Each member of the team had a hand-held blaster, more than a thousand bolts per gun, fighting harness, assorted grenades, launchers, protective vests, masks, and coms.

Not far away in the hastily rented warehouse snored the lim's driver. He'd been gassed and tucked away.

'Should we not have killed him?' Grok said. 'Gas is unpredictable.'

'Not that unpredictable,' Baldur said. 'Besides, the

fewer bodies we strew about, the more kindly a judge will look upon us, should we fail.'

'I do not intend to fail,' Grok said firmly, making the last checks on several small pieces of electronics he'd bought and modified for their mission.

'I am ready,' he said, draping bits of weaponry about his frame.

'Then shall we go on about our business?' Baldur said, doing the same.

King started the lim's drive, and the other three clambered in.

The warehouse door slid open, and Jasmine took the lim out at a slow hover, then lifted into the darkening sky.

They flew out of Tormal's capital keeping to traffic lanes, and within specified height/speed limits.

No one in the lim spoke, caught in their own thoughts.

Riss's mouth was dry, as it always was before action.

'Ten minutes to the prison,' Jasmine announced.

'My systems are ready,' Grok said.

Minutes crawled past.

'Go into your act, Jasmine,' Baldur said.

King keyed a mike.

'Anybody . . . help! Help! My driver's collapsed, and I can't fly this thing! Help! Oh, please, help!'

The com began squawking as various samaritans tried to cut in. Jasmine ignored them.

'Oh, help! I see . . . there's some kind of building ahead of me . . . I'll try to land it on that.'

An overriding blare came:

'This is Tormal Citadel! You are entering a forbidden zone. Identify yourself. Over.'

'Help me, Tormal! I don't know what my lim number is . . . but I can't fly, and I'm afraid to crash! Help!'

'This is Tormal Citadel. I repeat, you are entering a forbidden zone, and will be fired upon if you do not change your flight pattern.'

'I don't know how to do it!' Jasmine moaned, letting a note of panic creep carefully into her voice. 'Oh, please, don't shoot me! I don't want to die!'

'They're ranging on us,' Grok said. 'Proximity five kilometers.'

But Tormal Citadel stayed silent for a moment.

'As I said, robots perplex easily,' Baldur said. 'But you might want to perplex them a little more, Grok.'

'Oh, help me,' Jasmine said, artfully playing with the controls, and the lim obediently flopped from side to side, clearly in the hands of an incompetent pilot.

Grok touched three sensors, and a blast of static roared across the standard emergency frequencies, further confusing the situation.

A second device, originally intended to intensify radar imagery, went on. After Grok's fiddling, it now cast three images of the lim toward the prison.

A third, a dopplering device used in model aircraft competition to spoof tracking missiles, now power-jumped, 'cast artificial "window" in their flight path.

'Two minutes, maybe,' Jasmine said.

Over the static-wave, they dimly heard Tormal Citadel broadcast something.

But they never knew what it was, as the lim came down fast, dead center over the roof, and banged in for a landing.

Riss, Grok, and Baldur piled out, ran toward the gun turrets. As they'd hoped, the guns – a multiple-barreled auto cannon in each turret – had cutoffs installed, so no eager robot could shoot his fellow turret apart.

Baldur and Grok had small necklace charges around their necks. They flattened against the turrets, and draped a charge around the gun barrel, pulled a fuse. Grok thundered back to the lim as Baldur planted a second necklace charge, then followed him.

Riss had a larger coil of explosives, and wound it around the base of the fourth turret. She, too, set her fuse and doubled back to the lifter.

'Off and keep it very, very close,' she said, as she jumped back in the lim, and the door slid down.

Jasmine nodded, intent on the controls. She lifted the lim clear, slid it to the edge of the roof, and over the edge.

A blast of gunfire went overhead as two turrets tried vainly to depress their guns enough to reach her.

M'chel's eyes were on her watch's sweep second.

'And eight . . . six . . . four . . . three . . . two . . . bang.'

There were actually four bangs, three moderate, the fourth quite impressive.

King, needing no orders, took the lim back to the roof.

The damage was impressive.

Three of the turrets had their gun barrels blown off. The fourth had been torn out of the steel-and-concrete roof, and had vanished somewhere overside.

There were bits of the cannon's breech still intact, and, clearly, stairs leading down into the fortress.

'Just call me ebenemae!' Riss said. 'Do I know how to open a can, or what?'

No one bothered to answer. King got out of the lim, and crouched behind a ventilator, blaster ready.

The other three pulled on gas masks, slid headsets and throat mikes into place, and ran hard for the hole where a gun turret had been, and down its stairs.

All of them had small charges looped around their necks, guns in hand.

'About here,' Riss said, and slapped a charge against a door.

The three went down half a flight, and the charge went off, spinning the door into a hallway.

They ran back up, and into the corridor, ignoring the ENTRANCE FORBIDDEN sign.

They came to a pair of doors. One said: CONDEMNED PRISONER SECTION. ABSOLUTELY NO ADMITTANCE.

Riss blew the door open, and they ran down another corridor.

At the end of the corridor was a steel capsule, and in it, a man. He was speaking into a microphone.

Riss and Baldur knelt, launchers aimed, and fired at the capsule's window. Grenades arced out, crashed through the not very bulletproof glass, and went off. The guard grabbed his throat, convulsed, went down.

The raiders went down the hall, and Baldur dragged the guard's body out of the control capsule.

'About like other installations I have . . . hem, read about,' he said, fingers flying over sensors.

He pressed his mask close against the microphone the guard had been using, twisted a selector to a position marked CELLBLOCK.

'Inmates, get away from your doors,' he said. 'Goodnight, get moving!'

He jumped back out of the capsule, as a central door opened.

There were rows of cells, their doors sliding open.

Bewildered men and women, some half-dressed, stumbled out.

One of them was the man Riss recognized as Chas Goodnight.

'Let's haul!' she ordered.

'Right. But what about—'

A door came open, and a guard stepped out, gun in hand.

'Shit,' Riss muttered, kneeling, blaster up, in two hands.

She shot him in the chest, saw him fall, and she and Goodnight were running back to where Grok and Balaur waited.

'What about them?' Goodnight managed, jerking a thumb at the other prisoners.

'Good confusion factor,' Riss said.

They went back down the corridor past the control capsule, reached the door just as a stair door opened and four guards came out.

Very suddenly Chas Goodnight became a blur. Riss's gun was lifted, the guards' blasters were leveled. The blur smashed into one guard; spun, another was down; knocking a third sideways, and a fourth's neck snapped, the crack very loud to Riss's ears.

The blur came back beside them, then resolved into Chas Goodnight.

Riss one-handed a gas grenade off her harness, held one sensor down, pushed the other, and tossed the grenade into the midst of the sprawled men.

They went up the stairs into the shattered turret, were on the roof, pelting toward the waiting lim.

King was up, behind the controls as they rolled in, the lim already lifting clear of the roof.

She sent the lim diving off the roof, down into the valley below, then, at full, burn-out-the-drive-who-gives-a-rat's nostril speed, toward the small city where a well-paid merchant skipper was holding his ship on a ten-minute tick, supposedly awaiting last-minute orders from the ship's owner.

Riss was breathing as if oxygen was a new, delightful experience.

She unclipped her harness, sagged back on the seat, considered their prize.

Chas Goodnight was equally slumped against the jumpseat.

Even bearded and not that clean, Riss had to admit he was one of the more handsome men she'd seen.

He noted her attention, and smiled gently.

'Now, what I could do to a steak or three,' he said, and Riss's slightly romantic thoughts died.

Baldur must have been reading her expression, for he chortled.

'Thanks,' Goodnight said. 'I owe you.'

'That is correct,' Grok said.

'So what do I do to pay you back?'

'Nothing much.' Riss said. 'Just give us a good job recommendation.'

TEN

'This,' Friedrich von Baldur said, 'is a hell of a place.'

'Little joke?' Grok said. 'I think I have read someplace that Sheol equals hell?'

'Little joke,' M'chel agreed. 'Very little.'

Chas Goodnight was staring out at what the Foleyites, or however they labeled themselves, called the outskirts of a city.

Sheol. Population 5,000, days. Who knew how many, or was sober/straight enough to count nights?

If Sheol ever had a city planning board, they were never among those who were straight. Sheol grew as it grew, and no one cared, since the minute the lodes went dry, the miners would move on. Sheol's population would drop to five senile prostitutes, four bartenders with delirium tremens, three arteriosclerotic retired miners, two historians and one city manager.

Here were shacks, with large signs: LET US ASSAY, SELL YOUR SAMPLES; ADVANCE ON GOOD SAMPLES; GRUBSTAKE YOU AGAINST YOUR NEXT BIG STRIKE; and, as always in any mining town: PAWNSHOP. WE'LL TAKE CARE OF YOUR VALUABLES WHILE YOU'RE PROSPECTING.

There were lots with battered ships, some of which might actually be practical for mining, supply houses with used gear from those who'd guessed wrong, and new supplies for those who hadn't guessed at all yet.

Here and there were houses of the few citizens in service industries not battening off the asteroids.

As their rented lifter got closer to what passed for city center, there were streets entirely devoted to various forms of sin.

In the middle of one such blinking, flashing row of iniquities, some of which were yet to be invented, sat, like a prim maiden with her legs crossed in a whorehouse: MINER'S AID SOCIETY.

There appeared to be no one inside.

'Now this,' Baldur announced heartily, 'is my kind of place.' A delicate pink tongue came out, touched his lips. 'It smells of credits. Loose credits, just waiting to leap into our pockets.'

Reg Goodnight stared in incredulity.

'But I thought you were—'

'Rumors of my execution,' Chas said dryly, 'were thankfully exaggerated.' He looked across the desk, only approximately big enough to land a starship on, then around the paneled suite. 'Well aren't you gonna leap into your brother's arms, or go kill a prodigal sheep or whatever it was?'

Reg came around the desk, and embraced his brother.

M'chel thought it took a bit of study to tell the two men were related. They had the same lank bone structure, the same lean build. But where Chas's face was weatherbeaten, with easy smile lines, Reg clearly didn't get out in the open much, and he'd started to go a bit to fat. He was also balding a bit, and his fingernails were well dined on.

Where Chas wore a shirt and trousers an engineer or outdoorsman might choose, Reg was most carefully tailored and trimmed.

He looked exactly like what he was — a very sharp executive, who was also very harried.

He turned away from his brother, wiping his eyes with the back of his hand.

'You said,' he said to Baldur, 'that you had a surprise, and that it was personal. But I never dreamed—'

'That's the best kind of surprise, isn't it?' Riss said.

'Well, yes. Yes, of course,' Reg said, almost stammering. He turned back to Chas. 'How did you get out?'

'These people were kind enough to rescue me.'

'Well, thank you,' Reg managed. 'Thank you from the bottom of my heart. I assume you didn't do it for charity, and I'll be happy to meet any fee you want, to the limits of my resources.'

'We do not want any credits from you,' Baldur said. 'Only from Transkootenay.'

Goodnight turned suddenly cold, and now M'chel could definitely see the resemblance between the two brothers.

'Go on,' he said, voice flat, neutral.

'Should we have been more subtle?' Grok asked.

'Why?' Baldur said. 'There were no witnesses, and I was carrying an anti-bug.'

'That is not what I meant,' Grok said.

'I think what our furred friend means,' M'chel said, 'is should we have put it less blatantly than "in return for your brother's ass, we'd like to be at the top of the list for your security contract"?'

'Why?' Baldur asked again. 'We do not tart around; we do not expect him to do so either.'

M'chel looked at Grok, shrugged.

'Hell if I know if Freddie blew the pitch,' she said. 'I've never done this kind of business before, either.'

'Perhaps we should have let his brother negotiate?' Grok tried.

'That's a terrible idea,' M'chel said. 'We don't know if Chas has a silver tongue, and, as far as we know, as soon as we give him leave, he'll be off on his galaxy-wide thieving and couldn't give a rat's elbow if we starve.'

'Bit of a pity,' Baldur said. 'We could use someone of his talents.'

'Speaking of which,' M'chel said, 'where is our bouncing young bester tonight?'

'Out,' Baldur said. 'He asked Jasmine if she wanted to help him find a place where you might not be ptomained to death.'

'Just a lonely guy,' M'chel said. 'Wanting to keep a lonely gal from being lonely.'

She snickered. Chas Goodnight, on the flight from Tormal, had made it clear he was interested in Riss, and wouldn't mind waking up next to her at all.

Riss, being a polite sort, hadn't said that she'd had her days of pretty boys, and generally looked for a bit more these days, and had fobbed him off with the excuse she never fooled around on a job.

She also hadn't given her real reason, which was that on the flight she'd talked enough to Goodnight for her initial interest to fade, and to start thinking Chas had the moral makeup of a spider.

'With Jasmine?' Grok said. 'Now that might answer a question I've had.'

'Which is?'

'Whether or not she is a robot. I may have erred when I told Goodnight, when he asked where she'd come from, that Cerberus was her former employer, which service she left because they think her to be a robot.'

'What would sex have to do with it?' M'chel asked.

'Couldn't a robot – which I don't think Jasmine is – be programmed to screw like a mink?'

They were sitting very close together in a booth of a rather plush restaurant. The meal had been horrendously expensive, if not much more than adequate, and the wines had been worse.

Chas Goodnight leaned over, and gently nibbled on Jasmine King's earlobe.

'That feels nice, Chas,' she said, in her perfect voice. 'But it won't get you anywhere.'

'Why not?' Chas said seductively. 'Don't you want to be the first to help this poor boy recover from his near-death experience? Lovemaking is one of the best ways to reaffirm humanity.'

'That's true,' she said.

'Not to mention that'd be a great way for me to express my thanks to you for saving me.'

'That's true, as well,' Jasmine said. 'But no.'

'Why not?' Chas flushed, realizing he was sounding like a pouty adolescent.

'Because is enough of a reason, isn't it?'

'Well . . . I guess so.' Goodnight drank wine, tried again. 'You know, I studied robots some time ago.'

'That must have been interesting,' King said blandly.

'It was. Especially the Prime Directives.'

'In what way?'

'Remembering the First Directive,' Chas said. 'How is it? "A robot may not injure a human being or, through inaction, allow a human being to come to harm."'

'So?'

'Well, a psyche deprived is a damaged psyche, and therefore its owner would be harmed.'

'So?' King said again.

'Well, if a robot, say, were an incredibly lovely woman,

and she didn't want to make love to a good-looking man, thereby harming him, wouldn't that be a violation of the First Directive?'

'Yikh,' Jasmine said, drinking her wine and refilling it from the bottle in the bucket. 'Who would want to go to bed with a robot, anyway?'

'You didn't answer my question,' Chas purred.

'But what if that robot didn't have the First Directive?' Jasmine asked. 'Or the other two either?'

'That . . . that'd be impossible! All societies require robots to have the Three Laws programmed into them.'

'*All* societies?' Jasmine asked.

'Everyone that I've heard of does,' Goodnight said.

'And you've heard of every culture that happens to synthesize artificial beings? *Every* culture?'

Goodnight looked deeply into her eyes. They were clear, deceit free. But he felt a shiver touch his spine.

Jasmine smiled again.

'Besides, if I have to be honest with you, and I truly don't mean to hurt your feelings,' she said, patting his hand, 'I never go to bed with a man who's not as smart as I am.'

Goodnight looked amazed. 'But I've got a near-genius intelligence level.'

'Which you don't use.'

'What do you mean?'

'One instance,' Jasmine said. 'You got caught stealing, and were thrown out of the army. You got caught again, and were about to be strangled.

'Yet you propose to keep on the same track, even though your record hardly suggests you've made a successful career choice.'

Goodnight, his romantic mood shattered, glowered at her.

'You see?' Jasmine said. 'Not only won't you listen to

logic, but you insist on letting your ego get all bruised and battered in the process.'

'What do you want me to do?' Goodnight said. 'Join you people or something?'

She patted his cheek.

'You could do much, much worse.'

'I've decided,' Reg Goodnight said, 'to reconsider my original options for Transkootenay's security provider.

'I'll be honest, since there's only the five of you present, and admit a bit of my decision had to do with my brother deciding to join Star Risk, Ltd..

'Not to mention that Cer – one of the other security services I invited to bid on this project has been most dilatory in providing me with a prospectus.

'And your offer was most reasonable.

'I propose that I, meaning Transkootenay Mining, offer Star Risk, Ltd., a tentative contract for six months service. You can have your lawyers go over the contract as soon as it's drawn up, assuming you accept the general terms, but, in brief, I propose to offer you a traditional "no cure, no pay" contract.

'However, I do realize this is an expensive contract. The raiders are costing us a minimum of five million credits per day, which is intolerable, even for a company the size of Transkootenay.

'You'll be given half a million credits per diem, plus full expenses to the tune of two million credits per diem, said expenses to be vetted by Transkootenay's business office, for a period of six E-months, during which time you are to attempt to discover these criminals who are attacking Transkootenay Mining, its employees and representatives, destroying Transkootenay's equipment, and stealing valuable resources that are the legal property of Transkootenay Mining, as attested by a legally binding contract between Transkootenay Mining, and the Foley System Government.

'At the end of that time, this contract may be renewed, in six E-month intervals.

'Satisfactory completion of this contract will be rewarded with a minimum of ten million credits, plus bonuses for exceptional or early completion of the task.

'These sums will be paid by the Foley System Government, routed through Transkootenay Mining.

'Welcome aboard,' Reg Goodnight said sincerely.

'And may you do Transkootenay as much good as you have my brother.'

ELEVEN

An N-space transmission, coded with one-time-only pad:

UNWORRY ONE RISK. FOR UNKNOWN REASON TRANSKOOT IGNORED CERBERUS OFFER, SIGNED SECURITY PACT WITH UNKNOWN SMALLIE. NEW FIRM LACKS SHIPS OPS LOCAL INTEL. PLAN SOONEST OPS TO PUT THEM IN PLACE. HAVE AT LEAST SIX MONTHS TO CONTINUE AS PLANNED WITHOUT REAL INTERFERENCE.

TWELVE

The onscreen ship looked like a flattened pyramid, with its electronics suite mounted in two winglets stretching ahead of the central control area. Delta wings, for operation in-atmosphere jutted from the back third of the fuselage, and there were four enormous drive tubes.

'Eighteen *Pyrrhus*-class patrol ships, plus spares, and so on and so forth,' the young saleswoman said, trying to keep the excitement out of her voice. It had been a very dead day for sales before Friedrich von Baldur came into her office.

'Chamkani Starship Systems is delighted to be doing business with you,' she said. 'So, as a free bonus, we'll throw in any auxiliary ship you choose.'

Baldur smiled. 'Yes, I was advised your firm has such a generous policy, which is one reason I came here.

'I think I would like that converted transport at the back of the yard, the *Corsair*, I believe it is?'

The woman touched sensors on her screen.

Something that was either an ocarina carved by a deranged misanthrope or a starship appeared. Its control area sat atop the bulbous mass which narrowed down to a surprisingly small drive area.

'Yes, sir. Uh . . . that's a rather unusual craft,' she said. 'It was listed as a transport on the Alliance Registry, but it was actually an illegal conversion, done by a certain admiral, who was relieved in disgrace when he was discovered. It's most palatial on the inside, and mostly roboticized.'

'So what makes that undesirable, Miss Winlund?' Baldur asked.

'It's described here as rather wallowy inatmosphere, and its drive isn't adequate for the listed Gross Registered Tonnage, sir.'

'I do not plan on taking it racing, but rather to use as a headquarters for myself and my staff.'

'There's another thing. I probably shouldn't be telling you this, but I appreciate your order, and would hope to have further business in the future. It's considered unlucky.'

'How so?'

'After it was salvaged out by the Alliance, three of its five subsequent owners were plagued with an astonishing amount of trouble.'

'I believe you make your own luck,' Baldur said. 'But to get out from under the curse, I shall rename it.

'The *Boop-Boop-A-Doop* rings a bell inside me. It is an old Arabic phrase, meaning good luck to all.'

The saleswoman's eyes widened in surprise, then she recovered.

'*Boop-Boop-A-Doop* it shall be, sir. I'll have our repair shop replate the hull, and I'll put through a change of name with the registry.'

'Excellent,' Baldur said.

'Now, how will we handle the financial details?'

'Billing should be made to Transkootenay Mining in the Foley System, on the planet Mfir,' Baldur said. 'Their electronic address is—'

'Thank you, sir,' Winlund said. 'But I already have it here on my computer. Since we're the largest previously owned ship dealers in this sector, we've done business with the Transkootenay people on Mfir before.

'Will you be needing any assistance crewing up the patrol ships?'

'No,' Baldur said. 'Peace having broken out all over, we should have no troubles at all in that area.'

'Let's see now,' Riss mused. 'We'll need two thousand of those ship-to-ship missile systems. Can you provide them with a universal mounting and guidance system?'

'Ma'am,' the salesman said. 'For that size of an order, I'll design and build one myself. What else?'

'About the same number of your infantryman's basic armament and harness system, with five units of fire and grenades per system.

'A hundred heavy crew-served autocannon, with ten units of fire.'

'What about uniforms?' the salesman asked.

'I doubt if we could get our people to wear them,' M'chel said. 'Two hundred long-distance portable com systems.'

She thought. 'I suppose that should be all. I'll want them shipped ASAP to Star Risk, Ltd., the city of Sheol the world of Mfir, Foley System.'

'I'll get the invoice ready,' the salesman said, and bustled away.

'Quite a lot of death and mayhem there,' Chas Goodnight observed. He'd been silently watching the transaction.

'It should do,' Riss said. 'At least for a beginning.'

'So we're going to sell the miners these,' Goodnight said. 'What'll be the markup?'

M'chel considered. 'Fifteen percent on top of the price and transport should be enough.'

'If we wait until there's a couple of bodies bouncing

around,' Goodnight said, 'we can charge an obscene amount, plus fifty percent.'

'Fifteen percent will be enough,' Riss said firmly.

Goodnight shook his head.

'I'm not sure I approve of all this honesty going about lately.'

THIRTEEN

The port irised open, showing the strange colors of N-space for a moment, then they vanished, and there was the less stomach-wrenching hard glitter of stars and blackness of normal space as the liner dropped out of star drive.

Grok and King were one of the few passengers in the liner's main lounge, which was all old-fashioned red leather and fake wood paneling.

The other passengers were in their cabins, packing their bags, getting customs slips ready, or milling impatiently about the passageways near the locks.

The liner was luxurious and huge, but, since it stopped at the Foley System, obviously was that sector's puddlejumper, and was a little shopworn.

The steward approached with a tray, served Jasmine a blue foaming liqueur in a tulip glass, Grok a cream cake and water.

'To your health,' King said, lifting her glass.

'I did not know you could toast with a sweet,' Grok said.

'You're an alien. You can do anything you want.'

Grok grunted, adjusted his great bulk against the pillows of the couch he half lay on.

'Not true,' he said. 'The maid, when she came to make up our suite, gave me the strangest look.'

'She thought we were sleeping together,' King said.

'Why would we want to do something like that?' Grok wondered. 'These bunks they provided are small enough. I'm thankful you insisted we not book normal cabins.'

'I didn't mean we were sleeping together when I said she thought we were sleeping together,' King said dryly.

'Oh. You meant . . . what an odd concept,' Grok said. 'I doubt if our reproductive systems would be compatible.'

'Probably not,' King said, grinning.

'A small problem I am still having,' Grok said, devouring the last of the cream cake and licking his fingers. 'I do not understand just why you wanted me to come with you. I know little about hiring starship pilots, particularly those knowledgeable about ship-to-ship fighting.'

'You could call it what the old seafarers called "makee-learnee," but in reality I don't know much more about hiring fighter jocks than you do. But I have a name to track down who does know,' Jasmine King said. 'Another reason you could be here is to ensure I don't spend too much of the firm's credits on this liner, wallowing in the lap of luxury.

'But the real reason is to protect me.'

'From what?'

'From starship pilots.'

'Now I'm truly lost,' Grok said. 'Why would someone who is offering an unemployed flier a well-paying job, presumably at the task he loves, need protection?'

'You don't know pilots,' King said. 'I'll give you what used to be called a koan to meditate on.'

'I am familiar with koan,' Grok said. 'My race reads and contemplates many philosophers other than their own.'

'How do you keep a rocket flier from talking?' Jasmine asked.

'Am I to contemplate just that?'

'No. There's an answer,' King said. 'Tie his hands.'

Grok furrowed his already severely wrinkled brow, stared out of the great lounge viewport at the world they were approaching after their final jump.

'I do not get it.'

Before Jasmine could answer, Grok pointed out.

Flashing toward the liner was a vee-formation of small fighting ships, clearly attacking. Grok reacted in shock.

'But the Alliance is not at war with anyone that I—'

A speaker came on.

'All passengers,' a voice said calmly. 'We are approaching Boyington, preparing to make planetfall. As is usual, various freelance fliers are practicing their tactics on this ship. Do not be alarmed. I say again, do not be alarmed. We are in no danger.' The speaker should have keyed his mike off then. Instead, it stayed on for a moment, long enough for 'unless the silly bastards go and ram . . .'

Then the speaker went dead.

Jasmine started laughing.

'I cannot protect you, even though I am of a size,' Grok said, 'against spaceships.'

'You're not expected to.'

'Then . . . ?' Grok let his voice trail off.

'Never mind. You'll see once we're on the ground.'

'You have dealt with the people of this world before?'

'Never,' Jasmine said. 'I just assume all pilots are the same.'

Boyington might have been designed for pilots. Or not designed at all. A young planet, its central continent was mostly flat, weather temperate, seasons not particularly variable. The settlements were scattered here and there, with plenty of room for landing fields, firing grounds, and the like.

More important for fliers and their support teams, the citizens of Boyington were very aware of whom they ultimately worked for.

This didn't mean there was any evidence of civic planning . . . the streets were broad, but a house might have a bordello on one side and an engine building shop on the other.

King and Grok unloaded, picked up their luggage, went through a most casual customs, and waved to a lifter.

It was noisy – half a dozen small spitkit scouts were practicing what were still called touch-and-goes, in a time of antigravity, on a field just away from the main landing ground.

'A good hotel,' King said to the lifter pilot. 'After we check in, we'll need transport to the, uh, Bishop Suites.'

'Yes'm.'

'A quiet one,' Grok asked.

The pilot raised her eyebrow.

'Mister, you better get back on that liner if you want *that*.'

Grok grunted, clambered inside. The lifter wobbled mightily, then stabilized.

'Very well then,' he said. 'Damn the torpedoes and on to bedlam.'

'Wittgenstein on a pogo stick,' Grok exclaimed. 'You weren't jesting.'

King nodded, sidestepped a staggering drunk, went on into the hotel's lobby. Grok was behind her. He wore a full weapons belt, with grenade pouches and a holster. King appeared unarmed.

'We might be making a mistake,' she said, over the

roar of half a thousand drunks and fiends, and two bands, each playing a totally different kind of music. 'Today's the day the Alliance disability and pension checks arrive, so everyone's celebrating. But at least I'm pretty sure we can find our man here.'

'They do this every time they receive a check?' Grok said, watching a half-naked blond woman chase a completely naked blond man, pursued by a baying pack of men and women in flight coveralls.

Scattered around the room were other, nonhuman fliers, evidently content to watch mankind make an ass of itself.

'Every E-month,' King said, 'from what I heard.'

'How can their livers and eardrums stand up to it?'

A man roared up to her, shouting, 'And now, my lovely, you've met your dream match.' His flight suit was unzipped to his waist.

King sidestepped him, and nodded to Grok. The alien grabbed the man by the neck of his suit, whirled him twice overhead, and let go. Man and suit parted ways along his trajectory, and he vanished, screaming, into a knot of swirling pilots.

'As to your question,' King shouted, 'they don't worry about the future. Evidently the Alliance tests people for imagination before they let them into flight school. If you can envision flying into a cement cloud, or running out of fuel a thousand meters above your destination . . . you're out.

'Come on. Surely someone at the bar will know our man.'

She pushed her way toward the long bar, where at least fifteen octopoidal barkeeps were kept at a frenzied pace.

A man she'd pushed turned around, fists coming up. He saw King, and his eyes widened, and he extended his arms.

King ducked under them, was at the bar. A bartender came over, and she asked him something Grok couldn't make out over the din. He scratched his chin, then pointed.

She nodded thanks, passed a bill across, fought her way back out to Grok.

'He's in the Quiet Bar,' she said. 'Over there. On the other side of those idiots.'

Those idiots were a gauntlet of pilots of various sexes. Non-fliers were being ramrodded through the line, being groped, fondled, propositioned, and such. A few of them seemed to be enjoying it.

'I don't like that,' King said. 'Ask them to mind their manners.'

Grok moved a head up and down, growled, growl rising to a maniacal scream louder even than the bands, and he charged the line, arms windmilling.

It may not have been pretty, but it worked. Fliers scrambled or were knocked away. Others went down and were trampled.

The gauntleteers suddenly decided their sport wasn't that interesting, and scrambled for safety.

King strolled through the momentary open space, and into the Quiet Bar, Grok following.

'You notice,' he rumbled, 'I did not have to reach for a single weapon?'

'How pacifistic of you,' King said.

The Quiet Bar at least had no band. But it was a roar of conversations:

'. . . came down like owl shit from thirty grand, and they were still getting into their damned interceptors, so I double-launched, climbed back up, and . . .'

'. . . heard for certain the new McG Destructor'll be picked up by the Alliance as the standard light fighting ship, as soon as it quits blowing drives . . .'

'. . . I guess you *could* go for the contract, if you don't mind a quiet life. Nothing but bandits in the hills, they say . . .'

'. . . so the first thing you'd better do if you end up in one of those beasts is make sure the goddamned escape mechanism is set for humans. Otherwise, it'll blow you sideways through the frigging bulkhead, which'll sure as hell ruin the rest of your day . . .'

'. . . it's a sure buy, my friend. Specified right here no humans need apply, which means for you and me that . . .'

Grok noticed that, as in Jasmine's koan, everyone, indeed, was moving his hands around, as if they were aircraft.

King leaned over the bar, and the barkeep swiveled one of his heads toward her.

'Looking for Redon Spada.'

'Over there,' and the barkeep waved a tentacle.

Grok peered through the crowd to see what this perihelion of pilots might look like.

He'd expected some tall human, blondhaired, square of jaw, whose flight suit would be blazoned with dozens of unit patches, and momentoes of obscure, near-suicidal missions. She or he would be drinking in heroic fashion, perhaps yards of real Earth ale, shooting them back with raw alk boiling in dry ice.

Instead there was a slender, dark-haired man, wearing old-fashioned glasses. He wore a dark blue set of coveralls, and there were no patches on it. He was drinking what appeared to be a cup of tea, and carefully reading a sheaf of printouts.

'Uh . . . Mr. Spada?' King asked.

The man rose politely.

'I am he,' he said. 'Would you care to join me?'

Jasmine introduced herself and Grok, and sat down.

Grok saw a heavy bar stool that looked as if might bear his weight, lifted it over, and sat, towering over the two humans.

'I must assume you're not here because you're attracted by my devilishly handsome features,' Spada said.

King smiled, passed a business card across.

He studied it, nodded thoughtfully.

'You know, three E-months ago, I was so broke I was afraid I'd have to do something suicidal, such as reenlist, or take a job at a flight school.

'Now I have an offer from some police force somewhere to head up their skyspy program, another from some rather desperate rebels somewhere, and now you. Might I have the details?'

'I have eighteen Pyrrhus class patrol craft,' King said. 'I need pilots and the rest to go with them.'

'P-boats, eh?' Spada said. 'Perhaps not my first choice to use when looking for trouble . . . but I've flown worse. Far worse.

'Perhaps you'll give me a sitrep on your troubles?'

King obeyed, telling him about the Foley System.

'Interesting' Spada said. 'Quite interesting. What's the pay?'

'Five thousand an E-month. Cash. Not reported to any Alliance officials. Good for six months minimum. Bonuses when we win. Full insurance, and death benefits.'

'*When* you win. Not if. I like that approach,' Spada said.

'About these bandits. You've no idea what they want? Assuming they're not just plain gun-in-the-guts-for-your-credits types.'

'We don't know anything about them yet. Grok here is our SigInt specialist, so he'll be setting up various monitors.

'You'll be charged with keeping the miners and Transkootenay Mining as safe as you can, and finding out where these bandits base themselves out of.

'When you do, we'll launch a full strike against them.'

'I like the way you put that "as safe as you can,"' Spada said. 'That would suggest you know the realities of being able to patrol an entire asteroid belt with only eighteen ships.

'Since you don't know much about these bandits, may I assume they most likely look like everybody else in the Foley System?'

'They are human,' King said positively. 'At least all reports of contact say that.'

'Which means,' Spada said, 'we also must worry about infiltrators, spies, saboteurs, double agents and such.'

'That brings me to the second item,' King said. 'We'll need crews for these ships besides the pilots. Plus we'll need ground support – maintenance, supply, logistics, security, and the rest.

'We can't afford the fat an Alliance squadron would have. You have a budget of seven hundred and fifty thousand credits a day.'

Spada nodded. 'That's not much, these days,' he said. 'But on the other hand, these days there's a welter of ramp rats to be had. There's no problem with that.

'You sound like you're most experienced, Miss King. I suppose there's little benefit to be gained by bargaining.'

'You can try,' King said. 'But I truly think you'll be wasting your time.

'And there are others here on Boyington who have the Galactic Cross.'

'There are,' Spada said. 'But none of them are as pretty as I am.'

He was about to say more when a flier stumbled, fell toward the table.

Grok didn't see Spada move. But the drunk was somehow caught, and pitched sideways, to thud down on the floor.

'I *do* despise policemen,' Spada said, as if the incident hadn't happened. 'And rebels have a terrible tendency to not meet the payroll on time.

'Give me a day to consider. Then I'll be in touch, either way. I see you put your hotel's com number on your card.

'It might just be a pleasure doing business.'

FOURTEEN

The man backflipped out of the door, skidded on the rough aggregate that made up sort of a street, sat up groggily. He wore moccasins, the bottom half of an orbital spacesuit, nothing else.

'I told you once,' the voice from inside the Dew Drop Inn boomed, 'I on'y drink with people I like. There ain't no second warning.'

The voice was deep, resounding, but quite female.

The miner bleared at the door to the bar, blinked twice, then sighed and curled up for a nap in mid-street.

Riss and Baldur looked at each other doubtfully.

'Perhaps we should have brought Grok,' Baldur said. 'I am definitely opposed to combat as a recreational pastime.'

'You and me both,' Riss agreed. 'So don't stand in my way when I start running.'

'It might well be the other way around,' Baldur suggested, and they went in.

The bar was pretty standard for any workingman's joint: There were beer pumps every three meters; alk dispensers between them, the alcohol and beer reserves safely stowed somewhere beyond brawling range; and half a dozen barkeeps, all chosen for size, combativeness, and ability to talk away a fight, or be the first to swing a meter-long club as a last resort.

The only nonstandard item was an animated panel overhead, showing the asteroid belt, and blinking lights for settlements or mines.

The Inn had half a dozen men and women peaceably playing chess, either conventional or three-dee in the back, and one woman at the long bar.

She was a little less than a meter and two-thirds, in any direction. She wore her hair cropped short, as did most miners for convenience, a one-piece ship's coverall, and heavy boots.

In front of her was a plas bottle, half-full of a clear alcohol, a small vial with a tiny spoon, half a dozen twisted cheroots, and a glass of water.

Riss and Baldur bellied up, ordered brandy, water back, were served.

M'chel glanced at the woman.

'You wouldn't be L. C. Doe, by chance?'

'I am . . . and not by chance. A damned fine name I picked myself.'

'Buy you a drink?'

'Sure. Buy you a snort?' Doe rolled the small vial down the bar.

Riss hesitated, then opened the jar, took out a spoonful, inhaled.

She jerked a little.

'Pure quill,' Doe said. 'I'm tight with th' quack that makes it.'

Riss blinked, took a deep breath.

'Makes your heart go.'

'Makes *everyt'ing* go,' Doe said. 'At least, until you run out, and then everyt'ing is real, real slow.'

'Maybe I'll just stick to the one,' Riss decided. She passed the vial to Baldur.

'I better not,' Baldur said. 'I get nosebleeds quite easily.'

'Well, hooty-tooty,' Doe said, and took a noseful of the drug. 'I assume you came in looking for me.'

'We did.'

'Did you see that buttbreath I pitched out into the street?'

'We did.'

'When I'm on a toot, I generally don't like to deal with anybody. So, meaning no offense, unless you want to talk inconsequentials, take a hike.'

'It's about the Miner's Aid. Which you're president of.'

'Aw, shit!' Doe snarled. 'Goddamned business. But . . .' She looked down the bar. 'Bennie, gimme a sober.'

The bartender reached under the bar, took out a tiny bottle, and handed it to Doe.

'Damned shame,' she muttered. 'To have to go and spoil t'is nice, building high. But . . .'

She opened the bottle, drained it.

Doe shuddered, shook, and Riss thought for a moment smoke was going to roil out her ears. Her eyes reddened, and she swallowed hastily twice.

'All the joys of a hangover in ten seconds,' she muttered after a while. 'Plus a detox to boot.'

She swallowed again.

'It better be damned fine business, all I can say.'

'I don't know about fine,' Riss said. 'But it's important.'

She introduced herself, Baldur.

Doe examined them carefully.

'Maybe we better go find a quiet corner,' she decided. 'I assume I can drink a beer without it getting in the way of t'ings.'

Riss drained her brandy, tapped the top of the glass with a forefinger, and Bennie refilled her glass. He waved the bottle at Baldur, who shook his head no.

They found a table, away from the chess players.

'You notice I'm bein' particularly kindly,' Doe said. 'Here you are, Transkootenay's goons, and I'm talking to you, instead of pitching you out the door.'

'Which you could *try* to do,' Riss said.

Doe lifted her massive eyebrows.

'Girlie, are you calling me?'

'Nope,' Riss said. 'Just putting in a notice that I don't get pushed a lot.'

Doe considered.

'Now, a few minutes ago, I would've had your ass out in the alley. But now . . . especially since you've got business . . . we'll set matters aside. Besides, I t'ink I could take you, but you got a look in your eye suggesting I'd need a bit of repair myself.

'So set t'at aside. Although, I got to warn you, if you two are gonna suggest that what's going on is somehow the fault of Miner's Aid, t'at we're linked up with these high-grader bastards, t'en we'll go back to misunderstanding each other.'

'We are not in the business of wasting time,' Baldur said. 'Ours or anyone else's.'

'So talk,' Doe invited, leaning back, and letting beer slide down her throat. 'Although you note my suspicious nature, since there were a couple of pukes from – what was it? Cerberus something or other – snuffing around, saying t'ey were about to be the muscle in the belt, working for Transkootenay, and wonderin' if maybe us miners were getting cute, trying to drive Transkootenay out, and set up some sort of a Co-op.

'Shit. Transkootenay's not the worst outfit to

contract for, and damn few miners want to take on the headaches of bossin', least of all me. Tried it, hated it.'

'We had not even thought of that,' Baldur lied. 'What we are contracted for is to first provide security for Transkootenay and you miners; second, to find out who these "high-graders," as you call them, are, and deal with them in a manner that seems appropriate.'

'High-spoken gent, ain't he?' Doe said, lighting a ghastly smelling cheroot. 'And kinda cute, for an old fart.'

Riss hid her grin, while Baldur tried to bury his reaction.

'Hokay,' Doe said. 'I got your mission requirements, as t'ey tell me military sorts say. What do you need from us?'

'Not getting into accusations,' Riss said. 'But these bandits, whoever they are, seem to have some intelligence taps into your people.'

'No kid,' Doe said. 'But who it could be, or even where to look, I couldn't guess. Miners work alone, mostly, and when t'ey get in civilization, they run their mouths a lot.'

'If you hear anything, or have any ideas, we would appreciate a com,' Baldur said.

'I ain't experienced at playing counterspy,' Doe said. 'But I'll listen, and if it ain't one of my friends, well we'll see. You want anyt'ing else?'

'We do,' Riss said. 'As Mr. von Baldur said, we also are tasked to provide security for you miners. We'll be providing security flights, but we can hardly make the whole belt safe.

'So what we're proposing is to sell any interested miner a compact ship-to-ship missile system.'

'Holy dragon poop,' Doe said. 'I don't t'ink Transkootenay – or SysGov – are going to be dancing around you dumpin' flower petals when you tell t'em you're arming us dangerous wildasses.'

'We are not proposing to consult them,' Baldur said.

'Also,' Riss continued, 'we'll be selling, at not much over our cost, individual weaponry, and long-range com gear, linked to our command center.

'Later, when we have a target, or think we do, we'll make various autocannon available for site defense.'

'Whoooh,' Doe said reverently. 'You clowns don't screw around.'

'We don't have the time to,' Riss said. 'Now, I need some more skinny on how you miners operate, or, rather, how we can keep these high-graders from getting to you.

'You said you work mostly by yourselves. Would you be willing to pair up, or work in small groups, for better safety?'

'Not a chance,' Doe said firmly. 'We'd be watching everybody else all the time, waiting for t'em to steal our claims. Or trying to steal *their* claims.'

'I kind of thought that'd be the answer,' M'chel said. 'What about the idea of convoying miners to their claims from here, and picking them up when they're ready to come in?'

'That's a big negatory,' Doe said. 'Same t'ing applies.'

'Right,' M'chel said. 'Try an idea of mine. I've gone through the incident reports of miners getting robbed or killed. How long after they stake a claim, which I found out can be done by com to the Transkootenay office here in Sheol, have these women and men been hit?'

'Sumbeech,' Doe said. 'I don't think anybody asked that.'

'Would it be hard to monitor whatever frequency is used, and then go after the miner who's obviously found something interesting?'

'Hell no.'

'Then that's got to be changed,' Riss said. 'Can you convince miners to physically file their claims with Transkootenay, Miss Doe?'

'It's L. C., by the way,' Doe said. 'I can try, and I'd be listened to over some stranger. Especially when I point out t'at could be one way you get killed.'

'What next?'

'A big one,' Riss said. 'The high-graders base themselves somewhere. Nobody knows where. Would your people mind being a little nosy?'

'. . . Miners are pretty nosy anyway,' Doe's voice said from the tiny speaker. 'Problem is, if t'ey get too nosy, somebody's gonna bob it for them. Maybe with a blaster. But I can put the word out.'

There was a pause.

'I still can't believe,' Doe said, 'you're gonna sell us missiles. Real, live, shoot-back-in-anger missiles.'

Riss shut the recorder off, looked around the ultra-plush wardroom of the *Boop* at the other four members of Star Risk.

'That's generally all there is on the tape,' M'chel said. 'Hell if I know if we've got the miners on our side or not.'

'Probably not,' Jasmine said. 'I suspect it'll take something concrete before they get on board with us.'

'Yes,' Baldur agreed. 'Such as having one of these so-called high-graders in hand, while we apply some drug-oriented interrogation to discover what we need.'

'Or else just tying them to a table,' Goodnight said, standing. 'And pulling their frigging toenails out.

'Sorry, people. I'm off.

'Dinner with little brother. I've got a couple of questions to ask.'

'*Do* keep us posted,' Riss said sarcastically.

'I shall, I shall.'

'I, too, have work,' Grok said. 'There are circuits to be cast, SOI's to be written.'

Chas Goodnight boomed laughter. His brother, Reg, joined, ruefully.

'It would've been even funnier,' Reg said, 'if I hadn't been the one the cops came looking for, instead of you.'

'But see,' Chas said, 'I knew you had a solid alibi.'

'Yeah,' Reg said. 'Trying to convince that little redhead . . . I don't even remember her name . . . that she ought to leave the dance with me.'

'I knew she wouldn't,' Chas said. 'If I couldn't get anywhere, why should you be able to?'

'Damned tough assumption,' Reg said, and for an instant his smile vanished, then returned.

'Oh, well,' he said. 'Just part of being a little brother, I guess.'

Chas had noted his expression.

'You aren't still pissed at me for that, are you? If you are, I apologize. I beat my head on the floor.'

'No,' Reg said. 'I'm not angry. I wasn't, not really, even then. I guess I figured out early that big brothers do things like that.'

He poured more wine.

'To tell you the truth, the only time I got angry with you was in my sophomore year at Harvard, when the checks stopped coming.'

'I didn't have any choice,' Chas said. 'That was when they caught me, and the troubles started.'

'I know that,' Reg said. 'But it was a bitch to have

to quit Alpha Tau, and get a job. I never realized what snobs those bastards were – hell, I guess I was as bad – as when they'd come by the laundry, drop off their clothes, and hide their grins at seeing me, once one of them, now just another slavey in the working class.

'I got my revenge, though. Did you know that if you add a certain chemical to piss, take the liquid, and soak a smartass college puke's dress shirt in it, when he starts sweating, like say when he's trying to hustle some sister, that stink just *rolls* on out?'

Both of them broke into laughter.

'Ah, well, ah, well,' Chas said. 'I guess it's a bit of a miracle that we're both on the outside, and you, at least, are rolling in it.'

Reg turned serious.

'I'm doing all right, I guess. But I'm earning every damned credit, especially with these idiots running around killing my miners. And Transkootenay's not the easiest company to work with. They pay you well, but they don't cut you a lot of slack. Screw up, and it's the whisper of the ax.

'And they work your ass off. Look at me, Chas. I'm twenty-nine E-years old. No wife, no children, not even a home of my own. Hell, here on Sheol I don't even have a real girlfriend.'

'Would you *want* one, here on Sheol?

Reg's smile came back.

'Strong point, and maybe I should stop complaining.

'So tell me what you wanted to buy me dinner for?'

'First,' Chas said, 'To see if a big-time operations manager like you could get better service and food out of this joint than the last time I tried.'

He glowered across the restaurant at the maitre d'.

'You could and did, so now I know the hustle. From

now on, I'm Reg Goodnight's brother, and snap it up.

'Seriously, I had a couple of questions. Official type.'

'Go ahead,' Reg said. 'If you can do me one, small, subtle favor.'

'You have but to ask.'

'Well, if you people need things, especially high-item things—'

'Such as bangsticks?' Chas asked, amused.

'Those, but worse were the ships you people bought. I got a rocket from Transkootenay Central tearing my lips off. I had to do some fast explaining.'

'What are we getting into, the old expense account disallowed bullshit?' Chas Goodnight asked. 'I've got to say that kind of thing won't sit well with von Baldur. Or me, come to think about it.'

'No, no,' Reg said hastily. 'You'll still be able to buy whatever, uh, tools you need. But do me a favor, and check with me about suppliers. The company that supplied your ships is someone Transkootenay doesn't deal with, hasn't for some time.

'There's only a few big suppliers like them in this cluster, and we have our favorites.'

'You mean, Transkootenay takes a kickback from.'

'I can't say what Central does,' Reg said. 'I know I don't have my fingers in the till.

'Anyway, go ahead with your questions.'

'These bandits . . . do you have any idea where they operate from?'

'Nary a hint,' Reg said. 'Just like I told Baldur.'

'All right. Now a nasty one, all my very own. Is it possible that they could be tied in with the System Government?'

'Why on earth would they do something like that?'

'Oh,' Chas said, 'maybe they want Transkootenay to

do all the development, then find a way to break your contract, and slither in and collect *all* the geetus.'

Reg started to answer, then stopped himself, and thought.

'I was going to say not a chance, that SysGov wouldn't be thrilled at having to deal with these warty-ass miners. But . . .' He thought again. 'No. I don't think they're that sneaky. Or bright, come to think.'

'There's no sign, from any of the reports, that, say, the baddies are using the same kind of spaceships, or wear the same kind of suits or use the same kind of guns,' Chas persisted, 'like they might be Spec Ops types?

'I'm asking, because I used to do shit like that for the Alliance, and I assume the Foley System has some covert sorts of their own.'

'I don't think so,' Reg said. 'But I'll ship over the raw data on all of the bandit encounters, if you want, and you can go through them. You'd have a better eye for that kind of detail than I would.'

'Last question,' Chas said. 'Who's Transkootenay's contact in SysGov?'

'Why do you ask?'

'I'm grasping at straws,' Chas said.

'It's a woman,' Reg said. 'Good exec. In her fifties. Not a diplomat, but an administrator. Her name's Tan Whitley, and she's head of Offworld Development, on Glace.'

'Thanks.'

Reg looked at his brother carefully.

'Chas, are you going to stay with this Star Risk?'

It was Goodnight's turn to think.

'For the moment, I think so,' he said. 'At least while your ass is in a crack. After that . . .' He shrugged.

'Back to my wild, carefree life of crime, riches and

beautiful women. Especially if something better gets offered.'

'Check me on this for what we should be trying to figure out first,' Baldur told Riss and King.

'First, what is our villains' intelligence network like? We know they have something, since they are able to pick their striking points accurately. Second, are they running any double agents here on Sheol, or on any of the outstations? Third, what is their Signal Intelligence? Fourth, and quite possibly this should be first, what are their ultimate goals?

'Finally, where is their goddamned base?

'Did I miss anything?'

The two women considered.

'For the moment,' Riss said, 'I think that covers it.'

'So then, we shall begin by attempting to provide our miners . . . gad, but I am starting to talk like that paternalistic Reg Goodnight. *Our* miners, indeed. Anyway, we must start providing security for them, which hopefully will also provide openings to begin striking back.

'One other thing I just arrived at. When our Chas returns to the ship, I think I shall sequester him. Very few people, other than his brother, and a scattering of others, know his face.

'I think we should keep it that way. We may need to send a ferret down a rat hole, and I would prefer our ferret be as suspicion free as possible.

'How, where, and when we might do that, I do not have a clue at the moment.'

'But it's not a bad idea,' Riss said.

'I doubt if Chas will like being mewed up,' King said. 'But better a bitter bester than a blown, broken, battered bester. Right?'

'It's settled,' Riss said. 'You are a robot. Nobody human could have made it through that last sentence without breaking her tongue.'

Baldur looked slightly shocked, until King started giggling.

FIFTEEN

M'chel considered the snifter, took it from its gimbal mounting, lifted the stopper, and sniffed.

No. It didn't smell right, which meant it wouldn't taste good, either.

But she still couldn't sleep.

She decided to force a daydream that'd make her doze off, and curled up in one of *Boop-Boop-A-Doop*'s plush captain's chairs, and thought about the ship.

The admiral who'd had it converted to his rather luxurious tastes didn't deserve forced retirement, she thought, and yawned. More like keelhauling.

At least from the perspective of the Alliance taxpayers who'd inadvertently funded this barge.

If there was extravagance left off, she didn't know what it was, from the gold fixtures in all of the freshers, to the jet-tub, covered against spillage if, gods forbid, the *Boop* ever went weightless, to the tapestrylike wall coverings.

Even the control rooms – two, fore and aft – were luxurious. The ship was a little shy on weaponry, having only four chainguns in blisters and a single missile station. But that was all right, she thought.

The whole universe didn't *have* to pack a gun.

Name me a place you've been where one didn't come in handy, her mind challenged.

She hmphed that away, and considered who, if she were rich enough to run this beast as her very own, she'd share it with.

Her list of potential lovers ran out very quickly.

For some reason, she didn't like the idea of navigating it around the galaxy solo.

Face it, Riss. You're getting lonely.

Fine. So, since this is your goddamned daydream, who in your past would you mind playing bunkie with?

She ran back a year, didn't come up with anybody who fit her standards.

Damn, woman. You've been too long with inadequate loving. Perhaps you ought to—

The blast broke her thoughts, and she was on her feet, headed for the forward control room. Whatever it was, it'd been close enough to rock the ship on its landing skids.

She keyed a screen, swept the area, found where the blast had gone off.

Not far outside the yard, somewhere very damned close to Transkootenay's headquarters here on Sheol.

Riss ran for her cabin, slid into a coverall, lifted her always-ready combat harness from a hook on a bulkhead, had it on, picked up the blaster under her bed, and was headed for the lock, fingers automatically loading the weapon.

She was the first, but Goodnight, Baldur, Grok, and then King showed up shortly.

All of them except King were armed, and they went out the lock and down the ramp toward the scream of sirens and the roar of flames.

One of Transkootenay's buildings *had* exploded, and fire cascaded upward.

Baldur saw Reg Goodnight, gazing aghast at the flames, grabbed him by the shoulder.

'What happened?'

'Don't know,' Goodnight said. 'But that's . . . that was . . . the mine claim center. Gone. All gone.'

He was about to say more, then saw a helmeted policeman, carrying a long tube.

'What is it?' he called.

The cop started to ignore the question, then realized who had asked it.

'Some kind of rocket launcher, sir.'

'Let me see it,' Baldur said.

'Do what he says,' Reg said, as the cop hesitated, then passed it over.

'Recognize this?' Baldur asked the others.

'Sure,' Riss said. 'Used ones like it myself. Standard-issue Alliance bunker buster. 90mm, shaped charge. Makes a good-size hole in anything.

'If it's got white phosphorus back of the warhead,' she went on, 'it'll also raise a fire.

'Like this one.'

'Was anyone hurt?' Jasmine King asked.

'We can't find the watchman,' the policeman said. 'Other than that, no.'

'A nice, clean little shot,' Chas Goodnight murmured.

'Indeed,' Baldur said. 'Destroying all records of who owns what piece of real estate, and who is permitted to work that claim. It was a good choice of target, guaranteed to make any miner in the system suddenly realize he has nothing in the way of anything to hold him here.'

He motioned the others away from Reg Goodnight and the cop.

'And I think we can now posit what our opponents' final goal is: to close down Transkootenay's operation, and drive every miner out of the system, I would assume, so that these unknowns can then move in.'

'High-graders one, heroes zero,' Grok said. 'We should think about evening that count as soon as possible.'

SIXTEEN

It was weekend in Sheol and the bars were just warming up to a nice, loose rhythm.

No one was quite sober, no one was totally drunk when the eighteen ships dove in-atmosphere, coming straight down on the city.

They flared a few hundred metes above Sheol into four perfect fingers-four formation, with two other ships on high cover, and came over the city just above the rooftops.

Miners and citizens screamed, dove for cover, even a few prayed, all sure their doom was here, that the raiders were now directly attacking what passed for civilization.

Friedrich von Baldur stood outside the *Boop-Boop-A-Doop*, beaming proudly.

His belt com came to life.

'And how was that?'

Baldur keyed his mike.

'Very fine, Mr. Spada. Very fine, indeed. You've trained your crews well. Now you can bring it on home for a drink.'

'Fine for the others,' Spada's voice came back. 'Ask M'chel for me if this armpit's got anything interesting in the way of teas.

'Come to think, ask her if she wants to go have it with me. She can have alk if she wants.

'Spada, clear.'

As the ships climbed and came back into a classic Immelman, cut from secondary drive to antigrav, and, skids extending, settled in for a landing near the *Boop-Boop-A-Doop*, Sheol realized it was not going to be carpet bombed and strafed.

'Sonnovabitch,' a miner, drunker earlier than most, managed as he gathered Baldur into an embrace:

'We got us a space force!'

The pilots and the two other members of each ship's crew were quartered in a hotel Transkootenay owned.

They were allowed out into the streets, since none of them knew anything specific they could leak.

While they unwound from the series of jumps they'd made to reach the Foley System, Grok and a group of electronics techs went to work.

Each ship had a black box installed. None of the techs knew what the boxes were intended to do, and only Grok tested them to make sure they were operational.

The boxes had started life as Search and Recovery locator beacons, intended to 'cast screams for help when a ship was in trouble. Grok recircuited them so they still 'cast on demand. But instead of a plea for rescue, they broadcast various electronic signatures. These signatures could be varied, from those of mining ships to yachts to merchant vessels to Alliance warships. All of the signatures were quite 'real,' having been stripped from the current *Jane's*.

Riss had tea with Redon Spada, and a very quiet time it was.

'This here's Johnny Behan,' L. C. Doe said to M'chel with some distaste. The man was stocky, with a trimmed beard and hair. There were four others behind him. 'He doesn't drink, at least not to amount to much. And when he does, like these other parygons of virchoo, his mouth doesn't flap.

'I've used them for delicate work for Miner's Aid. They've volunteered to help, without knowing what they're volunteering for, just like you asked.'

'Ladies and gentlemen,' Riss said, 'thanks for your faith. Now you're going to go drinking, on Star Risk's tab. And then you're going to have a nice, quiet, invisible vacation on Glace.

'No risk, no pain, with pay.'

Miners on Sheol were a little surprised when a nice, quiet rock-shifter named Behan started barhopping. He still didn't drink alk, but he frequently took hits from an inhaler, which evidently was enough to put him in low orbit. Other miners asked for a taste, and were refused. Nobody got that offended, figuring Behan was just beginning his career as an inebriate, and didn't know all the rules yet.

He said he'd had it, right up to his pooper-pump, with these goddamned illegitimate high-graders, who liked to do it with their own mothers.

So what if they'd blown up the claims office? He knew where his claim was, richer than Jesus or Croesus, depending on how fried he was at any given moment.

And he, and some friends, were going back to work their rocks, go back to getting rich, and anybody who got in their way would have only himself to blame.

The news vids announced that Star Risk's patrol ships were off on a training flight to Welf, the system's innermost, mostly uninhabited world, for some shakedown drills.

signal from that dead asteroid, aimed as far as I can tell in the general direction of nowhere.'

His voice never got excited, but his helmet was on, faceplate sealed, while he touched an inship alarm sensor, and opened his mike on the TBS channel.

'Eighty-three,' he said then, through the intercom. 'Not that that means anything. I just told the others to spring about when I called a number, any number . . . ah, yes, there they are. Down "below" the elliptic.'

One screen, that had been showing little except a few asteroidal blips, suddenly flashed, and ten objects, trailing rainbow tails, indicating size and speed, appeared.

'Dopplering straight on toward us, like we're innocent miners,' Spada said, again switched channels. 'Decoys . . . stand by . . . stand by . . . I shall have you roasted, Dinsmore . . . *Break*!'

At his command, the five decoys went to full drive, the ship commanded by the to-be-unfortunate Dinsmore a bit in front, arcing 'around,' and straight into the oncoming ships.

Simultaneously, the other thirteen Star Risk ships, in three fighting formations, came out of N-space, and came after the raiders.

Spada's voice was calm, but M'chel saw a sheen of sweat through his faceplate.

Not that Riss was a picture of calmness. It was very seldom in her combat career that she'd had to just sit and watch, without a gun or a knife or a weapons sight to occupy her attention.

Grok seemed perfectly calm, although Riss didn't know how she would tell if he was excited or disturbed, watching several screens.

'We have a launch, skipper,' Spada's weapons officer, Lopez, said, also completely controlled. 'Three inbound. All acquired.'

'Stand by,' Spada ordered. 'We'll take them out, then I want a counterlaunch right after, before they have time to figure out they missed.

'I hope. On my command . . . *Launch*!'

The ship lurched a little as countermissiles spat from tubes. There were other missiles incoming from the raiders, and other patrol ships' missiles were going after them.

Screens showed little flashes, then nothingness where the incoming missiles had been.

'Main launch . . . *Fire*!'

This time, the jolt was a little larger as ship killers, almost an eighth as long as the patrol ships, flashed out.

M'chel heard a bleep in her suit speaker, then three others.

'All missiles have acquired targets . . . homing,' Lopez reported.

'Taking evasive action,' Spada announced, and his fingers touched sensors here, there on the control board.

The ship's artificial gravity was almost up to the veers and jumps. Almost. M'chel's stomach reminded her that it'd been awhile since it'd been abused like this, then shut up and concentrated on keeping things down.

Grok turned to her, and said calmly, 'It would appear my trickery has worked. Mr. Spada, if you'd now order your ships to enter X-One-One on their spoofery boxes?'

'X-One-One,' Spada echoed, and 'cast the order to the other patrol ships.

'That should really irk our friends,' Grok said. 'Instead of small mining ships, we should all now have the signature of small, wildly orbiting rocks.'

'Tracking . . .' the weapons officer droned. 'I have a counterlaunch . . . one of our missiles acquired . . . destroyed . . . a hit!'

The oncoming bandits, in spite of their counter-missiles, closed into what was almost a spear-wall of oncoming rockets.

'Strike . . . another strike . . . incoming missiles . . . acquired . . . destroyed,' the weapons officer went on, while Spada kept his ship dancing in irregular orbits.

'Firing' he said. '*Launch*!'

'Wups. They're turning, skipper. We've got them on the run.'

M'chel tried to interpret the screen, full of flashes and disappearances. There were five left . . . no, four.

'We have three on the run,' Spada reported.

'Go after them,' M'chel said. 'We want their base.'

Spada spoke quiet orders on the TBS.

There was another flash onscreen, then a second.

'We seem to be doing better than we should,' Spada said. 'We do want at least one survivor to track. I'll hope those missiles had already been launched before I issued my orders.

'If not,' he said ominously, 'then my junior birdman who got trigger-happy shall be in large shit. Pilots are a great deal easier to replace, and cheaper these days, than ships.'

Again, he went to the TBS, ordered two other ships to format on him, and the others to hang 'back' in the pursuit.

The last remaining raider flashed into N-space.

'A little late, friend,' Spada said. 'I have a tracer on your young bottom.'

Their ship went in, out of N-space twice more, and each time the fleeing raider's blip was onscreen.

Spada turned a speaker on, and an unintelligible chatter filled the compartment.

'He's screaming for help, I'd guess,' he said. 'But he's not completely out of control since his signal's in code. Now, all we have to do—'

Again, they came out of hyperspace, and there was a tiny flash on the blip.

'What the hell?' Spada said, touching buttons.

'That's strange,' he said. 'The bastard appears to have blown up. Look, here, on an infrared. Run it back a few seconds, and here. We've got a flash of energy, almost as strong as the drive, coming from the bow of the ship.

'And now, look at the prog screen over here. Unable to predict an orbit. That ship's now out of control.

'I wonder—'

'Close on that ship,' M'chel ordered. 'And stand by to let us out. I don't like wondering.'

The woman and the huge alien floated near what had been a warship, a former N'yar attack craft. The N'yar had been pacified by the Alliance more than ten years ago, but the ship still qualified as a modern killer on the civilian market.

It looked to Riss like an Earth cuttlefish she'd seen in holos, sleek from its stem to midsection. But there it blossomed out, alloy tentacles splayed.

The two pulled themselves closer, went into the ruins of the ship's nose.

'Interesting blast pattern,' Grok said.

'It is,' Riss said. 'Very interesting.'

'You have a theory?'

'Better. I have an explanation,' M'chel said. 'Now, let's see if the explosion left anything worth picking through.'

'There's no question,' M'chel said, turning away from the holo of the N'yar ship, 'the raider ship was destroyed by an explosion from within. We weren't within range at all.'

'An accident?' Jasmine King asked. She got up, went

to a sideboard of the *Boop-Boop-A-Doop*, poured chilled tea for herself.

'Probably not,' Baldur said.

'Certainly not,' Goodnight agreed.

'The ship was 'casting to its home base for support when it exploded,' Grok said.

'A booby trap,' Riss said. 'Put in by the raiders' leader, certainly without the knowledge of the ships' crews. Probably command-triggered.'

'Poor bassid shouldn't have hollered for Momma,' Goodnight said. 'Momma wouldn't've blown him up, otherwise.'

'I assume you shook down the wreckage.'

'You assume right,' M'chel said. 'The control room, and the crew, were shredded. The other compartments all had standard-issue Alliance surplus. No letters home, no nice little star charts with "we live here," no nothing worth talking about.'

'At least we have two more facts,' Baldur said. 'First, since the raiders made no attempt to challenge or seize what they thought were miners returning to their claims, we have further verification of my theory that the bandits are simply trying to drive Transkootenay away, for still unknown reasons.'

'I have a strange thought,' Riss said. 'Jasmine, would Cerberus Systems be evil enough to want to snatch up what Transkootenay's got, and they're running the raiders?'

King thought.

'They're *morally* capable of anything,' she decided. 'But I don't think they'd pull a grab. Word might get out, and that kind of thing would lose them more clients than whatever they could gain by ending up with the Foley System's goodies.

'I don't care how rich these asteteroids are, or if there's

some incredible discovery that's been made that the raiders are after.'

'Now there's something we haven't gone after,' Goodnight said. 'I've got all of the raw reports from my brother. I wonder if there's anything in common that the guys who got their ass shot off could've found?'

'Like what?' Riss asked.

'Like . . . hell, I'm not a geologist. God, diamonds, the apes of Ophir. But I'll see if I can find anything worth taking,' Goodnight said.

'Your second fact?' King asked Baldur.

'Thank you. We were veering. The second, obvious fact is that whoever is running this little operation wants to keep his little secrets, whatever they are, secret, which is the reason for the booby trap. Also, which is heartening, we now know that he or she actually *has* little secrets, which is what we should be going after.'

'*I'm* going after a drink,' Goodnight said, and went to the sideboard.

Baldur ignored him.

'Another thing that just occurred to me,' he said. 'We took zed casualties in this little battle. The oppo, assuming that each of those N'yar ships were half-manned, and *Jane's* lists them as having a twelve-person crew, took sixty losses. That may be no more than an unfortunate skirmish to the Alliance, but to anyone in the private sector, that's a catastrophe.

'So, if we hear no more of these bandits, we may assume they were merely a collection of free-lances, working for their common good. But if they are still strong for the fray, then we have a single opponent, with a defined, if unknown goal. Which, of course, will make our task a bit harder, and worthy of renegotiating our contract with Transkootenay.'

'I think we should give this unknown a name,' Riss suggested.

'It would be better than a vague him or her,' Baldur agreed.

'Call her . . . him . . . Murgatroyd,' M'chel said, suddenly remembering an archaic romance she'd read as a raw recruit.

'Murgatroyd?' Goodnight said with a great deal of skepticism.

'Murgatroyd,' Riss said firmly.

'Murgatroyd it is,' King said. 'So entered in our records.'

'Something else that should be entered,' Grok said. 'The score is now high-graders one, heroes one.

'Or better.

'I think we should attempt to further change the score.'

SEVENTEEN

Murgatroyd did, indeed, appear to have both an organization and a goal. Within the next week, two isolated mining stations were wiped out, and a small processing center was hit and badly damaged.

Two solo miners vanished, but that could have been by accident – mining isn't the safest occupation, on- or off-planet.

'Of *course*, we can provide security for you and your partners,' Jasmine King said in a soothing voice, almost a coo.

Off-camera, Chas Goodnight grinned, made credit-counting motions with his thumb and left hand.

'I'd suggest,' King said, 'that you first provide yourself with area safety. We have a missile and detection package I'm sure you'd be interested in, at a price far below any independent weapons dealer could provide, capable of covering the area around your asteroid.

'I *thought* you'd be interested,' King said, making notes. 'What about an autocannon for your mine?

'Ah. No, if you're still working the surface, without enough trace yet to warrant sinking a shaft, our autocannon isn't needed.

'Yet. We can discuss that at a later date. Also, you'll be

pleased to know that if your claim doesn't work out, our missile system is easily transportable to a new claim.

'Now, you'll also need personal weaponry, I would assume. No? You brought your own with you.

'What about communications gear? We've found that's a weakness for almost all of our clients, especially . . .'

'You did well on your first action,' Reg Goodnight complimented Baldur. 'Now, might I ask your next step?'

'Keeping the pressure on,' Baldur said vaguely, smiling into the com.

Goodnight looked slightly dissatisfied, and the conversation trailed off.

Baldur shut off the com.

'He is right, you know,' he said to Riss. 'We could use a bit of a plan, a general strategy against our foe.'

'No,' Jasmine King said. 'First we need to take care of ourselves.'

'I thought we were,' Baldur said. 'The bank account is comfortably afloat.'

'There are,' Jasmine said dryly, 'other dangers than bankruptcy.'

'Oh. Yes. That's true.'

'We're vulnerable in three areas,' King said. 'First and most importantly, especially to me, is the *Boop-Boop-A-Doop*. For it . . . her . . . we need vastly improved detection devices—'

'Which I am already working on,' Grok interrupted.

'As well as sector security when we're grounded.

'The second area of concern,' King went on, 'is the hotel with the flight crews.'

Goodnight winced. 'Shit. I never even thought about it.'

'I did,' Jasmine said. 'Finally, of course, we need to

protect our ships. I've already taken care of that. Transkootenay has agreed to give up their secondary landing field, and I've hired a construction company to build revetments for the ships, razor-wire and alarm the field, and again, Grok will provide electronic security.'

'Have I told you I love you lately?' M'chel said. 'You remember everything.'

'Of course,' King said. 'That's my job, isn't it?'

EIGHTEEN

The security guard scanned the various screens showing various angles on Star Risk's flight crew quarters, yawned.

It was a job, he thought. A dull, dull job. But it paid well and, if he kept his body out of the bars and his nose out of the jar, he'd be able to squirrel up enough for another grubstake, and get out where a man could get rich.

In the meantime, it was four hours till dawn.

He touched sensors, and the screens cleared, showed other views of the former hotel.

Exciting, he thought. Thrilling.

How frigging dull can things—

An indicator flickered, then returned to normal. If he hadn't been looking, he probably wouldn't have noticed it.

Probably nothing except that goddamned gorilla's circuitry hiccuping.

But, just for drill, he turned three screens, one infrared, on the area.

This time, the flicker was pronounced, and stayed on.

He zoomed in, saw two humans, both wearing some kind of suits . . . heat-shielded, he guessed, which was why they didn't show up when they somehow got through the outer perimeter.

Two men . . . both wearing heavy packs.

Even as he watched, one man was pressing sensors, and pillow alarms were going off in the guardhouse. He felt bootheels hit the floor above his head, faintly heard the clatter of guns being pulled from weapons racks.

The man hit another sensor, this one setting off alarms in the *Boop-Boop-A-Doop*, parked not far distant.

But the two figures were moving, moving fast, toward the hotel toward the man, toward the women and men he'd been hired to protect.

He grabbed a gunbelt, buckled it on, knowing how futile it was, and how it was almost certainly too late.

The first figure paused, and the second touched the first's backpack, here, there, and very suddenly the screen went blank, the infrared screen next to it went up through overload to black to blankness, and the ex-hotel trembled, rocked, as the blastwave shook it like a puppy shakes a rag.

The man dove under his desk, as things around him tumbled, crashed, The walls moved, swayed, and he was sure he was about to be buried alive.

Then the tremors stopped, but things around him, and on floors above him, crashed and emergency lighting flickered on.

But he was alive, and he staggered to his feet, made his way to the door, touched the sensor to open it. It was blown, but he didn't care. He had his hand through a crack, pulled, almost yanking the door out of its slot as the first of the standby guards came down the stairs, oddly crooked, leaning toward him.

'Somebody set off a bomb,' he managed.

'No shit, Sherlock,' the guard said. 'Where's your magnifying glass?'

'I do not understand,' von Baldur said. 'Somehow those

two got through the outer wire, I suspect with the help of others, who left them to their mission.'

He looked at the other Star Risk members.

'They run toward the hotel where they are going to plant their bomb. One fiddles with the other's pack, and both of them blow up.

'That makes no sense whatsoever.'

'No,' Chas said. 'It makes a deal of sense. And it shows that our Murgatroyd's a ruthless bastard.'

'Would you explain?' Baldur said. Riss was equally puzzled.

'You take two men, who you don't care if they come back, and you surely don't want to have interrogated. One you give a bomb in a pack to, and tell him that the button he's supposed to push, once he's got the bomb in place, has, say, thirty seconds before it goes off,' Goodnight explained.

'You give another pack to the second man, and tell both it's their escape mechanism. When *he* hits *his* button, the diversion starts. Maybe it's supposed to be smoke, maybe a fireworks display to blow out any available light or IR screens, whatever. He's supposed to hit his button right after the first man starts the bomb going.

'These two clowns wanted to give themselves as big a head start on getting the hell out of town as they could, so they decided they'd start the diversion *first*, then start the bomb timer.

'Both packs, naturally, had bombs in them, set to detonate instantaneously.'

'That is most nasty,' Grok said, and there might have been a slight note of admiration in his voice.

'Oh,' King said. 'I should have thought of it myself. Centuries ago, back on Planet Earth, a certain security service set up assassination plots like that, always using people they thought were dispensable.'

'Well, thank whatever anyone happens to believe in that the plot went awry,' Baldur said piously. 'Now all we have to do is find a new haven for our fliers, since that hotel is nothing but a scrap heap now, calm them down and put them back out in the skies, where they think they're safe.

'Wherever their new home is, I suppose we'd better offer improved security around, eh?'

'Our Murgatroyd,' Grok said, 'is proving himself a worthy opponent.'

'That he is. I don't think,' Riss said, 'I'm going to mind it at all when we finally nail him.

'Not at all.'

NINETEEN

The two ships came out of star drive, and flashed in on the asteroid from 'beneath,' beyond visual range of the three mining ships and the two prefab domes.

Their radars had only a moment to alert the tight-faced men and women inside the raiders that somehow, beyond their plans, they were being tracked.

Then two missiles spat from one of the mining ships. The first tracked perfectly, and crashed into the nose of the trailing raider.

It blew up, colors flashing brilliantly, then spun into the crags beyond the miner's camp, and its drive exploded.

The second missile may have been jarred by the first explosion, and went off behind the lead raider.

The pilot fought for control, thought she had it, then the ship wabbled on her, and the best she could manage was flaring her braking tubes as her ship spun sideways, hit hard on the asteroid, and rolled, bouncing high above the surface.

Finally, it grounded. There were three survivors, bruised, battered.

As they picked themselves up, suited figures came out of the domes, bounding dark figures coming toward the wreckage.

*

'Hang on, M'chel,' L.C. said on the com screen. 'I'll patch you t'rough.'

She touched sensors, and M'chel's screen in the *Boop-Boop-A-Doop* divided. L.C. filled half, behind her the Miner's Aid office. On the other was a grim-looking man in a spacesuit, without a helmet.

'Awright, Hank,' she said. 'You're t'rough to Star Risk.'

'What the frigging hells we need 'em for?' the man snarled. 'We got the bastards, and we're gonna give 'em a nice, fair trial then hang 'em. Slow.'

'This is Riss,' M'chel said. 'Star Risk. What the blazes is going on?'

'A couple ships fulla high-graders tried to hit us,' the miner said. 'They didn't know we'd went an' bought one a yer missile kits. Killed one ship dead, got three survivors from the other. We're gonna nuremburg t'eir asses in a few minutes.'

'Listen, Hank,' M'chel said urgently. 'We need those survivors. We need the information we can get from them, to get the rest of the raiders.'

Hank stared into his pickup, then said, very deliberately,

'My best frien' was one of those got theyselves killed by these bassids.'

He turned his head, spat, and the pickup cleared.

'Elsie,' M'chel said. 'Can you get Hank back, and convince him to keep those raiders alive until we get there? And I'll need coordinates.'

'I'll try,' L.C. said. 'But good luck on t'is one, lassie.'

M'chel Riss had seen a good number of bodies, men, women, and children. But she'd never seen three bodies like this before, unsuited, lying outside one of the domes, sprawled, their necks strangely elongated.

'You . . . hanged them?'

'Cert'ny did,' the stock miner named Hank said, not without pride. 'Like I promised.'

'Might I ask how, given the low gravity of this asteroid?' Grok rumbled. He and M'chel had scrambled in one of Spada's patrol ships, Riss feeling she would certainly be too late.

They were.

'Mel's ship's got a big cargo hold,' Hank explained. 'Enough for a good drop, like I saw on a vid somewheres. An' antigravity. An' there was a big beam near the top t' tie off the cable we used.'

Grok unslung the bag over his shoulder.

'Clearly, we shall not be needing this.'

In the kit were several varieties of 'yodeling juice.' If there's never been anything such as truth serum, there are many chemicals that will make someone babble uncontrollably, and a trained and skilled interrogator, which Riss was, can steer the flow into desired directions.

'No,' Riss said. 'Now, let's shake the bodies, and what's left of that ship.

'With our fingers crossed.'

'Pretty damned pawky,' Riss said, surveying the shipsuits, small amount of money, a Saint Michael's medal, and a few other effects. 'Can you make anything out of this?'

'No,' Grok said. 'However, Jasmine is a veritable fount of information. Shall we return with our trophies?'

'Very close to nothing,' King agreed. 'However, there's one thing that's interesting. Two of the bills, and three coins . . . held by two of the raiders, I see . . . come from Seth V.'

'Which is?'

'A bit of a jaunt from here,' King said. 'It . . . or rather its capital of Trygve . . . is known as a hiring hall, so to speak, for those interested in hiring freelances.

'Cerberus used to recruit there frequently.'

'How interesting,' Baldur said. 'I am starting to think we might have a rat hole to send our ferret down.'

'Don't be so complimentary,' Chas Goodnight said. But a slight, wolfish smile touched his lips.

Riss was staring down at the effects.

'No damned ID,' she said quietly. 'No letters, no cards, nothing. I can't believe Murgatroyd could do that job of making sure his troops go out sterile.'

'Did you ever consider,' King said gently, 'that most people who are willing to go mercenary don't *have* any ties? That maybe that's the reason they're in the trade they chose in the first place?'

M'chel smiled wryly, but a bit of a chill came to her.

TWENTY

The only warning was a bleat from a patrol ship:

'Star Risk Control this is Patrol Seven . . . the bastards got a frigging cruiser . . . onscreen, bouncing it to you . . . they got Eleven, one blast, goddammit, I'm at full power getting the hell out of—'

The com went dead, and no attempts to reestablish contact with either Patrol Seven or Eleven were successful.

But that first transmission had come through quite clearly.

'Son of a bitch,' Goodnight said softly. 'Murgatroyd *does* have a cruiser.'

Onscreen was a long, deadly ship. A scale said it was a thousand meters long. No turrets were protruded, but two open missile tubes told what had killed two of Spada's ships.

'This is not possible,' Spada said softly. 'I don't know how any non-government operation can find the bodies to crew a warship that big.'

'Don't be so sure about that,' Baldur said. 'I can think of examples where you're wrong.'

'Here could be the answer,' King said, reading from the *Jane's* fiche onscreen.

'The ship's ID'ed positively as a former Alliance *Sensei*

class. About a hundred years old, so Murgatroyd must've picked it up cheap. But here's the key. "Ship was intended to be crewed by less than 100 hands, and is extensively automated." So he wouldn't need to have as big a crew as the cruiser's looks would suggest.'

Spada was reading over her shoulder: 'Chain guns, five four-tube long range missile batteries, three close-range batteries, six tubes, planetary bombardment capabilities . . .'

He turned to Baldur.

'Boss, I didn't contract to go against something like this.'

Baldur stared at the screen.

'None of us did,' he said. 'I think it is time to have a chat with Transkootenay.'

'This is bad,' Reg Goodnight said. 'Not ten minutes ago, I had a com from one of the outstations. A ship . . . a very damned big ship, they said, blasted hell out of the station.

'I've got twenty of my engineers and assayers dead, and the station's a dead loss.

'I ordered them to get back to Sheol as fast as they could.

'Von Baldur, is there anything to stop that ship from savaging us, even here on Mfir?'

'I've got all of my ships either inbound, or in close orbit around Mfir,' Baldur said. 'They should be able to stop it . . . if it attacks Mfir.'

'But there's nobody at all protecting the miners,' Goodnight said.

'No,' Baldur said.

'What are we . . . you . . . going to do?'

'I want you to set a meeting up with that offworld development person, Tan Whitley,' Baldur said. 'This is escalating, and I think it is time to ask for the Alliance to come back in.

'This is not banditry any more as open insurrection.'

Reg Goodnight worried his lower lip in his teeth, reluctantly nodded.

'I'll set the meeting immediately.'

Glace was green, if not quite earth-green, and fair. But as usual, the first colonists had looked around, seen the beauty, and set out to ruin it as rapidly as possible. The planet, eager for settlers, had made sure there were no annoying statutes interfering with a corporation's right to despoil in the name of profits.

'Why,' Riss said, looking at the brown haze onscreen, 'doesn't anybody ever hire people like us to go in and put a few bombs down a few smokestacks?'

As Baldur brought *Boop-Boop-A-Doop* down on the main field, Chas Goodnight had a request.

'Awright,' he said, voice slightly pleading. 'I understand the reasoning for keeping me hidden back on Mfir, or in the belt.

'But there ain't no py-rates on Glace. At least, not any that haven't already settled in and gone legit.'

'Your point being?' Baldur asked, without taking his eyes off the control board.

'I, uh, would like to take advantage of the brief time we'll be here to see some of the local sights.'

'He means, get laid,' Jasmine King said.

'I'm shocked,' Goodnight said. 'Shocked, do you hear me, shocked. Such language. And I was gonna ask you to hit the highspots with me.'

'Why?' Jasmine asked. 'The answer would still be no.'

'This woman has no, I say again my last, no, romance in her soul.'

'He's evading the issue,' Riss said. 'Maybe we

should've left him minding the farm back on Mfir instead of Grok.'

'I thought you were on my side,' Goodnight said.

Riss didn't bother answering.

'Actually,' she said to Baldur, 'there really isn't any reason we can't let the poor lad out to kick up his heels. Assuming he's got protection against the clap and his shot record card's up to date.'

'Thanks a lot,' Goodnight said.

Baldur considered.

'All right,' he said. 'But it shall be just like in the military with a first pass for a young recruit. You are cleared to spend time within 30 kilometers of the ship, and must check back in no later than 1900, Zulu time.'

'That's not even dark!' Goodnight complained.

'Why do you need to be out after dark?' Jasmine said. 'You told us you just wanted to see the sights, which unquestionably are best seen by daylight.

'And,' she added demurely, 'women don't mind being kissed in daylight. You may trust me on this.'

'You see, Chas,' Riss said. 'We have your best interests at heart, and don't want you getting in any trouble.'

'Aw farpadoodle!' Goodnight snarled, but hurried back to his compartment to dig out appropriate ground-side clothes.

Tan Whitley reminded Riss of any one of several pay-masters she'd had to confront about underpayment during her years as a Marine, never to get satisfaction.

She was calm, collected, had all of the data she would bother to consider at sensor's reach, and, in the immortal military phrase, wouldn't say shit if she had a mouthful.

'I shall be frank with you, Mister von Baldur,' she said, in a colorless voice. 'The asteroid belt has been troublesome, most troublesome, to this government since Transkootenay Mining first approached us and secured a contract to exploit the region.'

'I do not understand,' Baldur said. 'It is my understanding that Transkootenay has provided you with quite handsome royalty payments over the past few years.'

'Credits are not everything,' Whitley said.

Baldur gave her a look of utter disbelief, tried again.

'Might I ask in what way Transkootenay has transgressed?' he said, proud of his alliteration.

Whitley frowned, but didn't comment.

'This entire lease has been quite embarrassing to the government,' she said. 'First there is the problem with the bandits which, I confess, I believe are actually among the miners brought in by Transkootenay.'

'They aren't,' Riss said. 'But let that pass.'

'Be that as it may. Transkootenay was unable to deal with their security problem by themselves, so we were required to summon aid from the Alliance. They arrived, did nothing, but sent us a rather monstrous bill for their services.

'Not to mention the various tabloids having quite a field day with the government's evident inability to keep the peace.

'Then Transkootenay hires you, which of course I suspect means we will end up sharing that bill. And *you* aren't able to solve the problem.

'Instead, you want us to once again scream for help from the Alliance.

'I can give you an answer right now, without having to consult my superiors, for they're aware, most aware, of the situation.

'The answer is no. We cannot afford to keep supporting Transkootenay and its out-system employees.'

'In other words,' Baldur said, 'you do not mind a little

piracy, as long as no one of the Foley System gets robbed
or injured?'

'I did not say that, sir. Assuming, which I don't necessarily do, there is some sort of rogue warship . . .'
Whitley looked as if she wanted to snort in total disbelief, '. . . running around the asteroid belt, I would
suggest you recommend to your employer that
Transkootenay should take the most logical route, and
withdraw from mining until these unknown people,
assuming they actually exist, and aren't a figment of a
creative graphics person's doodling, get tired of their
non-productive existence, and find a new system to plun-
der, or whatever it is they're doing.'

Goodnight sat in the central lounge of the *Boop-Boop-A-
Doop*, nursing half a bottle of brandy. He saw Riss, King,
and Baldur's expressions, grinned, and rubbed a hand
across his sandy crewcut.

'You people look as if things went as bad for you as
they did for me.'

'Worse,' Riss said. 'We got told, somewhat politely, to
pack our ass with salt and piss up a rope.'

'No help at all?' Goodnight asked, incredulous.

'None.'

'I don't suppose there's any way that any of us can
holler for help directly to the Alliance,' Goodnight said.
'I think I'm the only one who's hot with the authorities.'

'You think they'll respond to a request for assistance
from a lot of damned mercenaries, do you?' Baldur
asked.

'Since you put it like that,' Goodnight said. 'But what
about Transkootenay going to the Alliance themselves? I
imagine they pay their taxes, and are good upstanding
citizens wot don't need no stinkin' pirates.'

'I asked,' Baldur said. 'Your brother said that the first

thing Transkootenay would do is fire him. The second thing would be to replace us. And the third thing would be to bring in Cerberus.'

'Mmmh,' Goodnight said. 'Which might or might not do anything for the miners, but it'd sure play hell with our bank account.

'So what do we do?'

'What we do is go looking for Murgatroyd's base,' Baldur said. 'Once we find the base, then we have the cruiser's location, and can deal with it as we see fit.'

'That's a start,' Goodnight said. 'Now, where would, could, this base be?'

'I would suspect,' King said, 'it's probably not in the belt. I thought otherwise, until that cruiser materialized. A ship that size needs rather substantial logistical support. I'd suggest it's either out-system, or in a hidden base on one of the three settled worlds.'

'If it's not in the Foley System,' Riss said, 'then we're screwed. Our grandkids would go gray looking.'

'True,' King said. 'But I have some possible thoughts on how to look.'

'Which are?'

King shook her head.

'Things need to be narrowed down somewhat. I think it's time for Mister Goodnight's undeniable talents.'

'Why not?' Chas said morosely. 'I'm starting to think I don't have any other ones.'

'Might I ask what happened to you?' King said.

'I met this lovely. Young, beautiful, friendly, almost smart enough to tell when it's raining. Perfect for an afternoon's quick dalliance,' Goodnight said. 'She was most friendly, as I said.

'She invited me home with her.

'To meet her husbands.

'Husbands plural.

'Sheesh.

'Let's get off this goddamned world and go back out where all you've got to worry about is getting robbed or killed.'

TWENTY-ONE

'Of course,' Riss said, 'the first thing, before we send Chas out a-hunting our snark, is what his name should be.'

'I suppose one Goodnight per operation is all that should be allowed,' Grok said. 'Not to mention our client would hardly make Mr. Goodnight's resumé appear nice and innocent. Or, in his case, black and villainous.'

The Star Risk team were assembled, heavily in plotting mode, in the luxurious lounge of *Boop-Boop-A-Doop*.

'Exactly,' Riss said. 'Now, let me ponder.'

She felt a strange kind of glee, realized it was because she was masterminding something, without having to take the slightest risk. Now she knew why her controllers had sometimes been strangely elated about things.

'I love the way you people are playing with my future,' Goodnight said sourly.

'We are not at all,' Baldur said. 'We want to make sure you *have* a future, is all.'

'I mean,' Jasmine said, 'we want you alive to get laid . . . that's got to happen, sooner or later, doesn't it?'

'It is to laugh,' Goodnight said. 'Hah.'

'Now, should we just pick a name out of the air?' King said.

'No,' Riss said. 'Murgatroyd appears a bit on the efficient side. So I'd like to give Chas as much of a solid cover as we can. Maybe . . . Chas, since you'll be going in as what you are, a bester, what about a real name, who just happens to be dead?'

Goodnight's expression turned somber.

'I've got one better. What about someone who went missing on an operation, and is still carried as an MIA by the Alliance?' he said.

M'chel was about to say something sarcastic, then noted Goodnight's face.

'That'd do,' she said softly. 'I assume you have a name?'

'I do,' Goodnight said. 'Raff Atherton.'

'There could be no possibility this Atherton could show up suddenly and get a squelch on your plans?' Grok asked.

'Not a chance,' Goodnight said. 'I was carrying him out after we got blown, and then his head came off.'

'Oh,' King said. 'Might I inquire as to why he's not listed as Killed in Action?'

'His home world was . . . is . . . touchy about doing anything with the Alliance, and Raff's father was connected with the local politics. A bit of a shit, I'd guess, since he didn't seem to mind his son being allowed to just vanish, no funeral, no Official Report from the Alliance, for fear it'd hurt his own career.

'Maybe,' Goodnight said musingly, 'that was why Atherton blew out into the military in the first place.'

'All right,' Baldur said briskly, trying to change the mood. 'You know his background well enough to play the part?'

'When you're in a hide, waiting for somebody to show up, you have a lot of time to talk,' Goodnight said. 'I can fake it.

'But what have I been doing in the . . . uh, five years since I went MIA?'

'I think,' Riss said, 'we want an involvement in weaponry. Gunrunning. That's a fairly open trade, and something someone with your talents could drift into.'

'All right,' Goodnight said. 'Why are we running this operation, which is a long ways from Seth, which is where I'm going, right?'

'Because we're not going to dump you straight into the crapper without a bit of a verifiable background,' Riss said. 'Baldur, Jasmine, and I discussed it. If you start with an operation, then move on to Seth, you'll be a lot more credible.

'Now, why a gunrunner? You were along when we bought the artillery for this operation, and I don't recall you introducing yourself to the salesman.'

Goodnight thought. 'No. No, I didn't.'

'So you're going to do that now, as Atherton,' Riss said.

'And for whom am I gonna ply my semi-nefarious trade?'

'It seems,' King said, 'there's this charming little world named Mitidja. On it there's the Old Guard, trying to hold on to the government, which is dictatorial. Rebelling against them was one faction. They recently broke in half, so there's now two forces trying to take over the government.

'All three factions have death squads, guerrillas in the hills, plus there's the police force and army, which also want a slice of the action.

'The Alliance has declined to get involved, since all this is internal.'

'Wonderful,' Goodnight muttered. 'You're gonna throw me in the middle of *that*?'

'Worse, actually,' King said cheerfully. 'The Alliance

may not be getting involved, but it's put an interdiction on any of the three sides buying guns on the open market.

'Which means they're even hotter about anything that puts a hole in people or real estate showing up on the black market.

'The nearest world where the Mitidja folks can buy bangsticks is called Puchert.

'The government of Puchert isn't happy about being Arms Dealer to the Multitudes, but their government, while sort of democratic, is corrupt to the eyebrows.

'So on Puchert, you've got all three Mitidja factions, both official and underground killers, shooting at each other, plus terminating any arms dealer who's selling things to the oppos. Not to mention the Alliance, whose operations are also a bit on the scoundrelly side.'

'Double wonderful.'

'Better,' King went on. 'Not only do you have these homicidal folks, but there's some very large arms dealers who aren't fond of any competition, and don't mind putting a bomb in the shorts of said competitors.

'Plus my source says that our friends, Cerberus Systems, are building a presence on Puchert. Nobody seems to know who they're working for, nor what their ends are yet.'

'Maybe you can find out some data on Cerberus's plans while you're there, Chas,' Baldur said. 'And we can sell it to the highest bidder. We can always use a few extra credits, you know.'

Chas moaned, leaned back in his chair, ran both hands through his bristling crewcut.

'Why me, God?' he said. 'Why me all the time?'

He frowned.

'What are we going to do about paying for these guns I'm to peddle?'

'Don't worry about it,' Riss said. 'The deal won't get that far. You'll never make pickup, let alone delivery.'

'That's not very honorable to our salesman friend,' Goodnight said.

'I looked at what he charged us for the first lot,' Baldur said. 'He will get over his chagrin.'

'That's what I like about us,' Riss said. 'Our clear-cut morality.'

'But how am I gonna keep the deal from going that far?' Goodnight asked.

'You're not,' Riss said with a sweet smile. 'We are. When things get interesting, we'll just nark you out to some shooters and let you get out of town fast for Seth V.'

Goodnight stared in disbelief, then shook his head.

'All right,' he said. 'Nobody said ferrets didn't have to chance getting their paws bloody.' He turned to King.

'You figured out this scheme, these worlds?'

'With the help of some of my sources,' King said. 'Yes.'

'Tell me, Jasmine,' Goodnight said. 'Is there anything you don't know . . . or can't find out?'

'Certainly,' King said. 'For instance, when . . . or if . . . you're ever going to get laid again.'

Goodnight moaned again.

King smiled at the blank com.

'Still cautious?'

'Of course,' a voice clearly fed through a dehumanizing filter said. 'Why do you think I'm still in business?'

'Because you have the best ID around,' Jasmine said. 'Great craftsmen are always desirable.'

'True,' the voice said. 'Two IDs, then. One in the name of this Raff Atherton?'

Goodnight, at the next com, dickering with the arms salesman, told him to hold on, blanked sound and vid, and leaned over to King's terminal. 'Three. Just in case there's a screwup.'

'You're the subject?' the voice asked.

'I am.'

'How bulletproof do you want things to be?'

'Solid,' Goodnight said. 'Complete to library cards and some unpaid com bills.'

'That can be arranged,' the voice said. 'Of course, it'll cost.'

'Since it's my ass that'll be on the line,' Goodnight said, 'the cost be damned.'

'I like working for a man with your attitude,' the voice said.

TWENTY-TWO

Chas Goodnight came off the liner's ramp into the main terminal on Puchert, just as the bomb went off.

Fortunately, it was a building away, and only rocked the world around him.

Goodnight picked himself up from where he'd gone flat, brushed dust from his immaculately expensive casual jacket, and looked about at his fellow passengers.

Several of them had reflexes as fast as his, and were back on their feet, grinning sheepishly, cleaning themselves off, and avoiding others' eyes. Sure, he thought. We're all just a fine lot of businessmen.

He picked up his costly bag, and, whistling cheerfully, went on into the terminal, as sirens screamed toward the roiling smoke and screams.

Goodnight started toward a ground transport booth, stopped himself.

A bomb on arrival, he thought. A nice omen. Perhaps you should listen, Chas old boy, and reconsider your plans?

He went back out of the terminal, walked past a couple of buildings, to another liner company's ticketing offices, went in.

He smiled brightly at the rather attractive woman behind the counter.

'May I help you, sir?'

'You may,' Goodnight said. 'My business here finished a day early, and my scheduled flight out isn't for three days. The company said they can't change my reservation, so I thought I'd check elsewhere.'

He shrugged. 'I'll let my boss worry about getting the other half of the ticket back.'

'We'll be glad to try and help, sir,' the woman said. 'Where is your destination?'

Goodnight had scanned the Departure board as he walked up.

'There's a flight to Deneb XII in three hours,' he said. 'I can cross-connect for home from there.'

The woman touched sensors. 'There's still several compartments available on that flight. If I could see some ID, please?'

'Of course.' Goodnight reached into an inner pocket, took out the third false ID he'd had made, handed it across.

The smiling woman touched keys. Goodnight yawned, a weary executive who wanted nothing more than a drink and a quiet place to lie down, and off this world.

Just for a second, the woman's smile slipped, and her eyes flashed up at Goodnight, then down.

'Uh . . . just a moment, Mr. uh, Hathaway. My terminal's not behaving at all. I'll run your ticket again from the main desk.

'I'll just be a moment.'

Chas Goodnight smiled affably, and the woman went through a door.

Goodnight was moving, walking quickly, as if in a hurry to reach his gate, back out of the building before the police showed up.

So those bastards at Star Risk don't trust me at all, he

thought furiously. My own people set me up if I try to get off this armpit in my own direction, just because I don't fancy getting blown up.

Or murdered by some back-alley goons because they think I'm going to sell guns to their competition.

What does Star Risk think I am?

Suddenly he grinned, and started laughing.

I guess they know me, after all.

So much for the idea of resuming my career as a dashing jewel thief.

At least for the moment.

I suppose I might as well keep on working for Star Risk.

He wasn't that angry, actually, knowing that you only gave your ferret as much information as he or she had to have, and didn't trust him or her any more than you had to. That was the way the Alliance had worked, so that would be the way Riss handled things.

So he'd have to stick to her plan.

No problem. Goodnight could handle that.

He spotted a lifter, waved it down and got in, just as a battered lifter grounded, and two harried-looking men, obviously cops, jumped out, and hurried into the terminal.

I wonder, Goodnight thought still amused, just what kind of a thug that damned Riss made me out to be? She must've had a chat with the phony ID man after I stopped paying attention.

Damned sneaky woman, that.

She would have made a good bester, if her frigging morals didn't keep getting in the way.

'Where to, Chack?' the driver said.

'Whatever the finest hotel around happens to be,' Goodnight said. 'A man in my horrible position deserves nothing but the best.'

TWENTY-THREE

'Like that?' M'chel Riss held out her foot.

Jasmine King considered her toes.

'Maybe . . . a shade darker?'

'All right.' Riss turned the tiny paintgun on, put her foot back in the form, and resprayed her toes.

Jasmine giggled.

'It tickles me, not you,' M'chel said. 'What's so funny?'

'Have you always painted your toes?'

'Since I was old enough to shoplift old-fashioned polish,' Riss said.

'That's funny.'

'Why?'

'Marines wear boots, right?'

'You got that right. Jump boots, suit boots, running boots, dress boots, climbing boots . . . you name it, we got it.'

'And here you were, Major Riss, all spiff and proper a Marine, secretly knowing your toes, under all that plas, were nonregulation as all blazes.'

M'chel grinned.

'I guess it was kind of silly . . . but you don't get many ways of feeling feminine in the Corps.'

'So why'd you join?'

Riss put the sprayer down, refilled her glass of wine, scanned the various screens in front of her.

'Getting decadent,' she said. 'This is my second glass in what, three days?'

King extended her glass, and Riss filled it from the old-fashioned decanter.

'Our Freddie has quite a style on him, doesn't he? Crystal, leather, silk.'

'You were going to tell me how you got to be a boot-neck, and I think you're evading the issue,' Jasmine said.

'Hey! That's something we only call ourselves.'

Jasmine didn't answer.

'Awright,' Riss said. 'I was born on this little pissant world, mostly desert. My folks were trying to be farmers, but the only thing they seemed able to produce was kids.

'I was fifth out of nine. Which meant my career options were nil, other than hanging around the farm hoping one of the local yokels'd get sweet on me, and carry me off to the big city.

'Said big city, half a day's travel, had twenty-K inhabitants. Gosharootie, boys and girls.

'So there I was, as stuck as any girl has ever been.

'And then I saw a poster at school. The univee, in the capital, no less, which was better known for its athletics than scholarship, was offering a full scholarship.

'There was only one slight catch.

'It was in freefall relative work.'

'Which is?' Jasmine asked.

'Migawds and little fishies. Something you don't know,' M'chel said. 'Basically, you get in this lifter, which is open, so you're breathing off an oxy tank, and it goes straight on up to, oh, anywhere from three to ten thousand meters. Sometimes higher, in balls-out competition.

'You've got this antigravity dropper . . . you know what that is, right . . . on a harness.

'When you reach altitude, you jump out of the lifter, and start dropping. It feels like you're flying, once you get away from the lifter so you don't have anything to see suddenly going upward, but if you watch from the ground, you're coming straight down at seventy-plus meters per second.

'There's all sorts of competition – spot-accuracy on landing, team hookups, relative work, which is doing maneuvers with another person with her own dropper . . . as many things as you can think of to pass the time while falling to your death.

'You use the dropper, flicking it on and off, to adjust your rate of fall. Then, when you're, say, a couple hundred meters above the ground, you turn it on full.

'That drops your rate of fall to about a meter a second, and you land. Stand-up landings generally get bonus points.'

'That sounds like an outstanding way to get dead.'

'Not really,' M'chel said. 'Not unless you screw up, not allowing for ground wind, or maybe you get out of control . . . that's called Zeeing out . . . and get in a tight spin, black out and wake up a couple of meters underground.'

'So you saw this poster,' King said, fascinated, 'and you knew how to do this freefalling?'

'Nope,' M'chel said. 'But I managed to borrow a dropper from the univee, and my folks had an old lifter they mostly used for crop dusting and going into the coop for supplies.

'I taught myself.'

'And got the scholarship,' King said.

'And got the scholarship,' Riss said. 'It didn't hurt that the coach thought I was the, and I quote, "Cutest thing since socks on a hog."'

'What a *charming* analogy,' King said.

'Yeah. This was also a guy, and there were students on the team who said the same thing, who told me that freefall's even better than sex.

'Not that I would've known at that time,' Riss said, a bit primly.

'So falling out of perfectly good lifters paid your way through the univee?' King asked. 'I guess that was a well-earned education.'

Riss grinned, didn't answer. She didn't think it was necessary to tell King that in those days, she got violently airsick. So the lifter would take off, and she'd throw up in her helmet, hold it out in the slipstream to clean out the vomit, put it back on, and jump.

'So here you were with a diploma and . . . how many falls?'

'Somewhere over a thousand. And my degree was quite sensible – business psychology,' Riss continued. 'And the idea of going offworld was great, but going to work in some mega-corp in Human Resources, or whatever they'd call it, was right up there with public sodomy.

'And then I saw another poster.'

'For the Marines.'

'For the Marines.' Riss shrugged. 'Nobody ever said I was the brightest one in the family.'

'Have you ever gone back home?'

'Once or twice,' Riss said. 'But I really didn't fit in.' She shifted, a bit uncomfortable. 'Now, it's your turn to do the bio bit.'

'I was born of poor but dishonest parents,' King started, and an alarm blared.

M'chel was at the *Boop-Boop-A-Doop*'s control panel touching sensors. A screen cleared, and showed a happy Reg Goodnight.

'Riss, I just got a com from L. C. Doe. A ship of

bandits tried to jump an ore processor, and things didn't work out for them. We've got three prisoners, same as last time, but this time they're held securely. Doe's on her way to my office, and we're coming for you.

'With any luck, the bastards'll be ready to talk by the time we get out there!'

'We're on the way,' Riss said, already shrugging into her combat harness.

'Son of a bitch,' Reg swore softly, looking down at the wreckage.

'It looks like eit'er the baddies had someone keeping track a t'em, or else our code ain't as tight as we t'ought,' Doe observed.

The ore carrier, an obese collection of globes, connected with open strutting, never intended for atmospheric flight, had been struck hard.

Nearby was the raiders' ship that had hit the carrier in the first place. Its lock was yawning open, but that was about all that was left of the ship. Carefully set demolition charges had reduced that starship to small untidy piles of junk. That must've happened after the backup unit came in for a rescue.

'T'e assholes knew what t'ey was hittin',' Doe said. 'Look. Eit'er t'ey're readin' our codes, or t'ey got a snitch in Transkootenay's com center or somet'in'.

'Anyway, t'ey heard t'eir boys went an' screwed up, and were just waitin' for interrogation, and th' backup team, not trustin' anybody, come in to make sure nobody sang.

'T'ey t'rew a missile in, aimin' back on t'e drive to keep th' carrier on th' ground, t'en landed, opened t'e crew spaces up like wit' a can opener, an' went in, lookin' for t'eir own.'

None of the Star Risk people, Riss, King, and Grok, said anything as Redon Spada brought the patrol ship down on the jagged asteroid, not far from the wreckage.

Already suited up, five of them went to the lock.

'Keep an eye on the screens,' Riss said. 'They might be back to see if there's any buzzards picking over the ruins.'

Spada nodded.

They went out of the patrol ship, moving in careful bounds toward the wreckage.

It was just as Doe had said. The crew compartment, the forward ball, had been cut open almost surgically, probably with a heavy-duty laser.

Riss clambered through a hole.

There were half a dozen bodies scattered about the compartment.

'Five of t'em should be t'e crew,' Doe said into her interphone. 'T'at ot'er, over t'ere, he's one of t'e raiders.'

Riss went close, knelt. The raider was a woman, killed when a section of steel plating had sliced her almost in half.

'They hit the ore collector with a missile, then cut this pod open,' Reg said, explaining the obvious. 'They must've killed one of their own, rescuing the other two.

'*Goddammit*, but I wish we'd gotten here earlier!'

M'chel went through the woman's suit pouches, found nothing, then opened the suit up. It was very gory, and Riss was very glad she was breathing canned air.

'Oh, m'god,' she heard, turned, saw Reg Goodnight with a hand over his faceplate.

'Swallow fast,' she ordered. 'Puke in your suit and you could strangle.'

She heard convulsive swallowing, felt her own gorge rise. King was beside Goodnight, turning his interphone off.

Grok had paid no attention to the sideshow, but was

dragging the corpse out of the suit, trying to keep it from coming apart.

He went deftly, in spite of his gauntlets, through the pouches of the shipsuit she wore.

'Nothing,' he reported. 'Except a tattoo saying "Lucius." And a pair of plain gold earrings. The body's just like the others. They went out from their base . . . wherever that is . . . with no ID, no clues. I'll wager that, when we check the wreckage of the other ship, it's just as sanitized as this body. Murgatroyd runs a taut ship.'

There was a sound like an old-fashioned teakettle steaming. Doe was making it, standing, arms folded, over a pair of bodies.

'The bastards went an' made sure,' she said. 'Shot 'em in the faceplate when t'ey busted in.

'I ain't gonna protest no more if some of t'ese asswipes get t'eir necks stretched. Not no more I won't.'

TWENTY-FOUR

'Nice-looking yacht, that,' Chas Goodnight observed.

'Yeah,' the stevedore said. 'Guess it belongs to some pol or richie with a guilty conscience.'

'How you figure?'

'There's a two-man crew on duty around the clock. And there's a bull walking security, too.'

'Hey,' Goodnight said. 'Haven't we all needed to get out of town fast sometime?'

The stevedore laughed.

'ID,' the cop demanded.

Goodnight took out papers, handed them over.

The policeman looked at them carefully, handed them back.

'Sorry, Mr. Atherton. But there's a pair of fugitives we're after, and don't have a good description of.'

Goodnight smiled politely, went on into his hotel wondering if the cop had been telling the truth, or if somebody was interested in keeping tabs on a man who was interested in weaponry.

'Sorry, Chack,' the doorman said, calling him by what was the evident generic nickname on this planet. 'I don't know you, you don't got a card from somebody I know, you ain't that beautiful a people, you don't get into Suckers.'

'You know me,' Goodnight said, holding a hundred-credit note like a tube. 'Real well.'

The man took it, grinned.

'Now I think you're my long-lost brother. G'wan in. You just looking for talent, or you got a meet?'

'Now, that'd be telling, wouldn't it?' Goodnight said.

The doorman slid the door open.

'Got to compliment you,' Goodnight said, 'for honesty in labeling your joint.'

'Hey,' the man said. 'No need to lie when you've got all the action.'

'Guess not,' Chas said.

Suckers was built on three levels, the floors and walls iridescing in rainbow colors. There was different music on each floor, kept separate by baffle fingers on the ceilings.

Goodnight went up a slideway to the top level.

There were two men at the head of the stairs, paying no attention to the dancers weaving their way through the tables. The big room was about a quarter full.

'You looking for someone?'

'Got a meet with somebody named Thatch,' Goodnight said.

The men looked impressed.

'Over there.'

Thatch was a biggish man, carefully going to seed. He sat at a table with two young women, with big eyes and smiles and tiny minds. There was a crystal container between them, fumes roiling over the top.

As Goodnight went over, two men sitting at another table shifted their attention to him.

He held out his hands in the unarmed signal and they relaxed, very slightly.

The big man looked up at him, stone faced.

'Thatch?' Goodnight said. 'I'm Atherton.'

Thatch gestured with his chin, and the two women, smiles not moving, got up and slunk to another table.

Goodnight sat down.

'Want a drink?' Thatch asked.

'I drink when the business is taken care of.'

'Good policy,' Thatch said, and poured himself another glassful from the container.

'I understand you got some artillery to move,' he said.

Goodnight didn't answer, but took out a small black tube from inside his jacket. Thatch jerked, and at the other table the two men's hands went to their belts.

Then Thatch realized what Goodnight held, relaxed. His gun guards did the same.

Goodnight turned on the anti-bug, pointed it in Thatch's direction, then ran it under the table, and the chairs.

The device didn't buzz.

Goodnight turned it off, put it away.

'Yeah. Now we can talk, since we're both clean. I've got stuff for sale.'

'Like what?'

'Current-issue Alliance small arms, Krupp anti-missile systems, a lot of stuff, as new as you want, as used and cheap as you can afford. I've got just about anything short of ships. And if the price is right, I can probably arrange for those, too.'

'How legit is the paperwork?'

'The end use certificate's genuine. But you can't check it with the supposed user. That's snide.'

'Not a factor,' Thatch said. 'What about delivery?'

'I'd rather do a transfer in space,' Goodnight said. 'But if you can't handle that action . . . I'll deliver. I assume Mitidja?'

'Right.'

'The Alliance has a blockade going,' Goodnight said.

'Yeah.'

'We can probably slide through,' Goodnight said. 'But it'll be double the price if you want planetside delivery.'

'Too high.'

Goodnight shrugged. 'Somebody willing to chance eating an Alliance missile ought to be compensated.'

'I'll think about that,' Thatch said. 'Meantime, let's take a walk, and discuss some details.'

'Why not?'

Thatch and Goodnight, the two thugs trailing them, went out of Suckers, down the brightly lit boulevard. Thatch turned and went down into a dark side street, where a lim waited.

'Now, let's go for a little ride,' Thatch said. His voice was just a little gloating.

'Bad move, my friend,' Goodnight said. 'You shouldn't ever sell the lion's skin while the lion yet lives.'

'Huh?'

One of Thatch's bodyguards heard the sudden alarm in his boss's voice, went for a gun.

Goodnight's hand came up, brushed his jawbone, and the world got very slow. Thatch was shouting something but his voice was an incomprehensible squeak.

Goodnight had a tiny, flat gun in his hand.

He shot the first guard, following the first rule of close-quarter combat – the first one to move, no matter whether he's closest or not, is the first one you take care of.

He shifted his aim, put two small bolts into the second man's throat.

Thatch was turning, trying to run.

Goodnight shot him in the back of the head, then shut off his bester unit.

There was a man behind the wheel of the lim.

Goodnight jerked the door open, yanked the man out, shot him as he tumbled to the ground.

He was behind the controls of the lim, lifting it away.

'Now, I wonder just who those idiots were, trying to kill me? Guess I'll never know.

'And I guess that's it for being subtle. Time for the direct approach.'

Goodnight crept up behind the bored policeman, hit him hard with a knuckle punch in the side of the neck, eased him to the ground.

He went up the ramp to the yacht, touched its lock sensor, and was inside. The inner door yawned open.

Goodnight moved silently through the ship, down the main passageway, glancing into luxurious bedrooms, kitchens, toward the nose of the ship.

There were two people in uniform in the yacht's wardroom, yawning over a screen game.

One started to get up, froze when she saw Goodnight's gun.

'Excellent,' he approved. 'Just stay like that.'

He went past them, turning to keep the gun leveled, to the control room door, and slid it open.

'One-man operation,' he said approvingly, went back to the two crewmen.

'Who's the pilot?'

The woman, a sturdy-looking brunette, set her jaw.

'Fine,' Goodnight said. 'And you're the engineer, right?'

The man nodded imperceptibly.

'I assume this tub can run for a while without anyone in the power room,' Goodnight said. 'So you're going for a hike.'

'The hell he is,' the woman snapped.

'He can either walk off, or I'll drag his frigging corpse off,' Goodnight said calmly. 'His choice.'

'I'm going, mister.'

'Good.'

'And, believe me, I won't tell anybody what you looked like or anything. Please don't shoot me.'

'I've no intentions of that,' Goodnight said. 'But let's hike. I've got klicks to go before I sleep. You can come along with me, sister. I want to make sure you don't get in trouble while I'm out of the room.'

The man went down the ramp, looked back at Goodnight, then started running.

Goodnight touched studs, and the ramp slid closed, and the lock closed.

'Now, let's lift.'

'Without a flight plan?' the pilot said.

'You're making a test flight.'

'At this time of night?'

'You've got a weird owner. Come on, woman. If it comes to that, I can boost this pig out without you.'

The woman looked at him, at the gun, nodded jerkily.

'And while we're going,' Goodnight said, 'I'll see if there aren't a couple or three steaks worth thawing out. I'm ti-red, and need me some calories.'

'Nice docking job,' Goodnight complimented.

'Thanks.'

'That makes seven words you've said to me in the last four days,' Chas said. 'Are you starting to fall in love?'

The woman just glared.

'Now, if you'll hold out your arm, please?'

'What's that?'

'It's a wee syringe.'

'You're going to kill me.'

'Lady, if I wanted to kill you, I would've shot you back

on Puchert. You're just going to sleep for, oh, about two E-days. Then you're welcome to do anything you want.'

She started to pull her arm back. Goodnight touched the syringe's stud, and it hissed. She jolted, slid out of her chair. Goodnight eased her down to the carpet.

He went to the lock, checked the readout.

'I love nice civilized satellites like this one,' he said. 'No suiting up, no floating through vacuum, just a nice transition onward.'

The lock door slid open, and he went through it, down a long tube into the space station.

The station wound here, there and back on itself like a vast intestinal tract. It sat in the middle of a great deal of nothing. But it was very busy, the hub connection between a dozen systems.

Chas Goodnight, carrying a real-leather valise full of clothes that'd been just purchased, laundered, and the price tags torn off, went up to a ticket counter.

'You wish, sir?'

'Passage to Seaworld II, then a cross-connect to Seth V.'

The woman touched keys.

'We can do that, sir. But it'll be a little close . . . the Seaworld II ship departs in an E-hour, and it'll only give you about four E-hours on the ground before the Seth V flight.'

'Very good,' Goodnight said, handing over the Atherton ID. 'My boss wants me out there in a hurry.'

The ID went through the machine without a fuss.

Now, Goodnight thought, supposing I'd used the Atherton identity to get my ass offworld back on Puchert, instead of that third ID? Would that have worked? Or did Riss figure the only reason I wanted it was to be able to skate on Star Risk?

He decided somehow Riss must have had some kind of booby trap set on the Atherton ID if he'd tried to get cute, even if he couldn't figure out what it might have been.

Not that it mattered now. He'd done his villainy on Puchert, and made a nice, fairly loud, quite illegitimate exit that should be remembered.

When that pilot woke up, she'd hopefully sing like a bird. The authorities on Puchert, even if Thatch had been the undercover assassin for one or another of Mitidja's rebels, instead of working for the government or for Puchert itself, still wouldn't be happy with somebody leaving at least four bodies scattered around to irritate the citizenry.

It wasn't likely they'd chase him beyond the station. But anyone checking Goodnight/Atherton's credentials on Puchert should be satisfied with his scumbucketry.

'Your tickets, sir.'

'Thank you.'

'Have a nice flight.'

TWENTY-FIVE

'My poor last surviving bishop to King's rook one and check,' Redon Spada said.

'Uh . . . King to Queen three,' Friedrich von Baldur said.

'You can't move there,' Spada said. 'You're in check by my knight.'

'Damn it,' Baldur said. 'I lost my visualization. Wait a moment.'

He leaned back in the chair, stared up at the patrol ship's overhead.

'It won't matter,' Spada said. 'Wherever you go, it's my mate next move.'

Baldur's lips moved soundlessly.

'I cannot believe,' Grok said from where he crouched behind an improvised array that looked like an exploded vermicelli factory, 'that humans could ever have been bright enough to devise chess, but never to learn to play it properly. Either of you two should have been mated half a dozen moves ago.

'Let alone the way you stumble through keeping a mere two-dimensional board in your mind.'

'Thanks for the compliment,' Spada said. 'Why don't you go comb your fur for fleas or something?'

'I have never had any such . . . ah. We have some indicators,' Grok said.

Their ship and two others hung 'above' a convoy of four medium-sized freighters, escorted by half a dozen Star Risk patrol ships.

The convoy had been formed loudly and slowly, with just about every known frequency used to inform the world that there was a big cargo heading for Mfir, and any miner who wanted to make sure his riches wouldn't be stolen should get them to one of the three pickup points inside the belt.

'Blip . . . blip . . . blip. Three of them.'

A trio of warships had come out of hyperspace, on an intercept orbit for the convoy.

'Broadcasting on two, no four frequencies,' Grok said. 'Recorded. Ah. Now a fifth frequency. They've seen the escort and are hopefully signaling back into N-space.'

Baldur moved a throat pickup into position.

'All ships,' he 'cast. 'Stand by for jump.'

'And here are three more, and three behind them. We're outnumbered,' Spada said. He opened his own mike.

'Get ready,' he 'cast to his two mates. 'On command, we'll be going down to play patsy.'

'Wait . . . wait . . . ah-hah,' Grok said. 'They aren't taking any chances.'

Onscreen, a large echo appeared.

'And here is our cruiser,' Baldur said. 'The cast is all onstage, and now the play shall commence.' Into his mike: 'On the count of three . . . one, two, jump!'

The convoy vanished into hyperspace.

'Now, with any luck, they took off before anyone could put a tracer on them,' Baldur said. 'Very good.'

'And I've got the frequency that cruiser's using,' Grok said. 'Very, very good.'

'Maybe better,' Spada said. 'Let's get some, team.'

The three patrol ships, now alone in space with ten

raiders, went to full drive, and set an intersection orbit on the cruiser.

'Start tracking,' Spada said calmly. 'Nobody fires until my command or I'll have you hung by your thumbs. We're out of range . . .' He looked at his weapons officer, who shook his head.

'Tracking . . . tracking . . . remember, one launch, then jump,' Spada ordered. He could have been requesting a glass of water.

'In range,' Lopez said.

'Wait . . . wait . . . the idiots don't appear to have "seen" us,' Spada said.

'Closing nicely . . . I think we've pushed our luck . . . all ships, launch!'

Three shipkillers spat from their tubes on three patrol ships, flashed in and out of hyperspace, homed on the cruiser.

'Let's go home,' Spada ordered, not waiting to see what happened with the missiles.

'Transmitter dropped . . .' and then they were in the blurry colors of N-space.

'My curiosity is killing me,' Spada announced suddenly into his mike. 'You other two . . . we'll see you on Sheol. Let's jump back to where we were, grab whatever the transmitter's got, and then out of there.'

'One second, boss. Plotting . . . jumping . . .'

Baldur's stomach swam a little as 'real' space surrounded them, then vanished again.

Computers hummed, recording the data from the tiny satellite dropped by Spada.

'I got a visual,' Lopez said. 'Looks like one, maybe two hits on that big plug.'

'By George, I think we done it,' Spada said, and Bladur wasn't sure he could detect any excitement, even now.

'Running the 'corder from the telltale,' the weapons officer said. 'Yep. Big flash down by the drive section, and something, not as big a bang, amidships. I'd call the sucker wounded in action and whining.'

'Looks like,' Spada said. 'I think we can curl up with our blankies in the knowledge we put that bastard out of action for a little while at least.'

'Not to mention,' Grok said to Baldur, 'we've got logs on what frequencies they use, and maybe enough transmissions to break whatever code they're using.'

'Quite a good day for the heroes,' Baldur said comfortably. '*Quite* a good day indeed.'

'Indeed,' Grok said. 'Now, I'll make sure our young hero is in motion to where he's supposed to be going, and, if so, this will indeed be the best of all possible worlds.'

TWENTY-SIX

Seth V was a small world that might have been attractive if it ever stopped raining. But it seemed it never did, offering an endless variation of water down the back of your neck from torrential to misting.

If the sun had ever come out, which as far as Chas Goodnight knew, hadn't happened in the week he'd been frowsting about waiting for something to happen, the brightly painted houses along the twisting canals of the capital might have made it a tourist attraction, and the scattered islands of the southern hemisphere might have been destination resorts.

But that didn't happen.

And so Seth made its money from light manufacturing, electronics subassemblies, and farming.

And mercenaries.

It was a very big business for the planet, and they knew it.

One entire district of the capital, Trygve, where the police went in four-man teams, wearing combat gear, was set aside for the whores of war, and their customers.

A client could hire one tawdry hard case as a bodyguard, or put together a battalion-sized combat team, plus any and all of their gear.

If Boyington was the place to hire pilots, Seth was a

good place to fill out the rest of an army. It tended to cater to human or humanoids. There were other places to pick up soldiers who didn't mind breathing silicone.

During daylight hours, the district appeared almost normal, although there were clues, such as too many bars, surplus stores and, in common with every town outside every military base in history, pawnshops.

The restaurants were most exotic, offering fares from as many worlds as man had soldiered on for the past two hundred years and more.

Chas Goodnight nursed a cup of tea in one of them. It had a counter, four tables on the other side of a divider, and he was the only customer.

On arrival, he'd taken out one of the small batteries he had for his bester function, and used a pinhead to trigger a small switch. That turned the battery into a tiny transponder, sending a signal to his tracker, hopefully Grok, since he was the electronics expert.

Goodnight guessed Grok or someone from Star Risk was lurking on Seth V, because the switch had turned itself off after two days, hopefully signifying his position was transmitted.

The proprietor came past with a bottle, motioned it at Goodnight's cup.

'No thanks, Ygort,' Goodnight said. 'I'm watching the budget.'

'Do not worry, Mr. Atherton,' the man said. 'Someone come with money soon.'

'I hope so. Otherwise I'll have to go to work washing dishes for you in another couple of weeks.'

'You make joke,' the man said, without a smile. 'Very funny.'

The door opened, and a stocky man with constantly flickering eyes slid in, let the door close silently behind him. He saw Goodnight, sat down at the counter beside him.

'How's it going, Maffer?' Goodnight asked.

Hal Maffer's career was a bit hard to describe. He was a contact man for the free-lancers, trying to get a commission from both sides of a deal. Some swore he was slightly richer than God; others thought he was no better than a hand-to-mouth pimp.

'All right for me,' Maffer sad. 'Not so good for you.'

'What's the problem?' Goodnight asked, artistically putting just a bit of a whine into his voice. 'I give you where I want to work. I'm sure as hell got more skills than any of the pooptitties he . . . or she's liable to find here, and you can't hook me up?'

Maffer gestured at the café proprietor, who came over with the bottle.

'You staying clean by choice?' he asked Goodnight.

'Hell no.'

'I'm paying,' Maffer said, and Ygort took a glass from under the counter, half-filled it, poured into Goodnight's cup.

'You want water or ice?' Ygort asked.

'Why? Cold enough out already, and I took a bath this month,' Maffer said.

'So what's the problem?' Goodnight asked again.

'I could put it one way, and say you're over qualified,' Maffer said.

'So what?' Goodnight said. 'I heard somebody's hiring over to the Foley System, and I need to lay low for a while.'

'Yeah,' Maffer said. 'The client went and checked back on you, and they *would* like to talk to you back on Puchert.

'Lemme put it another way,' he said, draining about half his glass. 'The client thinks you're working deep cover for the Alliance, like as not.'

'What?' Goodnight pretended outrage. 'I been running guns for years, and a deal goes wrong, and I'm still supposed to be doing spookery?

'Bullshit, batshit and meshit.

'Jesus, I wish I hadn't heard good things about this Foley deal, not to mention my gut feel it's going to get better. You aren't helping since you say there aren't a lot of quality jobs going these days, where you actually might not have to throw down on the client to get paid.'

'Come on, Raff, don't pull my pud,' Maffer said. 'I know, and you sure as hell know, the Alliance has had you besters pull all kinds of shit for your cover.'

Goodnight buried a smile. Maffer was right.

'So I'm supposed to just sit there, rusting, running out of money, or until and if those pootlebrains back on Puchert track me down . . . and I don't have any idea what kind of extradition agreement Seth has got with anybody.'

'Not much of one,' Maffer said. 'But you *could* end up stuck and broke. You got anything else I could use to satisfy the client about your credentials?'

'Shit no,' Goodnight grumbled. 'What do I got to do to make him . . . her . . . think I'm a proper scumbucket? Rape a granny? Sell dope to schoolkids? Bugger my dad?'

'You're thinking in the right direction, my friend. Definitely the right direction.'

It occupied three offices in a nondescript, very modern office building in one of Trygve's outlying business districts.

The offices had a small sign: ALLIANCE PLANETARY LIAISON. A truly suspicious mind might have wondered why these offices were kilometers away from the Alliance consul.

Chas Goodnight had a truly suspicious mind.

It was about time, he thought, for APL to change its name, since there must be more people than just

Goodnight who knew the Liaison was one of the many covers for Alliance Intelligence.

It was near midnight, and he trundled down the building's corridor, towing an antigrav lift with brooms, mops, and other cleaning tools. Goodnight wore coveralls with MAINTENANCE SERVICES stitched on the back.

He knew no one ever looked at a janitor, let alone remembered one. The sleepy guard at the desk on the ground floor had barely glanced at him when he signed in.

The Liaison offices were locked, and Goodnight took a few seconds to make sure no one was inside, working late.

He still had a few scruples left, after all.

Goodnight turned the power on the lifter off outside the door, reached under the top tray, and flicked an old-fashioned switch. He still didn't entirely trust pressure sensors that, he felt, could flip back the other way or do other strange things. The solid click was a reassurance to him.

He went back down to the lift unhurriedly. He had plenty of time.

Goodnight had a bit of luck – the security desk wasn't manned. The guard must've gone to use the facilities, or out for a beer.

Goodnight didn't care.

He went out to where his stolen, small cargo lifter was parked.

Goodnight took off, and followed the traffic signs for a few blocks, then climbed into one of the highspeed lanes.

It was raining heavily.

Goodnight flew to a low knoll he'd picked out a day earlier, grounded the lifter.

He should have ditched the rig and walked back to his

hotel but Goodnight liked to see the results of his crafts-
manship.

They came in half an hour.

He'd gotten a pair of stabilized binocs from the glove
box, and was patiently watching the business district.

The building he'd left bucked, and flames seared out.
The blast wave reached him less than a minute later.

Chas Goodnight reached over his shoulder, and patted
himself on the back.

Certainly nobody else was there to do it. So now it was
time to turn his transponder back on.

Hell of a way you take to prove yourself,' Hal Maffer
complained.

Goodnight shrugged.

'Goddamned Alliance'll probably have a dozen inves-
tigators sniffing around, which isn't good for business.'

'Life's rough all around,' Goodnight said, unworried.
He had never been impressed with the Alliance's
gumshoes. 'So what'd the client say?'

'First was "Holy friggin' shit,"' Maffer said. 'Then he
said that all besters are crazy, but there's never been one
crazy enough to blow up one of his own offices.

'He's convinced all over the place that you're genuine.

'Man, that office must've had all the records on every
Alliance troopie that's come through in the past ten years
looking for free-lance work.'

'And I don't notice any of them offering to buy me a
beer,' Goodnight said.

'You think anybody's talking about what happened?'
Maffer said. 'I sure as hell ain't.'

'You're a good little clam,' Goodnight said.

'Yeah,' Maffer said. 'Now, here's the address for the
guy who's hiring for the Foley System. Get over to him
by yesterday.

'He'll have you out of the system in a day or so, which is none too soon for me.

'You could get in trouble, hanging around with you, Atherton.'

'I never have,' Goodnight said gravely. 'Always found me the best of company, too.'

TWENTY-SEVEN

'Ah,' Grok said in satisfaction. 'He is on the move.' He looked at one of the screens on Patrol Six. 'Moving our way, which would suggest that he's passed his testing, has been hired, and is now headed offworld.'

'Do you want me to turn off the transponder?' his pilot asked.

'No,' Grok said. 'When he hits the port, and we track him to a ship, and you put a tracer on it, yes.

'Murgatroyd is just professional, and suspicious, enough to sweep their new hires.'

TWENTY-EIGHT

There were only seven 'recruits' on the ship, a small obsolete Alliance destroyer escort converted to a fast transport. Goodnight was familiar with the type, since it was frequently used to insert and extract covert operators.

It would have about a fifteen-man crew, maybe twelve if it was skeletonized. Twelve people to carry seven around, Goodnight thought. That wouldn't be profitable from the perspective of someone running a typical crooked operation. Murgatroyd must be thinking like someone who's already very rich. Or someone who's got government experience. Which was one of the questions Star Risk had, and one of the reasons he was here, playing mercenary rogue.

Of the other six men and women who'd joined on Seth V, Goodnight classified one as a bully; one as a budding toady; two who, with their quiet calmness were clearly experienced soldiers; and the other two were wistful wannabees, who might have gotten some drill and wargaming experience with a territorial unit somewhere.

They were issued black ship's coveralls, boots, by one of the crew, and were told they'd get the rest of their gear when they reached 'base.'

Goodnight noted the crewman wore an identical shipsuit, without patches. If this operation was being run by someone – Cerberus Systems, some other system looking to horn in on the Foley System's goodies, who knows – they'd sanitized everything in sight.

Goodnight was glad one of the newbies asked where this 'base' was, to be cut off with an abrupt, 'You don't need to know that, troopie.' It was a question that might have been answered, and he didn't fancy exposing himself to anyone by asking it.

Goodnight found a bunk away from the others in the forty-person troop compartment, and settled in for a long doze, which he planned to interrupt only for mess call and the head. Goodnight had made many interstellar passages before, and knew they were either scary, or a deadly bore.

He was arranging his erotic daydreams when the bully growled in his ear.

Goodnight sat up.

'What do you want?'

'I think,' the woman said, 'we ought to organize.'

'Why?'

'So we don't get pushed around.'

'Listen, stupid,' Goodnight said. 'You took the job, right? If you didn't want to get pushed around, you could have stayed groundside, stroking your yingle until you ran out of credits and the local heat put you on some road gang in the rain.'

'I ain't stupid.'

'Yes, you are,' Goodnight said. He could have been more polite, but he didn't have the patience.

Besides, he needed some exercise, and had the feeling himself that he'd been manipulated more than he liked lately.

Instead of lying back down, he slid down from his bunk to the deck.

The prospective bully lifted her hands into a martial arts stance.

Goodnight's foot was already moving, snapping forward into the woman's gut.

She screeched, stumbled back.

Goodnight spun-kicked her feet out from under her, let her thud to the deck. When she tried to push herself up, he kicked her arms out from under her, and dropped, knees first, onto her back.

Air whuffed out, and she threw up.

'Disgusting,' Goodnight said. 'Now, I'm going to get up, and leave you in your own puke. When you feel better, I want you to clean up your mess.

'After that, you can leave me the hell alone. Pick on somebody your own size.'

The woman managed a nod.

Chas Goodnight clambered back into his bunk, and decided he would think about Jasmine King. In his dream, she'd be admiring and most cooperative.

Then a better thought came. Murgatroyd could be a woman, couldn't she?

If so, she didn't have to be some middle-aged skank with frizzed hair, did she? She could be young, rich, and somewhat oversexed, couldn't she?

Chas Goodnight wouldn't mind doing his snooping about in a harem, he thought. He'd never been in one, wondered what it would be like.

Especially if said harem featured female attendants. No, not attendants. Samplers, to report to Murgatroyd the quality of a man's wares.

Goodnight smiled, closed his eyes.

TWENTY-NINE

'What I've got,' Jasmine King said, 'is something. Unless it's nothing.'

'How informative,' Riss said. 'Let's hope it's something so I can get my heinie off this damned *Boop-Boop-A-Doop* and get in some folk's faces. Waiting for Goodnight to end up somewhere . . . and Grok tell us where . . . is getting elderly.'

'Calm yourself,' Baldur said. 'No one wants to go riding off wildly in all directions.'

Riss sighed. 'Go ahead, Jasmine.'

'I've got some interesting theories on where Murgatroyd might be based,' King said. 'That cruiser made me start thinking, as I said.

'Warships – big warships – need bases, maintenance yards, machine shops and all that. It's almost impossible to keep one functioning without some serious backup.

'Which means I don't see how Murgatroyd can have his base in the asteroid belt. Some nosy miner or one of our patrol ships would've spotted it.

'So we're left with out-system, or within the Foley worlds. Out-system would be the simplest for Murgatroyd to maintain, but there aren't any systems particularly close to us. Still, that's a maybe. I hope Grok and Chas clarify that problem.

'I took a look at the possibilities in-system. I came up with, I hope, an approach that would keep me from years of looking at satellite photos.

'I also put a limit on my search, not considering either Welf, since it's almost uninhabitable, or the three outer worlds.

'It seems that, about thirty years ago, Glace was in some disagreement with another system. Fearing war, they built quite a few bases. The diplomats made a settlement, so the guns never came out, and the bases were abandoned.'

'Ah,' Riss said, getting it.

'Exactly,' Jasmine said. 'What would be simpler than taking over an abandoned base somewhere? Especially if the base happened to not have any neighbors.

'There are . . . were . . . three or four bases, mostly intended for Early Warning, on satellites of the outer worlds. I haven't been able to find a location on them yet, but I'm still looking.

'Which is very interesting, in itself, almost like there's somebody shortstopping all data connected with those bases.' Jasmine slumped. 'And here I used to pride myself that I could find anything.

'The best I was able to find was that there were some four bases on Glace itself. Two of them are close to population centers, the others were deliberately sited next to nowhere, so if Glace was attacked the attackers wouldn't have an exact location for all of Foley's spacefleet.

'Again, I lack locations so far.

'The more I think about it, this whole damned mess . . . or, rather, the complete absence of information . . . suggests there's something rotten about those bases. For all I know, they never were built, but were just a way for some politicos to skim off graft.

'The whole thing reeks, but I guess we'd better do some kind of followup.

'I suggest that we put out patrol ships off Glace, and stud a few at the system's edge, in case Murgatroyd has taken up light housekeeping on one of the ice giants' moons.

'An interesting bit of trivia, by the way. One of the bases on Glace was abandoned before the threat of war was ended.

'I've got scattered data that suggests Glace was inhabited before human colonists by primitives, no details yet. Supposedly these aliens were relentlessly hostile, either on first contact or after they watched man make his usual mess out of things, and retreated into hidden places where they sulked and ambushed the stray outdoorsman.

'I find that most interesting.'

Riss hadn't been listening to the last, but was considering options.

'I'd think the outer worlds are the most likely,' she said.

'And I disagree,' Baldur said.

'I'll stay here and man the fort,' King said. She reached in a pocket of her shipsuit, took out a coin.

'You two might well head up the patrol ships waiting for Grok to arrive. Heads take Glace, tails the iceworlds.

'M'chel you're first,' and the coin spun through the air.

King caught the coin, clapped one hand over it, then lifted her hand.

'Freddie,' King said, 'pack your woolies.'

'Just my luck,' Baldur said. 'So much for lurking over the fleshpots.'

'Jasmine,' M'chel asked. 'How do you find these things out?'

King smiled, and her smile was distinctly beatific.

'You have but to look, my little sister, and all things shall be revealed.'

'Oh, horseshit,' Riss said, and started for her cabin to start packing.

THIRTY

The starship drifted down, toward a jungled cliff face, as if out of control and doomed.

Concrete grated, and two huge clamshell doors slid open, exposing an enormous hanger. The transport floated in on its antigravity, extruded skids, and landed, dwarfed by the huge Sensei-class cruiser nearby.

The great bay still held room for half a dozen more warships.

The transport's ramp slid out, and its outer lock door opened.

After a few minutes, Goodnight and the other six recruits came out, stood, blinking in the dimness, broken by glaring work lights.

Air-conditioning machinery hummed and, on the nearby cruiser, maintenance men and machines crawled over the ship's skin.

Goodnight sniffed the air. It smelt of mold and disuse. He'd expected to land on some dead moonlet somewhere, not here, wherever here was.

A voice boomed, and a cargo lifter shot out of a port toward them. It grounded, and its driver got out.

He was small, slender, dark complected, and had a small, carefully maintained moustache, and a very big voice.

'All right, you people,' he said. 'My name is Navarro. That's all you need to know. I'm your boss.'

'What's your rank?' one of the bewildered freshies said.

'No rank,' Navarro said. 'This is a job, not the army.' He touched a stripe on the right sleeve of his shipsuit.

'This means I'm a boss. Anybody with one of these who tells you what to do . . . you do it.

'Actually, I'm not a *real* boss. There's five or six of those. Believe me, you'll know them when you see them.

'When they say jump, you jump, and they'll tell you when you're high enough.

'Pile in this lifter, and I'll take you to the barracks.'

'A question, Navarro,' Goodnight asked. 'What are we going to be doing? The man who hired me was pretty vague about what our assignments will be, although he said you can get very rich.'

'I'll give you a briefing when you're in quarters. But I'll tell you that first, we'll sort you out as to what you can do. One of you's a bester, right?'

'I am,' Goodnight said.

'The others of you are what you are, which won't take long to find out. Initially, we'll use you for perimeter security around this base.'

'Who're we securing against?' one of the experienced soldiers asked.

'Against being found out by any of the oppos . . . but mostly against the Grays.'

'Which are?'

'Nasty, short, little frigging aliens that think everything out there is their turf, and just love nailing anybody who disagrees. SOP is kill 'em when you see them . . . which won't be often, since they come from the jungle, and we don't.'

'That's all?' the bully asked, her face pouty.

'Till we get you tried and true, that's all,' Navarro said. 'After that . . . there's always places for somebody offworld, when somebody zigs when they shoulda oughta zagged and gets her body bag issued. We always need troops for the raiding teams, anyone with experience in space, and like that.

'That's where you can get rich like . . . Atherton, right? Like Atherton said. Assuming you don't get independent and greedy, and start pocketing some goodies here and there, which can lead to a real short future.

'But first you got to prove to us you're good . . . and lucky . . . enough to make it against the Grays.'

The woman looked dissatisfied, about to ask something else, and then alarms screamed.

THIRTY-ONE

'Risk control,' Riss said into her throat mike, 'this is Patrol Three.'

The small Pyrrhus-class patrol ship was making high orbits over Glace's thick, unpopulated jungle.

'This is Control,' Baldur's voice came through the ship speaker. 'Go.'

'This is Three. We had Goodnight's beeper solid when the ship came in-atmosphere, tracked it, keeping just below the horizon, and the ship vanished.'

'Say again your last,' Baldur said from his ship.

'Vanished,' Riss said. 'Gone. Offscreen. Pfft.'

Her pilot, Dinsmore, flicked a glance from his controls at her, shook his head. Still nothing onscreen.

'Suggestions?' Riss said.

'Try a high-speed pass over where it vanished,' Baldur said. 'Then pick an arbitrary point near that, and start doing concentric circles.'

'Sweeping the jungle,' Riss said. 'That's a big, dull Rog. Patrol Three, clear.'

She looked at Dinsmore.

'You heard the man.'

Dinsmore nodded, put the patrol craft to full drive.

Solid green jungle reeled past them.

'Here we go,' he said. 'Close to where it ghosted on

us, anyway. On my count . . . four . . . two . . . here.'

Riss scanned her screens, even looked through the port. She saw nothing but a jungled valley, with a small lake at its bottom, and a tall, brooding cliff.

'Nada from nada is nada,' she said. 'Hokay, Dins, put us in a nice orbit around your point.'

'You realize we're making ourselves into a big, fat target,' the flier said.

'I realize,' M'chel said. 'Which is why I'm depending on your steel-trap reflexes and mind to haul ass out of here if any of these little needles or scales even flicker.'

'A definite affirm on that one,' Dinsmore said, putting the patrol ship almost on its side, as he cut the drive down to a mild putter. 'And here we go loop-de-loo.'

'Nothing,' Riss muttered as they finished the first circle. 'Go a little wider on the next one. Which'll put us over, not into, that goddamned cliff. I hope.'

Dinsmore nodded, fingers touching sensors.

Again they started around the search point.

'Hell, we ain't got . . . Shit fire!' Riss snapped. 'Get us out of here! I got indicators going nuts!'

Dinsmore slammed full drive, went to the sky.

'I have an incoming,' Riss said. 'Hard on our tail . . . closing . . . try to turn away and topple it . . .'

Dinsmore banked hard, and M'chel saw a whitish flicker out of the port, then an explosion slammed, pitched the patrol ship sideways.

'We're hit,' she said, caught herself on the obvious, and switched to uncoded transmission on the guard channel.

'Mayday, Mayday,' she called, a bit proud that her voice didn't sound the slightest bit excited. 'Holding the transmit button down. Mark this location . . . ship struck by missile . . .'

'We're losing power,' Dinsmore said. 'Passing through six thousand meters . . .'

The driver hiccuped and there was sudden silence.

'Time to go,' Dinsmore said, unbuckling his safety harness. 'Our antigravs'll never ease us in.'

'Mayday, Mayday,' Riss said again. 'Going down. Mark this transmission.'

The com hissed, and all its lights went out as the patrol ship rolled end over end.

Riss went flying, caught a stanchion, and felt her muscle pull.

Dinsmore shouted in pain as he hit a bulkhead with his side.

The ship antigrav went off for an instant, then back on, as the lights died, and emergency lighting went on.

'This one's doomed,' Riss said, shrugging into her combat harness. She fought her way to the pilot, and pulled him to his feet.

He screamed, bit his lip to hold pain back, and Riss muscled him to the inner lock entrance.

'Here,' she said. 'Into this.'

She forced him into a dropper as the ship pinwheeled again.

'Jesus, that hurts.'

Riss didn't answer, but slid into a dropper of her own, cursing herself for being careless and not adjusting the straps before they'd lifted.

She pushed Dinsmore into the lock, followed him, hit the cycle button as she saw smoke billow from a swinging compartment door. Air screamed around her.

Then she was hanging on to the outer lock door as, around her, green and blue alternated being ground and the sky.

She pushed Dinsmore, saw him tumble away from the

patrol ship, waited until the lock was facing down, and kicked herself out.

Just like old times, she thought, except that in old times your jumpship wasn't going gaga on you.

Riss was spinning left, pushed her right leg and arm out, and the spin slowed. She put both arms, both legs out, was stable, falling toward the jungle below.

She looked down, guessed she was about two thousand meters from the trees, dropping at terminal velocity.

Riss found the on sensor on the antigrav harness, gave it a squirt, slowed, hit it again, and was falling at a reasonable rate.

She looked around for the pilot, saw Dinsmore, obviously riding his dropper hard, five hundred meters above her, almost drifting.

Riss heard a roar, saw an aircraft flash toward her, had time to ID it as an in-atmosphere scout, started pointlessly waving her arms, thinking about rescue and a very long, very cold drink.

Above its engine-scream, the scout's machine-cannon roared. Tracer rounds drew a green streak through the sky, walked across Dinsmore's body. The flier didn't even have time to scream before he was almost cut in half, blood spraying down toward the jungle.

'Son of a dead-eyed bitch!' Riss snarled. Her fingers found the off sensor of the dropper, and she fell, tucking her arms, legs in, head down, dropping like a bullet, falling away from the killing aircraft.

She managed to turn her head, saw the scout diving at her, saw the trees starting to rush up, knew she was too low, and again flashed the dropper, twice, three times, and the scout was past her in a dive, bullets streaming in front.

The pilot of the scout realized how low he was, reversed his drive, turned his antigrav to full power. The scout wobbled in its dive, started to recover, and then it was too late.

'Auger your dirty ass straight on to hell,' Riss growled as the fireball rose above the trees, red and dirty black, no more than two hundred meters away, and the explosion almost tumbled her. 'Teach you to be such a murderous bastard.'

She promptly forgot about the scout and its crew, holding down the antigrav sensor as leaves, branches, reached up and the jungle swallowed her.

THIRTY-TWO

'Star Risk One, this is Star Risk Control. Do you have anything?'

'Control this is One. Orbiting the area Three Maydayed from . . . nothing . . . wait. Patching through from Ten.'

'Control, this is Ten. I'm over a narrow valley, and, at the bottom, I've got smoke coming up. Do you want me to close?'

'Ten, this is Control. Proceed . . . cautiously. Something out there bites. Switching channels.

'One, this is Control. Were you monitoring?'

'That's affirm.'

'One, give Ten an escort down.'

'Affirm.'

'Control, this is Ten. Orbiting smoke at angels one . . . something went in hard, and blew. No sign of life.'

'Ten, wait.'

Baldur turned away from the com.

'Grok, do we have anything?'

'No,' the alien said. 'The tracking station we planted on Goodnight isn't casting . . . or is blocked out. Nothing on the Search and Rescue frequency from either Riss or Dinsmore, Three's pilot.'

Baldur touched his mike.

'Ten, this is Control. Still negative?'

'Still negative.'

'One, this is Control. What about you?'

'Nothing, boss,' Redon Spada 'cast.

Baldur thought quickly.

'All Star Risk stations . . . RTB. I say again, Return to Base.'

Again, he looked at Grok.

'Keep the SAR monitor going.'

'Your call?' King asked.

'I think we have lost Riss,' Baldur said. 'And very likely Goodnight as well.'

THIRTY-THREE

M'chel Riss stood on a jutting tree branch under the top tier of the jungle, but still about fifty meters from the ground.

She contemplated descent, so she wouldn't have to think about Dinsmore's bloody death.

Come on, Riss, she thought. Bad guys do things like that. That's why they're bad guys.

She smiled wryly. As if good guys sometimes didn't get carried away and do some unnecessary strafing. Yeah, but they didn't brag about it. At least, not in her hearing.

This was getting most rapidly nowhere. She slung the dropper over one shoulder, opened one of the sidepouches of her combat harness, and took out a can of climbing thread, and clipped it into her harness. She sprayed a blob out, attached it to the limb, and gingerly started down, grateful she didn't have to use a doubled rope.

Ten meters from the ground she stopped, and waited for a few minutes. There were small-animal and flying-thing noises below, but nothing that sounded like a creature big enough to consider Riss cutlets.

She went on to the ground, put her back against a tree, and looked about her.

It was very lovely, in a gloomy sort of way, the overhead cover keeping the ground-level plants stunted. It could have been, if there were little signs, a botanic garden.

Of a very nonterrestrial nature. The green was muted, and frequently mixed with rust-red hues. The ground under her feet was soft, aeons of rotting leaves.

A small animal peered at her over a downed limb. If it weren't blood-red, with six legs ending in clawed paws, it might have been a squirrel.

She moved, and it sprang away, and vanished.

Next M'chel considered what was in her survival pouches. She knew very well what they contained, but that was SOP to keep away panic.

Then she heard the screech of aircraft overhead, recognized the sound of a Pyrrhus-class patrol craft. There was another whine.

Friendly.

She realized she was a little shocky, clawed into a pouch, took out her SAR beacon. She'd turned the switch on before noting the large crack along one side, and the exposed circuit board.

She turned the sensor on, rolled volume up to high.

Riss, ever the optimist, keyed the send sensor.

'Any overhead aircraft, any overhead aircraft, this is downed flier. Be advised there are hostiles in this area. I say again, hostiles in this area.'

She didn't give her name, for fear the unfriendlies were monitoring the Search and Rescue band, and could use it later to set a trap.

Nothing came back at her.

Maybe, she thought, the beacon's receiver was just broken.

She repeated her message, and heard the aircraft above go back and forth, then climb away, their drive-sound receding in the distance.

Well dingbing it and all that good shit, she thought. I guess I'll have to hike this one out.

She thought about leaving the SAR beacon on, decided it might just be making enough of a noise for whoever'd shot her down to be picking it up, and homing.

Riss thought of pitching it into the jungle, then stopped. No one in a survival condition should ever throw anything away, no matter how useless.

Riss found a GPS receiver in one pouch, turned it on. The screen lit, but was blank.

Wonderful, she thought. These bastards here on Glace don't even have positioning satellites planted. I'll bet they hunt with spears, too.

Riss sat down, took out an old-fashioned compass, treated herself to a bit of candy from one pouch while she drew a mental map around herself.

Over there . . . west, the way they'd come . . . she remembered there'd been a river that looked big enough to raft down. Somewhere down there . . . southish . . . should be that town they'd flown near.

It *would* be a hike. A week, maybe two weeks, maybe longer.

So what? Riss was used to hikes.

She got to her feet, picked up the dropper, and started out.

The journey of a thousand miles, whatever a mile was, starts with one step.

How goddamned cheerful. Find something else to think about.

Riss tried *not* to think about those implacable hostile aliens that King had mentioned, who could be lurking around her, behind every bush. She had enough troubles already.

Near dusk, she started looking for her RON – Remain

Overnight – campsite. She found a near-perfect one, a great tree with a fork about fifteen meters off the ground, not that easily reached by questing beasts. Nearby was a spring. She splashed water about liberally, but didn't dare take anything off.

She used a small heat tab, odorless and smoke-less, to heat a pouch of emergency rations.

One of Riss's darkest secrets was she actually liked E-rats, which would have made her an outcast in any military circle if she'd admitted to it. She would be partially redeemed by her fondness for haute cuisine, which she loved eating, if not cooking. Riss had realized early on she was one of those people naturally ungifted in the kitchen.

Her choice was a mystery meat with red pepper sauce, dehydrated greens that, from their texture and bitterness, told her she *had* to be gaining strength just by smelling them, a stimulating tea she decided to pass on until the morning since she wanted to sleep, and dehydrated berries that had seen better days. But she ate everything, used the salt in the rat pack as a dentifrice, and then clambered up the tree to her nice, flat branch.

Riss bundled up in her waterproof sheet, and tried to think Gentle Thoughts, one hand curled around her heavy Alliance blaster.

Going to sleep was easier than she'd thought it would be – she was a bit off her top physical shape.

She jolted awake sometime in darkness, hearing something snuffling interestedly at the base of the tree. It sounded big and nasty, but could well have been that six-legged 'squirrel' with a good voice box.

Riss thought about sending a blaster bolt or two down as a warning decided not, for fear of pissing the creature off if it were big, and also the sound of the gunshot would surely rouse alarm.

After a time, the creature went away, and Riss went back to sleep.

She didn't remember dreaming at all when she woke before dawn as her mental alarm went off.

Riss waited, gun ready. But there was no movement around her.

She went down the tree with her gear, washed again, had some sort of dehydrated egg, crackers, a high-protein pack flavored, for some unknown reason, with cinnamon, brushed her teeth, and went on west.

It was about midday when M'chel heard the screams. They were close, and agonized. Riss might have thought they came from no human throat, but she'd seen too much agony in her years in uniform not to know that any sound can come from a human throat, if the pain's great enough.

A sensible woman would have gone in the opposite direction, or at least doubled her speed along her course, not needing any more grief than what she already had.

Instead, she drew her gun, and, thumb on the safety, went closer.

She smelt smoke, and seconds later was on the edge of a small clearing.

Four men, wearing coveralls and heavily armed, were gathered around a fire.

Next to the fire a strange being was tied up. He was gray, about a meter tall, and wore no more than a breechclout with suspenders.

His skull was squat, prognathous, with a beetling brow. Coarse hair hung low over what little forehead he had, and down the back of his neck.

Not far from him was the most archaic weapon Riss had ever seen. It looked like something she'd seen in a museum once that shot stone balls, fired by a low-grade explosive rammed down the barrel. Beside it was a short spear, with what looked like a stone point.

There were two sprawled bodies at the edge of the clearing, one about the size of the 'man,' the other clearly a 'child.' The 'child's' neck sat at an awkward angle.

One of the men had a small iron bar, which he was heating in the fire. The alien was moaning, and Riss saw three brands burnt into the ET's leg.

The man picked up the bar using gloves, and leaned over the alien. He laughed, and the being screamed in anticipation.

The other three laughed even louder than the first.

Riss knelt, braced her blaster on her cupped hand, and shot the torturer in the back of the head. He contorted, brains spraying, and fell across the alien.

The other three spun, saw Riss.

'Playtime's over, boys,' M'chel said cheerfully. The first grabbed for a holstered gun, and Riss shot him twice in the chest. She pulled right, and blew the third man's face away, then put two more rounds into the last man's stomach.

She listened to the echoes of her blaster fire die away in the jungle, then went forward.

Riss kicked the dead man off the alien, who stared up at her, eyes wide.

M'chel took her survival knife from a pouch, snapped it open, and cut the alien free.

He, if it was a he, didn't move at first.

Riss stepped back.

He still didn't move, as if expecting a trick.

'Come on, dummy,' she snapped. 'Those assholes've got to have friends.'

Still nothing.

She growled, picked up the being's weapon, handed it to him.

He took it reluctantly.

Riss thought for an instant he was thinking about shooting her.

It took effort to turn her back on him, and start going through the corpses' gear.

She ended with four shoulder-fired blasters, the same number of pistols, enough bolt magazines for a small army, sixteen grenades, and one recoil-less bunker-buster.

Riss was looking for a nice, sturdy tree to smash the weapons on, when the alien touched her arm.

She looked at him.

Using the top pair of his clawlike hands, he picked up one of the pistols, and hugged it close. Then he set it back down, and looked at her.

'Dummy me,' she said. 'Sure.' She gave him the pistol then the other handguns, and the shoulder weapons.

He made a chittering noise, imitated firing one of them at one of the men, pointed off.

'Sure,' Riss said. 'Kill lots more of the bastards if you want.'

The alien came to his feet and limped to one of the bodies, that of the 'woman.'

He chittered again, slowly, and Riss anthropomorphicized sorrow in his tones.

'Come on,' she said. 'I'll give you a hand.'

A few moments later, Riss, carrying the 'child's' body over one shoulder, and the shoulder blasters slung over the other, followed the alien out of the clearing.

She wished she'd had a Star Risk card to pin to the bodies' chests, but figured their friends would be angry enough when they found the corpses.

It was a longish trudge, giving Riss time enough to figure out the alien had to be one of those primitive badasses who'd driven the Glacians from their base, which now had to be taken over by Murgatroyd and company.

Aliens didn't sit well on her tongue, especially since this was their world, so she thought a bit, and decided she'd call them 'trolls.'

The name came easily, as the skies clouded over and it began raining. Riss plodded on, hoping her alien lived under a nice, warm, dry bridge like legend dictated.

The troll turned off the main path, and pushed brush aside.

Riss saw the first guard, with a nocked arrow pointed at her chest.

'Her' troll squeaked severally. The other one shook his head, but didn't shoot.

Another guard, this one armed with a weapon as primitive as the first troll's, came from nowhere, then two, then half a dozen.

They were chittering away, and Riss didn't think they were making friendly greetings.

She counted thirty, perhaps forty of the trolls, in various sizes, all dressed similarly, all armed. She couldn't make out any signs of their sexes.

One came close, and fingered her arm. She looked down at him, and the alien spread jaws in what might have been a smile, made a pinchers with his claws, and mimed pulling off a piece of Riss's flesh and stuffing it in his mouth.

And I could have kept right on trundlin', Riss thought sourly. But I wanted an invite to Saturday night's dinner.

As the main course.

The camp was as primitive as any she'd seen on any world, or in her anthro studies: a tree-covered clearing, with huge boulders around it. The boulders concealed small caves, and a great slab sheltered a cooking fire.

Primitive, but effective, Riss thought. The rocks'd hide any infrared, the caves'd sleep dry and fairly warm, and the trees would block visuals.

She'd seen – hell, she'd *made* – worse herself in the field.

Her troll indicated a rock for Riss to sit on. She set the child's body down as reverently as she could, put the rifles on the ground.

It was as if the trolls noticed the weapons for the first time, squeaking away as if it were Crossmass or something.

Riss tried to improve her lot, indicated the weapons, then motioned to the trolls, with a smile.

There was silence.

Her troll came close, and held out his hand for her blaster.

Reluctantly, she gave it to him, thinking that if things didn't work out, he'd be the first to die.

Two trolls came out of a cave. Both carried short staves.

They rapped them together, and there was silence.

One indicated M'chel's troll. She decided he had to have a name, couldn't remember what any of her childhood trolls were called.

She pointed to him, and raised an eyebrow.

As if he'd understand that meant a question.

He pointed to his chest. Riss nodded. He squeaked twice, very shrilly. That might have meant 'Who me,' a name, or even, 'My chest, dummy.'

She decided Two Twitters would be name enough.

He turned away from her, and began chattering away to the two with clubs, pointed at the two bodies, and there was a moaning.

He motioned walking, then reached up four times,

indicating the men who'd caught him and killed his wife
and child. Riss was making large assumptions about age
and gender, but then, these were her trolls by right of
discovery.

He went on with his story, and there were gasps at the
torturing, then wide eyes when he was rescued, and Riss
heard murmurs that might have been sympathy.

Two Twitters finished, picked up one of the blasters,
and pointed. M'chel thought it might have been in the
same direction he had before.

Murgatroyd's base?

The two chiefs, if that was what they were, went to
one side, and consulted.

The argument went on for almost an hour, and it was
getting dark.

Riss, even though she knew they were debating her
fate, yawned.

It had been a very long day.

Then the two of them came back, and squealed to Two
Twitters. He swung his head to the side twice, then
turned, and picked up her blaster.

Holding it by the grip, he came toward her.

M'chel braced. He'd be the first to die, then she'd be
on the two guys with the clubs.

When they went down, she'd try running, hoping the
shock would scare the trolls long enough for her to break
free.

Two Twitters turned the blaster, extended it butt first
to M'chel then pointed the way they'd come in.

Riss stood up, holstered the weapon.

She bowed to the chiefs, to Two Twitters, started away.

Then she stopped, wondering what the hell was going
through her head.

Marines didn't retreat, goddamnit. Even ex-Marines.
At worst, they just advanced in another direction.

Besides, these shorties knew where the goddamned raiders hung their hats.

She turned back.

'Guys,' she said slowly, knowing the trolls weren't understanding a word, 'you can welcome your new advisor.

'I'm gonna show you how to get back at those pimps. Hell, I'm gonna show you how to get back for every frigging thing that humans have done to piss you off since First Contact.'

Major M'chel Riss's smile was not particularly pleasant.

THIRTY-FOUR

'Sit down, Atherton,' the woman said, not introducing herself, and Goodnight understood what Navarro had meant when he said the five or six 'real bosses' wouldn't be hard to recognize.

The woman wore a well-tailored, conservative civilian suit, and her long, dark-blond hair was curled on the back of her head. Goodnight guessed her to be in her mid-fifties.

And she oozed self-control and power.

Goodnight wondered why she'd gone foul of some law on some world or system, instead of being what she looked like – a very high official in the Alliance.

He wondered if that was exactly what she was, working under deep cover, then discarded the notion, even though the Alliance, to his personal knowledge, had done things far more underhanded. This operation didn't have, for one thing the top-heavy rank and structure so beloved by the Alliance military, overt and covert.

'You're a bester,' the woman said.

'I am.'

'We don't see many of those,' the woman said. 'The Alliance doesn't like to lose people they've put as many credits into as you.'

Goodnight shrugged.

'In my case, they weren't consulted. Things went wrong, and it was their damned fault. I don't mind getting killed by my own stupidity, but not when it's gonna be by the people who're running me.'

'A nice sense of loyalty.'

'A nice sense of self-preservation,' Goodnight corrected.

The woman allowed a wintry smile, looked at a hidden screen.

'When you were first available, on Puchert, we thought you could still be with the Alliance. However, you proved us wrong. Deliberately?'

'Deliberately,' Goodnight said.

'You besters are more than just modified muscle,' the woman said. 'Very good. I can tell you that we had immediate plans for you as soon as we realized you weren't a double. After a very short testing period, we intended to put you in charge of one of our raiding teams, in the asteroid belt.

'However, circumstances here on Glace have changed somewhat.

'When the transport you were aboard was approaching this base, it was somehow spotted by ships belonging to the free-lance security team working for our enemies.

'We destroyed the ship, but evidently there was at least one survivor.'

Goodnight held up a hand.

'I'm confused. What's this free-lance security team? And how do you know our ship wasn't seen by whatever military Glace . . . the Foley System . . . has got?'

'Transkootenay Mining has retained a small independent company, foolishly trying to save money, but all to our benefit. And we know . . . you do not need to know how, but it is one hundred percent . . . that the tracking ship didn't belong to Foley's own space force.'

Goodnight filed that for later contemplation.

'Fine,' he said. 'Go ahead.'

'These survivors of the crash managed to evade us, and seem to have linked up with the subhumans in the jungle, the ones we call "Grays."

'We lost a four-man patrol the day after we destroyed their scout ship, and six more of our security element outside this base have been killed.

'Killed and stripped.

'The Grays have always been our enemies . . . humanity's enemies . . . attacking our patrols and even listening posts when and where they can. But it was always smash-and-kill, no more than one man at a time, and that man or woman killed with the most primitive weaponry.

'These last ten were cleverly stalked and murdered with modern weapons, weapons taken from our dead.

'Somehow these survivors have managed to ally the Grays with their own designs.

'It's intolerable to have our flanks being nipped at like this, when we are almost ready to begin a final push to drive Transkootenay Mining from the system, and our final goals realized.'

Goodnight wanted to ask, 'Which are?', but knew better. He kept his expression bright, interested.

'There are no more than half a dozen Gray settlements in our immediate area. That's not a precise estimate, for these savages have a certain ability at hiding from our detectors.

'Be that as it may, we're putting together a hunter-killer team, which will be led by you and an experienced jungle fighter. Twelve men, and they shall all be experienced in ground combat.

'Your task will be to first find these survivors . . . we suspect three or four . . . and kill them.'

'What about the Grays?'

'Obviously any that stand in your way are to be destroyed. We do not wish to encumber ourselves with prisoners. When we have the survivors of that scout ship, the Grays will return to being no more than an annoyance.

'That's all. Navarro will provide you with whatever equipment you need, maps, and so forth.'

The woman stood.

Goodnight remained seated.

'Is there a problem, Atherton?'

'Well,' Goodnight said thoughtfully, 'I joined without too many specifications about my job description. But this assignment sounds not just interesting, but a little on the dangerous side.

'Perhaps we should reconsider some of the terms of my contract?'

The woman started to look angry, then smiled her cold smile once more.

'That can be arranged. And, if I had any doubts of your legitimacy as a mercenary, there are none at all now.'

The experienced jungle fighter called himself Siegfried. No last . . . or maybe first . . . name. But he appeared to know what he was talking about.

The other ten were a little less impressive. They *were* service experienced, but few of them had much in the way of combat, other than chasing dissidents in the hills on one-day patrols.

'What can you expect?' Siegfried told Goodnight. 'Hard goddamned times when most of the galaxy's at peace.

'A nice gawdawful war, and there'd be a lot more of us for rent with headbanging time.'

'Not to mention more competing for fewer jobs,' Goodnight said.

'Yeah,' Siegfried said. 'That's true enough. Maybe things are best as they is.'

As for equipment, there wasn't much in the quartermaster's for in-atmosphere combat, although a great deal of up-to-date gear for suit fighting.

Goodnight sorted through what there was, kept the eleven he'd been assigned from ladening themselves down with every comfort, and decided it was time for some real training.

He went over the maps, found an area not far from the base that was hostile, but not, at least by previous reports, all that hostile. He didn't want his soldiery to get immediately wiped out, especially when he was around.

Goodnight wondered how he was going to play this hand – certainly he didn't want to kill these survivors, whoever they were. Although he might have to, to keep from blowing his own cover.

He wondered if he would be able to turn his tracking device on and get Star Risk inbound for a rescue before things came to a head.

He certainly didn't want to flip it on until he was sure the base electronic monitoring couldn't pick up his signal, and then expose him.

Nor did he want to bring Star Risk in fat, dumb, and happy on this base and get their plows shot off.

He would have to wing it.

In the meantime, he and Siegfried had to teach his hammerheads how to move in a jungle, how to spot natural ambushes, how to set an ambush of their own, and all the other things that would be forgotten the first time something loud went off in their ears, but hopefully remembered when the adrenaline pulsed a little less.

They moved out of the base, with Navarro's assurances they were being tracked, and if anything went wrong, there'd be rescue on the way within seconds.

That told Goodnight not to start providing for his own rescue with the beacon.

These grunts weren't used to something as nasty as a jungle. They thumped into each other, loudly complained when they tripped, wanted to take too many breaks and those in nice, open, deadly clearings.

And they moved too damned fast, in spite of Siegfried and Goodnight's constant chiding.

They'd been out for a day and a half, with zed contact, when the woman Goodnight had on point, the least inept of his troops, was leading them up to a ridge crest where Goodnight intended to set up some sniffers and hopefully get a lead on some Grays to provide targets.

She froze, held her palm out, flat. The others took a moment to read the sign, then obeyed, and went down.

She touched her shoulders, then motioned toward the front.

Officer up.

Goodnight took that to mean him, and slithered up to the lead, past the team.

The woman's eyes were wide, and she pointed.

Goodnight dug binocs out of their case, turned them on, and scanned the jungle as directed.

He saw them, gathered around a promontory: five, no, six squat, dark-skinned nonhumanoids. Purely Stone Age, except for the very modern shoulder blasters three of them carried.

And, in their midst, a tall human in a tattered ship-suit.

The human had short, blond hair.

He turned, and became a she.

Goodnight hit the zoom button, and the she became M'chel Riss, and he barely suppressed a moan of 'Aw, shit, God. Whydaya gotta go and play games with me all the damned time?'

THIRTY-FIVE

L C Doe came through the lock of the *Boop-Boop-A-Doop* with a cagey expression, and a sample case in one hand.

The ship was parked on one of Glace's main fields, three patrol craft around it.

Jasmine King was sitting at a computer terminal, touching sensors, with a sour expression on her face.

'Doin' payroll, huh?' Doe asked.

King, who had been running probability studies on just where M'chel Riss and Dinsmore had been shot down, forced a smile.

'That's it,' she said. 'What brings you to Glace?'

'You know,' Doe said. 'Bright lights, big city, trying to get some bennies for my miners out of t'ese stumbling idiots t'ey call a government.

'And lookin' for M'chel. She 'round?'

'She's offworld,' King said. 'Tied up. Can I do something for you?'

Doe looked around the ship, as if expecting a large pink ear to be sticking out of a bulkhead.

'I got an idea.'

'Well, sit down, let me pour you a drink, and dump it on me,' King said, going to the sideboard and bringing back two glasses and a snifter.

Doe sat down, put the sample case down carefully next

to her, and poured her glass about half full. She looked astonished.

'Damme, but t'at's good Vegan brandy!'

'We pour nothing but the finest when we're on the client's tab,' King said.

'Good attitude to take.'

Doe took a printout and two small irregular mineral samples out of the case.

'T'is comes from the estate of t'e late Dmitri Herndon,' she said. 'Before your time.'

King frowned, then brightened. 'The miner who was murdered . . . sixth or seventh to be killed . . . almost certainly by the raiders.'

'Damn,' Doe said. 'You *do* know everyt'ing, like Riss said.'

She pushed one of the bits of mineral across.

'T'is is a bit of a diamond, cleaned up a li'l from its natural state. Herndon found traces, accordin' to his log book, which t'e high-graders missed, an' t'ought he was on to a diamond pipe. T'at's—'

'The natural formation of diamond in nature,' King said, 'generally found at great depths. With an exploded planet, you could expect to find such an occurrence everywhere.'

'Are you showin' off?' Doe asked.

King grinned. 'A little.'

'I'll bet you're a real kick in the ass on a date,' Doe grumbled.

'Anyway, I been goin' over t'ings, tryin' to figger what t'ese friggin' pyrates want. S'posin' Herndon, and maybe some ot'ers, found traces of t'is diamond pipe. An' t' baddies found out about it. Would t'at be enough to spark t'ese hog-futterers into somet'ing resemblin' motion, not to mention murder?'

King considered, finally shook her head sadly.

'Nice try, L C., but I don't think so. You figure these people have at least a hundred, more likely twice that on the payroll. That's a big overhead, and even having a lot of diamonds won't meet that kind of demand, even if they've got something as big as the Kimberly Memory, which is the biggest diamond found, out on Dietrich VII.

'Plus diamond prices are like gold. The people who deal in them keep the prices high by locking up their supplies, and letting them out onto the market little by little.

'I can't see anybody, especially criminals, going on an if-come like that.'

'Shit,' L. C. said. 'I was hopin' for a nice simple solution.'

'Aren't we all?' King said. 'As far as I can figure, it'd take having access to all of the minerals in the whole belt to make a decent profit for the high-graders. If there was another mining company lurking around besides Transkootenay . . . maybe they'd be working for that company. But I don't see anybody in the wings.'

'The hell wit' it,' L. C. decided. 'If I can't be a genius, I can at least be happy here in t'e big city. I think I'll get drunk. You want to come along?'

King looked at the clock on the bulkhead.

'Sure. Hang around ten more minutes, and I'll wake Grok up for his shift.'

THIRTY-SIX

The troll trotted up to M'chel, chittered quietly, and pointed south.

That was the direction the patrol had taken, another scout had reported in sign language.

She'd deliberately exposed herself, hoping to pull the patrol into the open, which had evidently worked just fine.

She'd given herself four nervous minutes, then left at a dead run, waiting for the screech of incoming artillery or rockets, or, worse yet, the dull thud of mortars.

Nothing had happened, and she'd resumed breathing.

Her six acolytes thought the tall person's game was most fun, especially since equally strange games had given them a chance to kill some of their enemies.

Maybe this game would be the same.

'How many?' Riss tried, then sighed, knelt, picked up some twigs. She pointed south, and the troll nodded, or at least made the sideways lurch of the head Riss had arbitrarily defined as a 'yes.' She put down one stick, got a nod, another, then another, got eight, getting increasingly enthusiastic nods each time.

She chanced another stick, got more enthusiasm, the another, and got no reaction at all.

Nine members of the patrol.

Maybe.

She'd learned not to go beyond eight per count. The trolls did have mathematics. To the base eight. Which meant counting their fingers on each hand.

Beyond that was 'many.'

That was the same number the first scout had reported leaving the cavern.

She'd made tentative gestures trying to represent a backpack radio, got more nods of yes.

Which meant a qualified maybe.

But she was learning to do the best she could with what she had.

It had taken a full week – arbitrary seven days by M'chel's decision – for her to learn she'd never be able to speak the primitives' language. She remembered what a language school instructor had told her once, that civilization could be defined by the simplicity of language. Primitive people, contrary to what most thought, didn't speak primitive tongues of 'oogs' and 'aarghs.' He offered the example of one language that had seven different variations on dead game, from 'tasty' to 'edible' to 'trap bait.' All people used a language to give them what they needed. A journey, for instance, might be 'one day,' 'two days,' and such up to the amount of traveling a tribe was accustomed to. Such as 'three days.' Beyond that would be the equivalent of 'your children may see it,' or 'beyond lie the gods.'

The trolls had guns, which must have been taken from the first settlers and back-converted to black powder and roundish rocks, forgetting about the rusting charges in the butt magazines, the electronic circuitry, and the trigger. All that was needed was a tube, a small hole in the side of that tube, and a roughened part of the barrel they could scrape a flint across to fire the powder inside.

She couldn't figure how they'd discovered making

gunpowder, wondered if there'd been a renegade centuries earlier, then realized she'd never know.

The problem was they seemed to think the noise of the gun going off was as likely to kill as the ball, so they'd point a gun in the desired direction, close their eyes, and yank the trigger.

It took another week to teach them to use the Alliance blasters as intended, instead of giving them to the tribe 'gunsmith' for drilling and tapping.

Riss had thought it would take a century to teach the trolls any sort of tactics.

She was completely wrong here – they'd instantly understood her 'games,' and after counterambushing and 'killing' their teacher twice, were ready to go to war.

Riss had started simply, drygulching a straggler here, an unwary sentry there. The trolls were most adept at killing, but it took some time, and some cuffed heads, before she could convince them not to dance around their trophy and give the other humans a chance to return and take revenge.

Her first patrol had been to backtrack a patrol and find the location of the cleverly hidden base. She'd waited, watching, for three days, until the cavern had creaked open, and spat out a pair of patrol ships.

Now she knew where Murgatroyd's base was. She corrected herself. One of Murgatroyd's bases. Hopefully the bugger with the cruiser. Or maybe the only base, if she was lucky.

All she had to do was get word to Star Risk to blow it apart.

Not to mention picking her up.

'Next week,' she murmured, 'we're going to learn how to build a starship out of a rock.

'C'mon, troops. Let's move, with our fingers crossed.'

*

Chas Goodnight woke just before dawn, and found he was the only one in the patrol awake.

Siegfried, who had relieved him, and who'd been relieved in turn by the snoring momentary noncom next to their com man, was sound asleep.

Goodnight cursed, and kicked Siegfried hard in the thigh.

The man rolled up, blaster in hand, blinked, looked around, and understood. He mouthed an obscenity.

'Get them up,' Goodnight whispered, pointing to the bodies sprawled around the edges of the clearing.

Siegfried nodded, started off, but was a little late.

A grenade arced in from just beyond the tiny perimeter Goodnight had carefully set up when they'd RONed the night before. His troops, evidently all tired out, had eaten, and then curled up, still certain, in spite of casualties of the previous two weeks, nothing could happen to them.

They were supposed to have kept one-third alertness.

The grenade went off, and tore the sleeping about-to-be-ex-noncom's arm off.

The com operator stammered awake, sat up, and a stone spear spitted him.

Men, women, were standing in the clearing, fumbling with their weapons.

'On me!' Goodnight shouted, as a spear clanged past him.

He triggered bester, took four giant steps and dove for the largish rock he'd picked out the night before as his own personal retreat.

Then he turned off, and the world slowed.

Siegfried was running toward him, and Goodnight laid down a chatter of fire behind him. He could have thought he was aiming carefully at brush, not wanting to hit Riss, if she was out there.

But he would have been lying – the goddamned Grays left nothing to see, nothing to shoot at.

There were six of his troops still up, running toward him. One tripped, and a rock, probably fired from a sling, smashed her skull.

The five survivors made it to the rock, and pulled back, two firing, three moving, leapfrogging each other.

But there was no more shooting, no more spears.

Goodnight found a position, waited.

Nothing.

Then, ignoring the terror and hatred in the other five's eyes, he ordered them back to the ambush.

He hoped the Grays weren't lying in wait.

They weren't.

They had what they'd come for – all the weapons and ammo abandoned.

Plus Goodnight's com.

'Any Star Risk Station,' Riss said into the mike. 'I say again, Any Star Risk Station, this is Romeo India Sierra Sierra. I say again, Romeo India Sierra Sierra.'

She waited, sweating. Beside her, Two Twitters crouched, proud that, of course, his personal totem could talk into boxes, and, most likely, fly like a bird if she chose.

'Romeo India Sierra Sierra, this is Star Risk Control.' Riss recognized Grok's voice. 'Please authenticate with us what floor home station on Trimalchio is on.'

She thought desperately.

'This is Romeo,' she said. 'Forty-three. I say again, four-three.'

'This is Control. Where are you, M'chel?'

'I've got to make this quick. This damned com, which I took from the baddies, has crystals for tuning, which is why I'm on the frigging main distress freq, in clear.'

'This is Control. Trying to locate your position. Have rough.'

'I had to improv an antenna to get out of this valley. Base is about in center of valley, concealed in cliff face. Guesstimate from mine up one zero, right niner.'

'You are very garbled. Understand that last as up one zero, lost second coordinate. Please say again, over. Please—'

Riss shut off the com, hearing the screech of incoming rockets.

She grabbed Two Twitters, who squeaked protest, flattened.

The rockets slammed in around her, and the rocky outcropping she was hiding in sang to the rain of shrapnel.

She got up, saw the com with a large chunk of alloy through its center, grabbed Two Twitters under one arm, and ran like hell as she heard another salvo crashing down.

'Goddamnit,' she swore, ignoring Two Twitters's protests, 'and goddamn me for being a sentimental bitch, you heavy bastard. I shoulda covered the com, not your fat ass.

'Now there'll be nobody left to save me but me.'

THIRTY-SEVEN

'So what do we have?' Baldur asked.

'First, of course, that our M'chel is still incarnate,' Grok said. 'Second, we know the base is in some sort of a cave. However, what we lack is Riss's location when she 'cast. All I have is a single compass heading.

'If I project that out, I get a great number of valleys. And I still haven't been able to get the location of all of those bases we want that might give me a second point to use.'

'Not good,' Baldur said. 'But, at least as you say, Riss is still out and about. Nothing from Goodnight. I am assuming that he did not do anything outrageous such as join Murgatroyd.'

'I'd think not,' Grok said. 'Or else someone would have tried to get a bomb or other nefarious thingie in on us.'

'Troubles, troubles.' Baldur sighed, drumming his fingers on the control board. 'All right. Contact all Star Risk ships and bring them here to Glace. We shall ignore the asteroids until we get our own back. Grok, put a monitor on that distress frequency, and if we get anything more, we shall get ships off at once and hope we can get a better fix from the air. Better. We shall keep a constant patrol in the air along that line of transmission.

I do not think we have to caution the pilots about being most careful, with Dinsmore lost.

'Damn, but I wish I had hired a few more ground pounders for whatever rescue will be required.'

'Speaking of asteroids and such,' King said, from her console to the side of the main control board of the *Boop*, 'Reg Goodnight's made three attempts to contact you today.'

'And I have nothing for him.' Baldur sighed again. 'But I cannot evade him forever.' King passed him the com number, and he touched buttons.

The screen cleared, and Reg Goodnight looked up from a printout.

'Goodnight. Ah. There you are, Mr. Baldur. Scrambling. I'm preparing a status report for my headquarters, and since you haven't filed anything with me in three weeks, I need to know what's going on.'

'Our covert operations are proceeding smoothly,' Baldur said. 'And our security teams are working excellently in the asteroids. You will note there have not been any attacks on your miners in some time.'

'Would you care to be more specific about your undercover work?'

'Not on an open channel,' Baldur said. 'Not even with a scrambler on.'

'Might I at least ask why you're on Glace, instead of Mfir?'

'I am afraid,' Baldur said, 'the same answer must apply. Perhaps if you came here, in person?'

'I certainly haven't the time,' Goodnight said. 'I'm not terribly pleased with your work at the moment, Baldur. I'm no soldier, but I know defense can do no more than put off a problem.'

'True,' Baldur conceded.

'I'm not making any threats, nor am I putting Star

Risk on any sort of notice,' Goodnight said. 'But if there aren't results in the very near future, I'm afraid we may have to review your contract.' He smiled politely, shut off.

'Thank you,' Grok said. 'That was all that I needed.'

'Come on, M'chel,' King said. 'Kick some butt and get us some good news.'

Baldur nodded.

'As they used to say, baby needs a new pair of shoes.'

THIRTY-EIGHT

There were more than a hundred trolls huddled in the rocks.

If this was a romance, Riss thought, this grand conclave of all local aliens would have been held at night, with flashing firelight, dancers, howls of approval.

Not with Murgatroyd's goons having air superiority, roving patrols, infrared, and amplified light technology.

Instead, the meeting was held about midday, when the forest was still in the heat, napping, and sentries could hear any patrols approaching for hundreds of meters.

And there was utter silence, the silence prized by any jungle resident not quite the size of a *T. Rex.*

Riss grinned at her thoughts. What local aliens? *They* were the natives, remember? She . . . and those murderous bastards in that cave . . . were the aliens, and pretty damned alien at that.

M'chel, who still hadn't mastered much of the trolls' language beyond a convenient cheep or two, stood, to make the most important speech of her life, so far.

In silence, with only gestures.

Head sweep. *All of you.*

Point to herself. *Know me.*

Hand sweep including herself. *We.*

Hand drawn across throat. *Kill.*

Hold up a combat harness taken from a raider corpse. *Raiders together.*

The trolls came to their feet, shaking their fists in silent approval.

Pick up a blaster. *There are guns you like and need.*

Pick up twigs, drop a handful. *Many of them.*

Point to Murgatroyd's base. *In the raiders' base.*

Pick up another handful of twigs, drop them. *There are many raiders.*

Hand across throat. *To kill.*

Pick up knives, other loot taken from raiders' corpses. *There will be loot.*

Point around. *For all.*

Two fingers moving. *We go to.*

Point again to Murgatroyd's base. *The raiders' base.*

Pick up spear, jab with it. *And kill them.*

Pick up the raider's harness. Point again at the base, shake head, point around at the ground, shake head. *No more raiders, no more humans in your valley.*

Hold out arms, turn twice, then hands point around at the trolls. *The valley will be all yours.*

Some puzzlement, then the trolls got it.

Again, they were on their feet, waving their arms, all in utter silence.

M'chel Riss had her army.

The doors to the cave opened slightly, and eight men and women came out.

They were a little nervous, but not as nervous as they could be if they'd been told to patrol the jungle. This was fairly simple, not to mention safe, duty.

They were to relieve the two four-man guard posts fifty meters beyond the cave's entrance. There were two other posts atop the cliff, reached by ramps, but mostly the base was secured by electronics, both aerial and in the ground.

Everything was mostly routine. There'd been no alarms going off for two days, after an annoying series of false alarms that had kept ground security on edge.

They were starting to wonder just how good their much-vaunted bester, and his combat-expert assistant, really were, since they hadn't been bringing in many kills of late.

The optimists figured they'd driven the Grays back out of the valley, or killed enough of them for the others to lie low.

The pessimists, who of course called themselves realists, said the damned aliens were just waiting for another chance, waiting until everyone got complacent and happy again, and then they'd start picking people off again, like they'd done before.

The replacement guards went down the trail, as they did every eight hours, around a bend, and out of sight.

The two women on the cave gate controls waited for the eight they'd relieved to come back.

Instead, a blood-covered figure staggered up the trail toward them. He/she'd been badly wounded, so badly the controllers couldn't tell if it was a man or a woman.

The figure dragged a blaster by its sling, stumbling, almost falling.

The controllers touched sensors, and the gate swung open a little more.

One woman ran out to help the casualty.

The bloody figure straightened, and shot the woman in the face.

The figure vaulted past the falling corpse, and gunned down the other controller, who was frozen in shock.

Riss took a moment to wipe off some of the blood — not hers, but one of the cut-down guardshack replacements, who'd died as silently as the ones they'd come out to replace – and looked at the inside of one of the cave's huge doors.

Just like any other hangar setup.

She thumbed a grenade, pitched it underhand into the rear of the door, where hydraulic lines snaked, jumped back and went down.

The grenade went off, and hydraulic fluid sprayed in all directions.

Riss came to her feet, went through the door, shouting, and half a hundred of her trolls, her Grays, came out of invisibility in the brush and ran after her, into the heart of the hidden base.

Even though she knew what to expect, she still stood a moment in awe. There were two ships in the hangar – one the enormous Sensei-class cruiser she'd been hunting, the other the transport Goodnight had arrived on, looming out of the dimness.

Riss saw a gaping mechanic, killed him, brought her blaster up, and sent bolts chattering up toward a petrified work detail on a platform next to the enormous cruiser.

A bolt cracked past her head, and she dove for cover behind the transport's landing skids.

She saw the man who'd tried to gun her down as he took aim again, killed him, shot his fellow as he bent to pick up the man's gun.

Then small gray figures were tumbling past her, and spears floated through the air, found targets and brought them down.

Guns slammed behind her, some the trolls' archaic projectile weapons, others modern blasters taken from raiders' corpses.

Sirens in various shades of panic started screaming, and men and women darted about like residents of a molotoved ants' nest.

That was what she'd expected, figuring Murgatroyd would have no more than a handful of soldiers with close-in experience. There'd be more supply clerks, ship mechanics, medics to wag the dog, and none of them would have signed a contract that mentioned throat-slitting as a required talent.

Loudspeakers began blaring, and, just to confuse things further, Riss blew a couple of them off the hangar walls.

Smoke curled, wisped from the remains of one, and she put another couple of bolts into the area on general principles, then rolled, diving, as two men shot at her. She sat up, and a third bolt crashed into the steel/concrete, a bolt from behind her.

Riss rolled twice more, fired more or less blindly, saw someone duck back into the hatch of the transport. She shot at him, missed.

And where the hell was Goodnight? She hoped she, or one of the trolls, hadn't killed the bastard.

Through the screech of the sirens, she made out two announcements: 'Fire in fuel depot'; then 'All personnel, prepare for evacuation.'

One of her trolls was looking at her in what she thought was a bewildered fashion, then the top of his/her/its head sprayed off. Another troll wailed, shot blindly, then crouched over his/her/its mate, and was killed in turn.

Riss saw the sniper, blew his chest apart, then ran hard for the transport's ramp.

She went up it at the double – the hangar floor was entirely too hot.

M'chel vaguely noticed people pelting up the ramps of the cruiser, didn't have time to worry about them, barely dove into the transport as the lock hissed closed.

Remembering her old attack training, she reflexively

went for the nose of the ship. Someone stuck a head out, yeeped in horror, fell dead as Riss killed him.

Then she was in the control spaces, and there were four men and women, mouths open, perhaps to say something, perhaps to scream.

She chattered a burst across them, jumped over their collapsing bodies. Ahead was the control room, and there was someone in a pilot's seat. She shot him.

Riss glanced at the controls, hoping she'd vaguely recognize something that could be made to do something, or maybe a weapons station to take over that would add to the madness outside.

She saw nothing familiar, decided any havoc was good havoc, pulled the trigger on her blaster, aiming at the panel, listened to it fire once, *clack* empty, realized she'd burnt through more than two hundred rounds coming into the base.

She slid another magazine in place, held the trigger back and let the blaster bounce rounds around the control room.

There were internal sirens going off in the ship, and the control panel was flashing a pleasing amount of red. Then the ship groaned, and one of the landing skids folded up.

The ship slammed to the deck of the hangar, rolled, and M'chel was thrown into a chair, fell heavily.

She got up, flash-thought a girl like me's getting too old for this nonsense, went back for the airlock.

If there were any living troops in the transport, none came out of their hiding places.

The lock was jammed, and Riss slung her blaster, spun the emergency manual controls, and the lock groaned open.

Chas Goodnight crouched just inside one of the hangar

tunnels above the cruisers, calculating the odds. Every now and then, just to make sure he still looked to be on the side of the angels, he shot at one of the scuttling Grays, missing each time by about a meter.

On the other side of the tunnel mouth, Siegfried and three of his patrol troopies lay prone, shooting as they dared.

The speakers blared, commanding evacuation, and Goodnight was looking for a chance to order a strategic withdrawal and haul ass for the cruiser.

Except that . . . he wasn't sure whether he should stay under cover. Except that . . . if he started gunning down raiders, somebody would certainly gun him down. Not to mention the Grays were hardly likely to realize he was sort of on their side and would be targeting their spears at his nice, soft hide.

So he shot and wondered.

The cruiser's secondary drive whined into life, and Goodnight smelt gawdawful smells.

'Look!' Siegfried called. 'Over there.'

He pointed to the transport, and Goodnight saw Riss slide out and down the ramp, jump the last two meters to the floor, kneel and shoot down a couple of raiders.

'Goddamned bitch traitor,' Siegfried spat nonsensically, lifting his blaster.

That settled that.

Goodnight, not without regret, since the man was a bit on the competent side, shot him through the heart.

The other soldiers had time for a wide-eyed look of astonishment, and Goodnight rolled a grenade between them, back-flipped, and went into bester.

Nobody knew what it was like, except those who'd been there. In bester, you were warm, safe, and the king of the world. At least as long as you didn't run into a machine with faster reflexes than you'd been given.

Sound went up decibels, and Goodnight ran for the nearest set of stairs down to the floor.

He shot as he went, not aiming, intending to cause more upset and poor morale.

Goodnight ran toward the transport, just as the cruiser lifted on its antigravs. He ducked under the massive ship as it floated toward the hangar mouth.

He thought of putting a few rounds straight up into the cruiser, didn't think they'd punch through the armor, and besides, if they did, he sure as hell didn't want the damned thing falling on his head.

Goodnight went around a pair of Grays, who'd just realized the blur was sort of human, which meant sort of an enemy, and then he was past them, almost slipping on the slick floor, then behind the nice, safe, solid ramp, and out of bester.

'I figured it was you,' Riss said calmly.

'You owe me.'

'Okay. I owe you. For what?'

'Somebody was trying to blow your silly frigging head off, and I went and—'

Riss had her blaster up, snapped two shots.

'We're even now,' she said.

'I didn't see that,' Goodnight protested.

'I'm a woman of my word.'

'Yeah,' Goodnight said, squirming closer under cover. 'And, by the way, what brings you to these parts?'

'My trolls wanted to go a-looting . . . *Shit* that was close!' Riss growled, sending a burst out.

'And so you thought of me,' Goodnight said. 'How touching.'

'Yeah. Is this place gonna go up?'

'Hell if I know. The automatic fire extinguisher ain't automatically fire extinguishing,' Goodnight said. 'Can you get your . . . trolls, you said, we call 'em Grays . . .

under control, or are they gonna stick around maiming, tearing, and ripping til the place blows up?'

'Good question,' Riss said. 'I think we'd best just sit here, nice and close to that door, until all the humans are dead or the flames get too big to take, and then plan what comes next.'

'That's what I grew to know and love about you revolutionary leaders,' Goodnight said. 'The tight control you have of your troopies.'

'And of course you counterrevolutionary swine have everybody in lockstep.'

'Weeell, there *were* a few things we were still working out.'

'Shut up,' Riss said, 'and take care of those three idiots who're trying to work around our flank.

'You got any idea where that cruiser is heading?'

'Nary a one,' Goodnight said. 'I hadn't wormed my way that far into their affections.'

'Then you best start thinking about your debriefing. Baldur's gonna be in the mood for some fingernail pulling, and he'll practice on yours if you don't have something nice and concrete.'

'Not a problem,' Goodnight said smugly. 'I can lie my way through anything. So let's go looking for a com and call up the rescue squad.

'And as long as we're at it, let's tell 'em to bring half a dozen steaks.'

THIRTY-NINE

Ten miners had formed a coop to work a smallish asteroid that was rich in high-grade industrial ores, and silver as well, but was on the outer fringes of the belt.

When the raiders showed, they'd closed their stake and gone back to Sheol to rethink matters.

After Star Risk was signed on, and began offering serious self-defense tools, the miners had invested in two autocannon, and gone back to their claim, restaking after the mining office was destroyed.

They set up shifts to man the guns, which were so automated it took only one man to operate each weapon.

The miners kept someone at the guns' control panels for three E-weeks, eternity to a civilian when nothing happens.

The raiders seemed to be driven back, and hadn't struck in quite a while. So the miners, seeing no profit in sitting behind a gun, let things slide.

They did buy a radar warning system, and hooked it up. Since they were shallow-pit mining, they figured that would give them time enough to reach the guns if they were attacked.

They were wrong.

The huge Sensei-class cruiser approached the asteroid from the far side, closing to within twenty kilometers.

The raiders launched a missile, with a camera instead of a warhead, and drifted it up on the asteroid. Within two shipdays the raiders had a schedule for the miners. They were hardworking, reliable sorts, and held to a definite shift.

When their determined 'night' came, they retired to the three small domes they'd built a hundred meters from the pit, close to the guns and their ships.

No one was awake to see the monstrous cruiser lift over the asteroid's near horizon, nor to see the four missiles spray fire as they were launched.

The four missiles, skillfully guided by operators on the cruiser, homed on the ships and domes.

They struck and exploded nearly simultaneously.

The cruiser's crew didn't bother landing to make an assessment. Their camera-carrying missile told them enough.

The raiders' ship jumped into N-space, was gone.

There were no survivors on the asteroid.

It took an E-week before a passing lone wolf miner orbited by, looking for a little of their bonded rye and somebody to talk to in person instead of a chat link.

Neither he nor anyone at Transkootenay noticed the cruiser's strike had left the mine pit quite untouched.

FORTY

'You do not have any idea where that cruiser might have gone off to?' Baldur asked.

'Not a one,' Goodnight said. 'Other than Murgatroyd obviously has another base, since we haven't seen that bugger for a week.'

'What's your analysis?' King asked.

'Simple,' Goodnight said. 'That base in the jungle was used to hide the cruiser, and was the relay point for any new hires, where they could be issued gear, evaluated, and so forth. I assume they also would have some sort of screening . . . hypnosis, babble juice or something.

'They never used anything on me because I was just too damned valuable, and I'd made my bones by blowing up the Alliance's MilInt office.'

He snorted. 'Not that either of them would have worked anyway.'

'You have been trained to overcome those devices?' Grok asked, interested.

'Of course.'

'We veered back there,' Riss said. 'You didn't finish why you thought the jungle base wasn't the only one.'

'The best reason,' Goodnight continued, 'was that nobody went a-raiding from there, and that boss who interviewed me implied that the raiders had something closer to the belt.

'It wouldn't have made much sense, anyway. Glace doesn't seem to be very damned civilized, and these Foley System dwots don't seem to be able to get their finger out, but sooner or later somebody would have seen ships booming out and back and vanishing into the undergrowth.'

'Now let us consider that woman . . . one of the quote five or six bosses end quote . . . you met.

'Any ideas on who she might be?'

'Nary a one,' Goodnight said. 'Other than she had clout . . . I don't mean just with Murgatroyd . . . and was used to it.'

'Could you IDkit her?' Grok asked.

'Of course,' Goodnight said.

'I'll arrange to acquire one,' Grok said.

'If we get anything useful from you,' Baldur said, 'then I shall do some quiet looking about.'

'You'll get something useful,' Goodnight said. 'Gawd knows this whole rigmarole has to produce something useful.'

Riss nodded. 'Maybe we should have let you stay on the job.'

'Maybe,' Goodnight said. 'But you weren't monitoring my bug, so who knows if anybody would've picked it up if I'd turned it on whilst being evacked on that frigging cruiser into the hinterlands.

'Never more to be heard from by Civilized Society, except for shadowy rumors about Bloody-Handed but Deliriously Handsome Goodnight the Super Pirate, who'd taken over from the Inept Murgatroyd.'

'So the end result,' Riss admitted, 'is that we didn't get much from shaking that hangar down. Murgatroyd runs a very clean operation.

'We still don't know if that cabal of five or six or however is Murgatroyd, or if there's a single entity above
them.

'By the time the fire and my people got through, there
wasn't, *most* unfortunately, anybody left alive enough to
interrogate. Not that I think they would've known anything particularly helpful.

'A pity.' Her voice was very cold.

'By the way,' Goodnight said. 'What about your
trolls?'

'We lost seventeen killed, more hurt,' Riss said. 'I
sign-suggested we could provide some medicos, and
almost got speared for my kindness. They prefer their
own medicine, whatever that may be.'

'It's a shame that there's no way they could just be left
alone to stay nice and uncivilized,' King said.

'If I were rich,' Riss said, 'I'd buy their whole damned
valley and deed it to them in eternity. But it's so far back
of nowhere I don't think we have to worry about a sub-
division coming in any time.

'And at least I happened to check with our friendly
local arms dealer, and found a whole batch of museum
pieces and powder and shot that'll help the trolls stay
solitary.'

'Which purchase, I would assume, you charged to
Transkootenay?' King asked.

'Of course,' M'chel said. 'Do I look that honest to
you?'

FORTY-ONE

The Miner's Aid Society meeting was louder than usual, less chaotic than usual. There were about five hundred miners packed into the building, almost double the usual number for meetings.

For once, there were only two items on the floor.

A miner had introduced a measure calling for 'the withdrawal of all members from the Foley System until Transkootenay Mining is able to guarantee our security, given that the company hired has failed in its contract.'

'Withdrawal to where?' L. C. Doe asked.

'To damned near anywhere,' the miner said. 'Me, I'm heading back to Rafael II. Crappy place, ore nowhere near close to what we're cutting, but you don't get a rocket up your ass either.'

'Easy for you,' another miner said. 'You've been damned lucky in your strikes. Some of us . . . like me . . . Don't have a pot to piss in or an airlock to throw it out of.

'And damned if I much like the idea of cutting and running.'

'Boy heero,' the first miner sneered. 'You want to get killed, you're welcome to get your dick shot off. Me, I'm motivating right on out of here.

'And I want a vote on the measure I just put on the floor right now.'

The vote was taken, and barely failed, 270 to 245.

'Nice to see such champions,' the first miner said. 'Me, I'm still gone.'

'You won't be alone,' another miner called. 'I'm even with Transkootenay, and sure as hell see no reason to stick around.'

When the shouting and screaming died, about twenty miners announced they were pulling out.

Doe tried to stop them:

'What're we gonna do? Up stakes and let t'ese friggin' high-graders know t'ey've won?'

'I think that pretty well describes it,' a miner said. 'Or you could say haul ass in terror. Remembering that I'll still *have* an ass to haul.'

'I like it when it's late and nice and quiet like this,' Riss said, pouring Redon Spada and herself another cup of herbal tea. She and the other Star Risk members were sprawled around the wardroom of the *Boop-Boop-A-Doop.*

'I like it better when I'm off the ground, in deep space and there's room to see 'em coming,' Spada said.

'I can understand that,' Goodnight said. 'I always think when it's quiet the shit's about to hit the fan.'

'Be silent, Chas,' Baldur commanded, 'and pay attention to the IDkit.'

'Awright, awright.'

The others watched King as she scrolled bits and pieces of the human face into the holograph sitting above the small computer.

Goodnight was muttering, 'Maybe, no, no, good gawd no,' as he considered the various projections.

'Mr. Spada,' King said, her eyes never leaving the kit, 'you like it out there in a ship. Doesn't it get lonely?'

Spada smiled humorlessly.

'*Life* gets lonely, doesn't it?'

Grok snorted. 'You humans spend so much time feeling sorry for yourselves. Consider me, without a fellow being for how many light-years?'

'You don't have to be here,' Baldur said.

'*None* of us *have* to be here,' Riss said. 'But we are.'

'Which brings up the question of why,' Grok said.

'You act like there's some kind of choice in the universe,' Goodnight said, a trace of bitterness in his voice.

'Of course,' Riss said, surprised. 'You don't think so?'

'I haven't seen any free will wandering around lately,' Goodnight said. 'Look at the way you people railroaded me neatly into going to Seth.'

'I'm shocked,' M'chel said. 'Utterly shocked. You don't mean to say you considered other alternatives rather than giving your all to the loyal sorts who kept you out of the death chamber?'

'Baah,' Goodnight said.

'I agree with Grok,' King said. 'What do you think it's like being thought of as a robot?'

'I beg pardon?' Spada said.

'Our Jasmine, because she's too beautiful and smart, is sometimes considered by some to be an android,' Riss explained.

'Are you?' Spada asked. 'If you don't mind me being nosy.'

King smiled blandly at him. Spada shrugged.

'All right,' he said. '*That's* lonely.'

'It doesn't have to be,' Goodnight said.

'No,' King said. 'You can always roll over and spread your legs to anyone who thinks screwing an android might be sexy, thinking the Three Directives somehow pertain.'

Goodnight winced visibly, and Grok made note.

'I think,' Grok said, 'the subject might well be changed.'

Riss was about to agree when the com buzzed. Baldur moved the pickup so it covered only him, touched the sensor.

'Star Risk, Baldur.'

The screen showed Reg Goodnight, lips pursed in obvious anger.

'Have you heard about the Miner's Aid meeting an hour ago?'

'I have not,' Baldur said.

Goodnight gave him the details, including how many miners had decided to break their contracts.

'Not good,' Baldur said calmly.

Goodnight got angrier.

'All you can manage is "not good"? That's a hell of a note, Baldur. I can tell you, and you can pass it along to the rest of your scalawags. I've been doing all I can to keep Home Office from ordering you discharged, and you say "not good."'

'I could remind you of our contract,' Baldur said.

'Contract schomtract! If we decide to abrogate the contract, you can damned well sue us in Alliance Court, which should take the case in about five Earth years. Not that I think Transkootenay would lose any such suit, since we would have good and sufficient reasons, such as incompetence, to invalidate the agreement.'

'You could do that,' Baldur said. 'Assuming you are prepared to accept the immediate consequences, which could be significant.'

'Am I to take that as a threat?'

'I threaten no one,' Baldur said.

'All right,' Goodnight said. 'I think we should both calm down, and discuss this problem rationally.'

Baldur was about to say he was quite calm, caught Riss's quick head shake.

'Very well,' he said. 'What do you have in mind? I

hardly think Star Risk is capable of chaining these miners to their pickaxes.'

'Of course not,' Goodnight said. 'But I must tell you, I must see some very solid improvements in the situation in the very immediate future.'

'Fortunately,' Baldur said, 'we already have some good news on the way, which I am not prepared to talk about at the moment.'

'Hmmph. Have you any leads on that damned cruiser?'

'We are developing some very satisfactory leads.'

'Weasel words,' Goodnight snarled, then visibly brought himself back under control. 'The proof is in the eating, so we shall see. I hope you are telling the truth.

'Is my brother still offworld on whatever mysterious errand you dispatched him on?'

'No,' Baldur said. 'In fact, he is sitting right here in our ship, preparing some reports.'

Baldur swung the pickup toward a bulkhead, gestured at King to shut down the IDkit. She obeyed, and Baldur turned the com to Goodnight.

'Good evening, brother,' Chas said. 'You don't sound happy.'

'I'm not,' Reg said. 'And if you don't improve your work, I'm afraid you'll be drawing welfare quite shortly.'

'Now, now,' Chas said calmly. 'Have faith in me.'

'In you I have faith. In your friends . . . well, at one time I could have said I trusted their competency as well. But now . . .' Reg Goodnight let his voice trail off.

'We're very close to some very interesting developments,' Goodnight lied. 'Including that cruiser's new base.'

'I hope so. Can you tell me where you've been for the last, what, E-month?'

Chas Goodnight shook his head.

'Not over an open com I can't.'

'Well . . .' Reg said. 'I'll keep Home Office happy as long as I can. But if you weren't my brother . . .'

'I could have been your aunt,' Chas said.

'What? What the hell are you talking about? You're getting as weird as your friends.'

'Now, Reg. Go have a glass of hot milk or something. Everything'll work out fine.'

'It had better,' Reg Goodnight said ominously, and blanked the com.

'I'm surely impressed by you,' Spada said. 'Star Risk seems to be able to do very creative thinking.'

'You mean, we lie well,' Jasmine King said.

'I'm polite about things like that.'

'Don't bother,' Chas Goodnight said. 'If we don't get our thumbs out, I think we're in big trouble.'

L. C. Doe left the Miner's Aid, starting for the Dew Drop Inn, determined to throw the toot of all time. Goddamned gutless bastards that were her self-appointed charge. Cut and run at the slightest setback.

Then she caught herself. She didn't go out into the belt very often, having most of her work here in Sheol. It was easy for her to growl at those clowns out there behind a rock drill with nothing but worries and bills, waiting for somebody to creep up and blow their shorts off.

All right, she thought. So much for sympathy. She'd better start coming up with a plan to keep the trickle of people fleeing the system from becoming a tidal flow.

And sitting over a bottle and a little jar wasn't the way to do it. She'd proven that to herself time and again, which was one reason she'd had to name herself L. C. Doe, back when her name was . . .

Hell she'd almost forgotten it.

She turned back, to sit and brood in her tiny apartment over the Miner's Rest.

Brood, and puzzle at something that was niggling at the back of her mind, something she should have figured out some time ago.

Nothing came.

Oh well. Maybe one little shot of busthead in her tea might help.

No, it wouldn't.

Doe grinned at herself.

Evidently she'd never, ever learn.

She didn't notice the man who came out of the shadows behind her with a knife.

FORTY-TWO

Redon Spada's attack ship hung just beyond the asteroid belt, waiting.

Lopez, his weapons officer, half watched the screen behind Spada showing Doe's rather impressive funeral.

It might have looked ridiculous – the archaic hearse was followed by a motley of vehicles, from lifters to ore carriers to actual wheeled vehicles. Beside the vehicles were men and women on foot. The procession was long, almost two kilometers, maudlin and raucous.

Baldur and the other execs of Star Risk could handle the formal mourning. Redon Spada rather thought Doe might appreciate a little blood on her casket before it went into the fires.

He had no idea at all where the raiders were now based, but had done a little target analysis, and found the majority of ship attacks had come in a certain sector of the belt.

With two wingmates, he'd had lifted from Sheol two days ago, and spent the previous 'day' scattering sensors to the limits of the Pyrrhus-class ships' pickups.

Then all he had to do was wait.

And hope that he, and Star Risk, would be lucky. For a change, they were.

A screen blipped, and a computer chuffed a printout.

Spada scanned it.

'Very sloppy,' he said. 'That's the same approach they used about six months ago. Four ships, N'yar built, exiting N-space, orbit projected . . . very fine.'

He keyed his mike.

'All Star Risk elements . . . slave to me, and set target as indicated. You might as well get your head down as well. Estimated time to contact . . . two hours or so.

'Clear.'

'You're sure,' Baldur said disappointedly, staring at the IDkit holo.

'I'm sure,' Goodnight said. Both of them still wore formal black, fresh from Doe's funeral. Neither had wanted to stay around for the drunken wake, especially given the likelihood of running into Reg Goodnight, and getting another readout. 'You expected maybe Czar Catherine of all the Russias, or whatever system she supposedly ran amok in?'

'I was hopefully expecting her to look like a Foley System official named Tan Whitley,' Baldur said. 'Who is Foley's head of Offworld Development.'

He sighed. 'But life is never that simple for a struggling young entrepreneur.'

King giggled. 'Young?'

'At least in thought, my love. Now you go and pack.'

'For what?' King said. 'Deep space? A trek through a jungle?'

'More dangerous,' Baldur said. 'We are going to Glace after I report Major Progress to that hellhound Reg Goodnight, where we shall check into a very expensive hotel, assuming that benighted world has such an entity. You are to be my mask, playing the part of a mistress of an aged roué, while I do some snooping in my area of specialty.'

'Which is?' Goodnight said. 'I mean, besides being a dirty old man.'

'Pah, sir,' Baldur snorted. 'Unlike some we might name, I remain a perfect gentleman. The area of which I speak is corruption, its most seductive reek, and those who flock around it.'

The raiders had hit their first target by the time Spada and his wing closed on them.

Professionals, the Star Risk fliers gave no more than a passing glance to the screen showing the rubble where a small mining claim had been set. They saw no signs of a ship, figured the lucky miner had been off to Sheol to mourn Doe.

Spada had all four raiders on his screen, set a closing orbit.

'Right up their bums,' he said. 'They'll not be looking back, but, like good pirates, ahead for more loot, although it doesn't appear these gentlemen are wasting time looting on this run.'

He waited, motionless, the only sound the ship's hum. After a few minutes, he opened his mike.

'All Star Risk elements. Plan is as follows. I'll launch on the forward ship, divert to the one to its left if I hit. Risk Five, take the far left raider; Six, the one to the right. Break contact if anybody hollers for help. Acknowledge by clicks, begin your own downcount, fire when you're in range. Com silence until the bangs stop banging. One, clear.'

Two mike-clicks sounded from the other ships.

'Now, sir,' Spada said, 'if you'll give me a closing count on range.'

'Yessir,' his weapons officer said, his hands poised over launch sensors. 'Time to contact . . . forty-seven seconds.'

Again, silence.

'Engineer,' Spada said, 'I'll appreciate your close attention over the next few minutes, in case we have to go chasey.'

'Rog, skipper.'

'Seventeen seconds.'

The only thing that existed for Spada was that blip onscreen. Unconsciously, he began deep, slow breathing, as if he were about to go to the mat with his enemies.

'Four . . . and three . . . and . . . they saw us!'

The four ships star-burst away.

'This is One,' Spada said. 'Keep your targets.'

Then he forgot about the others, trying for his own launch.

The first raider was jinking wildly, its computer obviously setting random orbits.

'Well within range, sir,' Lopez said.

'Launch one when you wish,' Spada said. 'Stay on guidance. I'll deal with his friend.'

'On guidance, sir.' The weapons officer put a missile helmet on. 'Launching . . . now!'

The patrol ship shuddered as a missile fired. The weapons officer's eyes were closed. The front two fingers of each of his hands played on sensors controlling the guidance vents of the missile as it chased after the first raider.

Spada opened his screen's range, found the second raider.

He watched it for a moment, then tapped sensors quickly.

'Engineer . . . I'd like full drive,' he said calmly.

'Full drive, sir.'

Spada watched for an instant, added a proximity detector to the onscreen data. He gnawed at his lip – the other ship was pulling away from him, even at full power.

Again, Spada opened his screen's range. He saw a distant planetoid. He touched sensors, and lines ran back and forth to the planetoid and beyond.

A small smile came and went on Spada's face.

He changed orbits, opened another screen just on the raider.

Spada waited a few seconds, nodded in satisfaction without realizing it, made a small course correction.

'Closing . . . closing . . . impact!' the weapons officer said, and Spada noticed a flash on another screen.

'One down,' the officer said, pulling his helmet off.

'Then get on this one,' Spada said. 'He'll disappear behind those two dumbbell-shaped chunks of rock, realize he's closing on that big asteroid there, which we're going to just skim, I hope, and change his orbit to' – he touched the keys, and a dotted red line appeared on screen – 'to come out just there.

'I hope.

'On the off chance I'm right, I'd like to have a missile waiting for our friend. Your launch time is about—'

'Nine seconds, I figure.'

'Close enough, mister. Launch on set and forget, just in case I'm wrong, and put on your little hat so we can have another option.'

The control panel beeped.

'Target acquired,' the weapons officer said.

'Time to launch?'

'Three seconds,' the weapons officer said, then touched a sensor and the ship jerked a little. 'On its way.'

He put the helmet back on, changed the selector to another missile.

'Standing by on three for your command,' he said.

Spada didn't answer, concentrating on his screens and instruments.

He was assuming that the asteroid they'd skim 'over'

had little if any gravity, not enough to pull them into an intersection orbit.

On the main screen, it looked as if they were about to smash into it.

A collision light blinked, and a gong started bonging.

'Goddamnit,' Spada said, concentration momentarily broken, 'shut that off!'

'Alarm off,' the weapons officer said, proud of his tonelessness.

'I don't think we hit the—'

A screen flashed, went dark for a moment.

'Cancel that insecurity,' Spada said.

He put up a real-time screen, saw the debris spinning away from a dying fireball.

'And that's that.'

He spun the ship on its axis, went back the way they'd come.

'All Star Risk elements. Report.'

'Star Risk One, this is Star Risk Five. Scratch one villain.' The pilot's voice was excited, triumphant.

'This is One. Congrats. Transkootenay is buying tonight,' Spada said.

'This is Six . . . got the skiddy little bastard!'

'All Star Risk elements. We did our paybacks for Elsie. Now, let's jump for home and appropriate adulation.'

FORTY-THREE

'I think,' Jasmine King said, as they rode the powered ramp down into Glace's main port, 'I could live happily in the wilderness, or in a great city. It's the small towns that would drive me out of my mind from boredom.'

'A metropolis like this one?' Baldur asked, a bit incredulously.

'Of course not,' Jasmine said. 'Nor like Sheol either. I was thinking more like Trimalchio.'

'Yes,' Baldur said. 'Trimalchio, indeed. As for your wilderness, pfah to Walden. Perhaps one day we shall make the grand score, and not have to journey about to pissant little worlds like this one.'

'We'd be bored inside a month,' Jasmine said.

'Probably true,' Baldur agreed.

The two had made an outsystem jump on one of Transkootenay's courier ships, then transferred to a plush liner to return to Glace.

Behind high-piled, matching luggage recently bought, and carefully aged by Baldur to look like the property of well-traveled wealthy before they boarded the liner, Baldur examined the customs form with a proper amount of hauteur. Then, under 'Purpose of Visit,' wrote 'Research,' very neatly.

'Research?' the official asked.

'Yes,' Baldur said. 'I am preparing a small monograph on Primitive Human Settlements.'

'You mean like Glace?'

Baldur sniffed. The official reddened, thought of searching all their luggage, decided he might get himself in trouble, and satisfied his anger with a hard-slammed visa stamp.

'And what did that accomplish?' Jasmine said, as Baldur waved for porters to carry their gear out to a waiting lim.

'Nothing, really,' Baldur said. 'Perhaps it was a residue from thinking about Trimalchio, and a nice Earth Bordeaux with, perhaps, a lobster diablo.'

'Well, we shall have to see what we can do to satisfy your desires, won't we?' Jasmine purred, making sure she was in earshot of a porter, and snuggling ostentatiously close to Baldur.

He lifted an eyebrow.

'Are we getting a bit too much into our role? Remembering that one should never allow emotion to enter into one's job.'

'The nice thing about going undercover,' Jasmine said, 'is that whatever one chooses to do to maintain your cover should be set aside and forgotten when the assignment is complete.'

Baldur's eyebrows seemed fit to climb well into his receding hairline.

'Was that satisfactory?' Jasmine said.

'It was,' Baldur said, 'although the main course had certain bad memories for me.'

The meal had consisted of fish roe on toast bits, freshwater crayfish, buttered small vegetables that could have been potatoes, a strange greenish vegetable that was

alternately hot and sour, a salad of wild herbs, followed
by a cheese course, and a dessert wine.

He considered the penthouse suite they'd booked, and
the lights of Glace below it, then his dinner companion,
who was wearing the sheerest of negligees.

'In all respects,' he said, 'starting with the company.'

'I thank you, sir,' Jasmine said, sipping her wine.
'Apropos of nothing, one thing I appreciate about older
men is they take their time.'

'We have to,' Baldur said. 'There are certain physio-
logical limitations that come on us in our declining
years.'

'Still, it was nice that you didn't attempt to ravage me
the minute the porter left us alone.'

'Never be in a hurry unless you have to,' Baldur said.
'But that is a predilection of youth.'

'Of course,' Jasmine said. 'It goes by so quickly. But
you must tell me why you have bad memories about the
meal . . . and why you ordered what you did.'

He sighed. 'I recollect when I was a young officer.
Very young. And I had somehow cozened a woman out
to dinner with me, and was prepared to spend my entire
month's wages on a dinner with her, in the hopes that
romance would follow.

'So I was being in my most debonair mode, holding
forth skillfully, keeping silent at the right moments.

'And as I was making some particularly brilliant
point, I attempted to crack one of those crustaceans we
were dining on.

'Since they were in butter sauce, they were a bit
greasy, and my finger slipped.

'The creature went spinning through the air, and
landed in the middle of an admiral's dessert at a nearby
table. It was a baked ice cream, and the langoustine did
not improve its appearance any, nor did the streak of

dessert across his impressive rows of medals help the admiral's demeanor.

'I was so chagrined that, when I took the lady home, I declined her invitation to come in, returned to the base and drank myself into insensibility.'

Jasmine was giggling.

'Why I continue to order dishes like that is not so much their savor, but to attempt to banish the memory, so far without success.'

Jasmine leaned across the table, patted his hand.

'Poor Friedrich.'

'You may call me Freddie, if you choose, since everyone else does it behind my back,' Baldur said.

'One might think,' King said, 'there might be more efficacious ways of destroying that memory.'

'You have one in mind?'

'I just might,' King murmured.

Friedrich von Baldur, immaculate in morning whites, with a very tiny but impressive medal rosette in his lapel, went whistling into Glace's most disreputable tabloid holo, asked for the political editor.

The receptionist blinked, then remembered one of the journalists who sometimes reported on a political scandal sent Baldur to Ric Knie's office.

It was cluttered with printouts, terminals, reference screens, and rather lewd holographs.

'You wish?' Knie asked.

Baldur took out the picture of the raider leader who'd talked to Goodnight.

'I'd like to know if you know who this person is.'

Knie flickered, covered.

'In exchange for a name, would you be willing to tell me why you want it? Someone doesn't usually come to our charming publication, known for its honesty and honorable ways, unless there's a scandal attached, which of course we would be very interested in.'

'There could be,' Baldur said. 'In the fullness of time.'

'You expect me to trust you?'

'Certainly,' Baldur said. 'Because if you do not tell me, I shall be forced to inquire elsewhere, guaranteeing that your publication, and you yourself, will be somewhat out of touch when the story breaks.'

'When, not if,' Knie mused. 'You have a deal, Mr. Dapper but Nameless.'

'I am sorry,' Baldur said. 'It is just that at present my name would be meaningless to you.'

'The woman in this picture,' Knie said, 'which looks mightily like an IDkit construct, is named Mar Trac. She is nicknamed "The Terrible." Currently she holds the portfolio of Minister of Development in the shadow cabinet of the party that's out of power, and clamoring to get back at the public trough.'

'How very, very interesting,' Baldur said. 'I think I must seek her out for an interview.'

FORTY-FOUR

Chas Goodnight glowered at the stack of microfiches, stared around the *Boop*'s conference room as if expecting a miracle.

'I hate paperwork,' he sniveled.

'And who does not?' Grok asked. 'Don't we all wish to be free spirits, moving as the wind takes us?'

'Have you been reading human poetry again?' Riss asked.

'As a matter of fact . . .' Grok said, a little sheepishly.

'If you're gonna be vapid,' M'chel said, 'come help me brood about where that goddamned cruiser is, which is the key to everything, as far as I'm concerned.'

'You know,' Goodnight said, having ignored the interchange, 'there's no reason we have to be sitting here on Mfir, is there? I can analyze all these goddamned contact reports my goddamned brother finally sent over anywhere in the galaxy to see if there's any commonality that'll give us a target, right?'

'You have a scheme?' Riss asked hopefully. 'I could do with some action, too. Spada and his flyboys are the only ones out there tootling around looking for trouble.

'I could even use some playtime,' she went on. 'Freddie and Jasmine are off being rich bitches on Glace, and we're stuck here.

'And that stinking cruiser is still nowhere to be found.

'I don't even have anybody to drink with after L. C. went and got herself murdered.'

'Howzabout we go mining?' Goodnight said.

'And what will that get us?' Grok said. 'I assume that you are thinking about going out there and playing Q-ship, with Spada's ships lurking in the wings. But the chance on us being the poor sods the raiders choose to hit is statistically nonexistent. Not to mention what troubles we'd be in if they did hit us if our ships happened to arrive a little late.'

'"We" is not an operative word,' Goodnight said. 'I was thinking more along the lines of M'chel and I.'

'Leaving me to sit here opening the mail,' Grok said.

'I hope, Chas,' Riss said, 'you aren't having any impure thoughts about you and me out there all alone back of beyond.'

'No, no, no,' Goodnight said hastily. 'You've slapped my paws enough. At least for the moment.'

'Do you have any specific idea on what we'd accomplish?' Riss asked.

'No less than what we'd get done around here,' Goodnight said. 'And we'd sure as hell get a better idea for the field, wouldn't we?'

'True,' Riss said.

'And I've always been lucky at finding trouble when I go looking for it,' Goodnight said.

'Both of you are intellectually stunted,' Grok said. 'You, Chas, are just looking for an excuse to go out and get your adrenaline going. As are you, M'chel. From him, I'd expect such gloriosities. I thought better of you.'

Before Riss could come back, the com buzzed.

Riss went to the console. 'Star Risk.'

Baldur's face was onscreen.

'Scrambling 413,' he said. His image blurred.

Riss touched sensors.

'Scrambling 413,' she echoed, and Baldur's face reappeared.

'I have an ID on Goodnight's Murgatroyd,' he said, without preamble.

Goodnight came out of his chair, and was hanging over Riss's shoulder.

'Good day, Chas,' Baldur said. He held up a picture.

'That's her,' Goodnight said. 'Ninety-five percent positive.'

'I did not think you made those sort of mistakes,' Baldur said, and told the three on Mfir about Mar Trac.

'I have a meeting set with her tomorrow,' he went on. 'I am pretending to be a possible contributor to her party's campaign, which my sources say will be most expensive if they hope to take the current administration out in the next election.'

'If she . . . and her compatriots . . . are the brains behind the raiders,' Grok asked, 'first, do you have any theories on what their plans are? And second, what are you planning to accomplish by this interview?'

'I am not sure if Trac's party is involved, or if she is just developing a scheme of her own. I shall know more tomorrow. As to your second question, I think my plan is quite simple, having nothing more elaborate. I plan to tell her the truth about what I know, and see what happens after that.

'It might be compared to a child stirring an ants' nest vigorously.'

'Ant?' Grok asked.

'An earth insect. Lives in colonies. Bites anyone who troubles it, en masse,' Baldur explained.

'Don't forget your analogy tomorrow,' Riss warned.

'I am not,' Baldur said.

'Something I don't understand,' M'chel asked. 'Why

did you go to a sensationalist holo? Or doesn't Glace have anything better?'

'I picked the *Scandal* quite deliberately,' Baldur said. 'First, politics is not their area of expertise. I do not want anyone digging about, trying to run ahead of me in this matter until I am ready. Second, they assume I am as venal as they are, so there should not be any of these worms inquiring about our activities on Mfir until matters grow a great deal hotter.'

'If you say so,' Riss said skeptically. 'By the way, Goodnight has an idea.'

'Speak away, young Chas,' Baldur said.

'I want to buy a ship,' Goodnight said, 'and go mining. Which means looking for trouble and contacts. I'll take Riss with me.'

'Which accomplishes what?'

'It gets me . . . us . . . out in the field,' Goodnight said. 'Second, there's something niggling at me in these contact reports, and I can't figure out what it is.'

'That is a most thin pair of ideas,' Baldur said.

'Maybe,' Goodnight said. 'But it'll make my brother think we're out there kickin' ass, or at least looking for ass to kick, and get him off my back.'

'There is that,' Baldur said. 'I've reported my progress to him just now, without, of course, naming names.'

He considered.

'Why not,' he decided. 'Also, we could use an additional ship that isn't obviously a combat one.

'Go outsystem to the same people we got Spada's ships from for your craft, so you two can come in clean. As I recall, our salesperson . . . her name was Winlund, by the way, said Transkootenay's credit is good.'

'Thanks,' Goodnight said, then frowned. 'Uh, I don't want to get you involved in nit-peddling. But Reg told me he was a little pissed we used that company. Said

Transkootenay hadn't used them for a long, long time, and he didn't want the paperwork to get his ass in a sling back at the home office.'

'You are not causing troubles by your caution,' Baldur said. 'Right now, we want to make as few waves as we can. Again, go offworld, but pay for it out of one of Star Risk's accounts. Our accounts are fat enough so we can pick up the tab, then bill Transkootenay directly.' He suddenly frowned.

'What's the matter?' Goodnight asked.

'Nothing,' Baldur said. 'Something flickered at me, but it is gone now. If it is important, no doubt it shall come back.

'Have fun mining, children,' he said. 'Oh yes. If there's any conflict, Riss is in charge. She is far less flighty than you, Mr. Goodnight.

'Strike it rich. And try to get in trouble. Clear.'

The screen blanked.

'So that's the way it shall be,' Grok said. 'I have to sit here, twiddling all four sets of thumbs, and you go out for adventure.

'As for your analyzing those contact reports with the raiders, why don't you leave them here, with me? I have a far more analytical mind than you, meaning no offense, Chas. Plus it'll give me something to do, besides puzzling over some other matters.'

'Nope,' Goodnight said. 'You may have a nice, analytical brain, but I've got something better.'

'Which is?'

'A criminal mind.'

FORTY-FIVE

The lim overflew carefully irrigated orchards of fruit trees, what appeared to be corn, vast fields of not-quite-Earth green grass, and grazing beef animals, taller than cows, with heavier legs, forward-pointing tipped horns, and shaggy coats.

'Virtue is, of course, its own reward,' Jasmine King said, admiring the land below.

The privacy screen between them and the driver was closed, although both she and Baldur were far too sophisticated to believe they weren't being listened to.

'Obviously you and I chose the wrong profession,' Baldur said. 'Perhaps, one day, it might be appealing to have such a . . . spread, I think is the word, I suppose because it appears to spread forever.

'Ah. I suspect I see our destination.'

The lim dropped down toward a compound with tall wooden fences in irregular lines. Baldur pointed to the automated guard towers here and there, and didn't need to say anything.

The central buildings were also unusual, dug in so their roofs were no more than two or three meters above the ground.

'Nice, entrenched development, good protection

against an air strike. A true sign of a clear conscience,'
King said, and the lim landed.

Four men came out to meet them.

Baldur got out, favoring one leg, and using a thin cane
for a support.

Baldur evaluated them. Fairly professional, he
decided. Especially since there wasn't the hint of a gun
showing.

He saw movement from a cupola, guessed these four
probably weren't even carrying weaponry. An autocannon
in that cupola would provide more than enough security,
even if it might be hard on the greeters. But that was
what they were paid for.

'Mr. Klinger, welcome to Mar Trac's home,' one man
said. He'd eyed King, figured her for nothing more than
a rented bimbo, ignored her.

'Yes,' Baldur said. 'This is my companion and *advisor*,
Choly Wells.' He put emphasis on the word 'advisor,'
and suddenly the man became vastly more friendly to
King.

'Please come inside,' the man said. 'It's hot, and I'm
sure you could use a cold drink.'

'Indeed,' Baldur said, and followed the four. Two went
first, the others behind Baldur and King.

They went through a large, hand-carved door, stopped
by a metal arch.

The first man bowed Baldur through the arch, an
obvious detector.

Baldur casually leaned his cane against one side of the
arch, went through, holding his arms out. There was a
click.

King did the same, also received the metallic
approval.

Baldur picked up his cane, marked the four down a
notch in his estimation for not noticing it hadn't gone

through the detector, followed them into a vast living room.

The house was very masculine, all dark wood and leather.

King wondered if that was Trac's personal taste, something she used to keep men feeling secure when they had to deal with a woman, or if she'd bought the property as it was.

The man, who didn't introduce himself, offered the Star Risk pair alcohol, was declined. He smiled thinly, and poured iced fruit juice.

The two sipped in silence. The guards made no attempt to make casual conversation, and Baldur marked them down another peg.

They were halfway through their drinks when Mar Trac made her Entrance, down an elaborately worked staircase that led below.

'Mr. Klinger, Miss Wells, I am Mar Trac,' the woman said. She wore a simple, very expensive, gray suit and dark shoes. Her hair was short, styled. The only jewelry that showed was a pair of tiny earrings and a surprisingly large, old-fashioned timepiece on her right wrist.

'I am pleased to meet you,' Baldur said.

'Your assistant said you would have matters of possible interest for me.'

Baldur looked pointedly at the four security men. Trac nodded them out.

Baldur sat down on one of the leather couches, very much at ease.

'I do have something that I think you should find interesting. But begin with the fact that my *partner* lied. I am actually Friedrich von Baldur, head of a security firm called Star Risk, Ltd. Perhaps you have heard of us.'

There was only the tiniest jolt from Trac.

'No, I'm afraid I haven't.'

She moved one hand to her timepiece.

'Please do not summon your bodyguards,' Baldur said. 'I assure you, I mean no harm. At least, not at this time.'

'All right,' Trac said. 'I'll listen . . . for a minute . . . before I have you removed.'

'First, let me advise you I advised certain journalists of my intention to visit you, so it would not be worth your while to deal with me in any sort of a physical manner.'

'I, sir, am a politician,' Trac said. 'Not a goon such as yourself.'

'You are also one of the conspirators heading a murderous conspiracy in the asteroid belt.'

'That's a lie!'

'No, it is not,' Baldur said. 'But let us not go back and forth on the issue. I came here for two reasons. First, to warn you that I am breathing very close down your, and your fellows', necks.

'Second, I hoped to get some idea on what you, and your fellows, are hoping to achieve by this conspiracy to ultimately defraud the government that you are temporarily not a part of.'

'You evidently weren't listening,' Trac hissed. 'I have no idea what you are talking about, and now I demand you leave my home.'

Baldur stood.

'Thank you for your time.'

'I advise you,' Trac said, 'to not repeat your slanders anywhere, or you'll be faced with the full extent of the law.'

'Thank you for the advice,' Baldur said. 'In exchange for which, I shall offer you some.

'The Foley System, rather barbarically, retains capital punishment as a penalty for, among other things, conspiracy to commit murder and murder, not to mention high treason.

'You might wish to prepare for the inevitable consequences when we catch up to you.'

'And you, Mr. . . . Beller,' Trac hissed, deliberately
garbling Baldur's name, 'should be very careful, as I said.'

Baldur nodded, and he and King went out, and got
back in the lim.

'That was quick,' the driver said.

'As I thought it would be,' Baldur said. 'Back the way
we came, and, if you would do us a favor, please fly at a
low altitude, and full drive.'

'Sure,' the driver said. 'Why?'

'I would not want to upset you by discussing things
that might make you worry.'

'You don't have to. My brother was in the military, on
an antiaircraft unit. And there's more than a few people
on Glace who've somehow ended up with their own
interceptors or AA weapons.

'You want me to do a few jinks as we go?'

The lim was already airborne.

'That might not be a bad idea at all,' Baldur said. He
turned, smiled at King.

'What do you think of our brief encounter?'

'I'm not sure what we accomplished, other than
making Trac angry.'

'That is enough for a starter,' Baldur said. 'Anger short
circuits the intellect. Also, the mere fact of being exposed
to sunlight sometimes makes beetles and other loath-
some insects scuttle about in an interesting manner.'

'I wonder what Transkootenay and Reg Goodnight are
going to think about what you did,' King said.

'It shall, no doubt, be interesting,' Baldur said, leaning back. 'What's even more interesting is what we
should be having for dinner this evening. Staring down
at all those cattle makes me think fondly of some seared
beef, perhaps in a pastry shell.'

'I thought for a minute,' Jasmine said, 'you were going to warn her about how sloppy her thugs were, not checking your cane.'

'Now, as I have said before and will no doubt say again, in the words of an ancient Earth rogue, 'Never smarten up a chump.''

FORTY-SIX

Grok growled, which was his race's way of yawning, realized he was getting stale, and his com to a friend in a division of Alliance Research wasn't likely to be answered in the next few hours, got up from his console, went out of the airlock, arming the alarm, and nodding to one of the guards patrolling Star Risk's compound.

Bored, he thought he'd wander down Sheol's main street. If a drunk miner didn't shout an insult Grok could take offense at, there was a small diner near the end of the open district that could provide him with an excellent bowl of vegetable broth.

Waddling importantly down the middle of the sidewalk, he was halfway to his destination without a fight in sight when the raiders slammed in.

Grok went flat, rolled behind a lifter as they came down the street, bare meters above the ground, their cannon flashing.

Glass shattered, steel broke, and the ground heaved as bombs cascaded down.

The raiders came in twin vee-formations, and their target was clearly the miners' section.

They made a full pass, climbed, and came back, strafing this time.

Behind them came the long-sought cruiser. Its bulk

made it appear to be moving majestically, slowly, although it was moving as fast as the patrol ships.

Its nose was suddenly wreathed in smoke as missiles flashed out. Buildings rocked at the explosions.

The cruiser jolted as the blast rolled back into the sky, corrected, and fired another salvo of missiles.

Grok rolled over, looking up, as the ships broke for space.

Seconds later, two of Star Risk's patrol craft banked overhead, as sirens howled and wounded women and men began shouting, screaming.

Smoke, flame boiled around Grok, and there was a blast as something, somewhere, exploded.

'A little late, my friends,' Grok said to himself. 'But perhaps just as lucky for you.'

He came to his feet, decided he could have his soup later. No doubt, if he'd survived the attack, Reg Goodnight would need someone to rave at for this latest outrage.

Plus the rest of the team would probably like to know Murgatroyd wasn't folding any tents, not that Grok had the slightest idea why a villain should waste his time doing something like that.

FORTY-SEVEN

Baldur and King were finishing their meal which Baldur had rated short of sumptuous, but still palatable.

'Your standards on Trimalchio have spoiled you,' King said.

'Not so,' Baldur said. 'I always was a food snob, even when I was poverty stricken, and forced to live by begging. Or, worse, to eat military rations.'

'I have a question,' King said. 'It's been three days since we met Trac. Why are we still on Glace?'

'I'm not sure,' Baldur said. 'But I have a feeling that we haven't thoroughly explored the situation here, and there's other things that may well happen.'

King was about to ask more when she saw a man filtering through the crowded restaurant toward them.

He was tall almost emaciatedly thin, but with a broad chest and large hands. He walked with a bit of a limp, and the side of his face had clearly had major reconstructive surgery.

King had time to kick Baldur and hiss 'Trouble,' when the man was on them, holding out his hands in the universal 'I come in peace' sign.

'Good evening, Jasmine,' he said in a low, rasping voice. Evidently the surgeons hadn't been able to do that much toward rebuilding his vocal cords. 'Colonel von Baldur.'

Baldur smiled politely. 'I do not believe I have had the pleasure, sir.'

'This,' Jasmine said, and in spite of her best efforts her voice was hard, 'is Walter Nowotny. My former immediate supervisor with Cerberus Systems.'

'Ah,' Baldur said calmly. 'Would you care to join us, sir? They have an extraordinary brandy here. Aged in, strangely enough, real wooden casks formerly holding a fortified wine.'

'I would be delighted.'

Baldur summoned a waiter, ordered.

'So how do you like your new career?' Nowotny asked Jasmine.

'Fine,' King answered shortly.

'It is, of course, due to you that I have a promotion and a new field assignment,' Nowotny said.

'I'm sorry to hear that.'

'Jasmine, can't we just agree that you and I have differing personalities, and that we should be able to get along as fellow professionals?'

'I don't think so,' King said. 'You are a proper rat bastard, and I have no intention of ever relaxing around you.'

'Tsk,' Nowotny said. He sipped his brandy.

'You are right, Colonel. This is an exquisite brandy, although my tastebuds aren't what they should be.'

'Nowotny,' Jasmine said, 'happened to get shot in the face by one of his agents after he told him Cerberus was abandoning him to the government they'd hired him to betray. As for the limp, he never told me what double-cross that came from.'

Nowotny shrugged. 'I didn't predict the man's propensity for violence, and paid for my omission. It is,' and his voice rasped even more, 'a mistake I've not repeated.'

'Since your presence seems to be disturbing my colleague,' Baldur said, 'might I suggest you go directly to whatever business you came here for? I don't mean to be rude, but Miss King's digestion is a bit more important to me than courtliness.'

'I can do that,' Nowotny said. 'I'll be brief. When Transkootenay hired you, there was a great deal of laughter at Cerberus. We felt you . . . meaning Star Risk . . . had taken on too big an assignment due to your straitened circumstances.

'We were surprised when you made a bravura effort, and have performed far better than anyone could expect.

'However, circumstances have gotten much more serious, and matters are larger than I think you and your colleagues are able to deal with.'

'Oh?' Baldur said noncommittally.

'There is an enormous amount to be gained here in the Foley System, not only by its natives, but by other people and companies as well.'

'Cerberus being one, of course,' Baldur said.

'Of course,' Nowotny said.

'So you are behind the raiders?'

'Great gods, no!' Nowotny seemed honestly shocked. 'Such is not at all the way that Cerberus does business. But I will admit that Cerberus has a certain interest in events that will most likely transpire in the future.'

'You are employed by Mar Trac and her schemers?'

Nowotny lifted an eyebrow. 'I'm slightly aware of Trac's existence, but no more. Not at the moment, anyway.'

'I am not sure whether I believe you. But continue with your proposal, assuming you have one.'

'Very well,' Nowotny said. 'I'll get to specifics. I think Star Risk has been fairly well compensated to date. You now have several millions comfortably in various accounts.'

Baldur didn't respond.

'You could, if you chose, withdraw from the Foley System on one pretext or another, without losing the slightest amount of face among the other small companies whom you compete with. Especially since Transkootenay is not entirely pleased with your performance. Correct?'

'I will not argue with that,' Baldur conceded.

'The question is, can Cerberus entice you to do just that, before the situation becomes serious, and you and your personnel will face real danger?'

King started to say something, caught herself.

'Cerberus proposes to sweeten the pot,' Nowotny said. 'We will double your existing bank balance, and pay off any expenses you may incur pulling out.'

'That is a handsome offer,' Baldur said.

'I would assume you could convince your colleagues to accept it,' Nowotny said, smiling.

'They might,' Baldur said. 'But I shall not present it to them. We were hired for a job, and we shall perform it until it is complete, or we are discharged by our client.'

'That's not the most sensible decision you could have reached,' Nowotny said.

'Probably not,' Baldur said. 'But it is the only one that shall be made.'

Nowotny drained his snifter, stood.

'I really think you . . . and your partners . . . should reconsider. Perhaps forthcoming events will change your mind, or perhaps Cerberus should approach them directly.'

Baldur nodded his head abruptly. Nowotny smiled again, and left the dining room, without looking back.

*

'I promise,' Jasmine said as they walked through the lobby of their hotel, 'I'll not tell the others you behaved in such a morally upright fashion when you told Nowotny to shove it.'

'It was not morality so much as simple professionalism,' Baldur said. 'Not to mention I suspect Cerberus would find some way to avoid paying us the promised bonus.

'However, given Nowotny's threat, there is a matter I should take care of.'

He bowed to her, went to the main desk.

'Yes, Colonel Baldur?' the smooth, unctuous clerk asked.

'I would like to go to our rooms without using the main entrance, but rather the service lift and entrance,' Baldur said.

'I'm sorry, sir, but that's *quite* impossible for any guest—'

A bill was passed across.

'Yes, Colonel,' the clerk said, inclining his head slightly. 'I'm delighted to be of service. I'll have someone from housekeeping bring a passkey.'

'Are you being paranoid?'

'After meeting that poisonous bastard, not at all,' Baldur said, sliding the slender bar of plas into the slot of the service door, around the corridor's turning from their suite's entrance.

'And what are you expecting?' Jasmine asked, as Baldur opened the door.

He didn't have time to answer as an explosion rocked the room. Jasmine was knocked away, almost going down, and Baldur had her in his arms as the walls shook around them, things ricocheted back and forth, and dust billowed.

He pushed her down, went on top of her.

When no secondary explosion came, he sat up, and helped her up. Jasmine's eyes were wide, shocked.

'A bit more sophisticated than I thought,' Baldur said. 'Probably triggered by barometric pressure change, I would guess. Our opening that service door would be enough to trigger such a device. The center of the blast would, of course, have been at the normal entrance.'

There was a thunder of feet coming down the corridor toward them.

'Now it is time for us to act surprised and shocked, like all innocents caught in loud bangs should behave,' Baldur said.

'The worst thing about people trying to kill you in polite society is all the damned reports you have to fill out,' Baldur groaned.

He went to a window of their new suite, looked out at the sun coming up, and yawned.

'Police, secret police, the press, Grok,' he said. 'Everyone wants to know just what happened.

'Not that we know anything. Hell, I am not even certain that bomb was intended to kill us.'

'It was,' Jasmine said, her voice still shaking a little, 'rather an incredible warning.'

'True,' Baldur said. 'Just what I would expect from Cerberus. Or, come to think of it, Mar Trac.'

He looked at Jasmine.

'Are you all right? They *did* miss us, you know. And I am sure staying here under a false name is safe for the night . . . sorry, morning. We shall be headed home by this evening.'

'No,' Jasmine said. 'This is the first time Cerberus has tried to kill me. I'm not going to sit here and be calm and make little jokes about it. I want to hunt down that frigging Nowotny and finish up what that agent didn't get right the first time, and shoot off the rest of his face.'

'Ah. Well, sleep knits up raveled sleeves and all that.'

'No,' King said. 'I won't sleep.'

'Perhaps I could offer other soothing measures?' Baldur said. 'Even if our masquerade is now thoroughly shattered and I suppose we must now take responsibility for our actions?'

Jasmine went to the window, took several deep breaths, then turned back.

'Yes,' Jasmine said. 'Yes. I think I need something like that.'

FORTY-EIGHT

'Might I ask you something?' Riss asked.

'You might,' Chas Goodnight said from where he slouched behind one of the mining ship's two control boards.

'You're sitting here running those frigging reports when you're not back in the hold lifting rocks for exercise,' M'chel said, a touch heatedly. 'So why me? This ship can run by itself, almost, and I could've been back on Sheol, looking for that damned cruiser of theirs.'

'I like your company at least because you're easier on the eyes than any autopilot I know,' Goodnight said. 'Plus, I might need somebody at my back.'

'Now there's an admission of humility,' Riss said. 'I didn't know you besters ever admitted to needing anything or anybody.'

'Other than massive amounts of protein and spare batteries, we normally don't. But I also might need someone to bounce ideas off of.

'That is, if I ever have any,' Goodnight said.

Their mining ship, cynically named the *Busted*, had been picked up on the cheap a system away from the Foley worlds Mining ships went for a considerable amount new, not much used, since they were generally either dumped when a successful miner made an upgrade, or the financing entity repossessed one from an out-of-luck digger.

The ship was an ovoid, sitting on long, extendable legs. Its central hold had a huge airlock in the ship's hull so equipment and ore could be lifted in and out on hydraulic platforms. Its control cabin and sleeping chambers sat in a secondary dome forward.

It was small, not more than seventy-five meters long, and was about averagely ugly.

It had also been armed after purchase, with a pair of missiles hidden in pods along the hull and a 40mm chaingun in the nose with a breakaway cover.

Riss decided to do what Goodnight had done, went back into the hold and exercised for a couple of hours, hoping her subconscious would give her another angle that might lead to Murgatroyd's cruiser and then base, which would produce Murgatroyd, whoever she, he, it, or they was, on a platter. Hopefully.

She thought of meditating, but couldn't stomach the idea of just sitting. She decided she'd suit up and go for a walk.

Actually, she would go for a bound on the near zero-gee surface of the asteroid the ship sat on. Goodnight had found a tiny world with a nice, convenient abandoned claim.

'I think that's close enough to actually having to do the work ourselves, don't you?'

M'chel had found a basic manual of mining in the ship's cabin, studied it, then gone out and put some of the forsaken gear to work.

'You really expect to find something?' Goodnight had asked. 'If you do, I get halfies.'

'Nope. On both counts.'

'Then why bother?'

'Why not?'

Riss could have answered honestly, and said she was always fascinated by a trade she knew nothing about, which is why, over the years, in times of Marine boredom, she'd taught herself the basics of photography, commercial art, accounting, historical research, Ping-Pong, and other seemingly useless, at least to her, trades.

But one ship-day of drilling, blasting, picking, and loading ore had made her decide she'd prefer a breadline to the back-destroying task of mining.

She went to the fresher, cleaned up, hating the ultrasound stall that substituted for real water, went back into the control room and announced her intentions.

'Hang on a shake,' Goodnight asked. 'I think I've got something.'

'I thought you thought you had something three ship-days ago, when you were growling around about people trying to kill Freddie and Jasmine. Not to mention some four hundred-odd people murdered in Sheol by Murgatroyd's strafing run.'

'I was wrong. Now, don't disparage. Take a seat over there, and consider this screen here.'

He darkened the cabin lights, and a large-scale map of the asteroid system appeared on the screen.

'Consider this. The red dots are where the raiders have hit. Nice and scattered, so we wouldn't have any idea where they might come from.

'Except for over here. Notice there's a nice wedge that's free of scabies?'

'Maybe there's no miners around there,' Riss suggested.

'Considered that, checked around. I'm now adding, in green, the number of claims that I could pick up from whoever's running Miner's Rest these days.

'I didn't go to Brother Reg because he told me they still haven't gotten the earlier claims substantiated when the records building went kaflooie, and I somehow know it'd be a pain in the ass to try to get the master files, which are supposedly somewhere on Glace. So I run with what I brung.

'Next I super on top of everything, in blue, a nice little miner's hell here, which has the romantic name of Asteroid 47 Alpha, short for its full nomenclature, two ore stations, and one freighter port for transshipment, which means the sector's at least got some workable ores.

'Doesn't make sense, does it?'

'No,' Riss said. 'Unless back of that is where that damned deepspace base of theirs is.'

'Thought of that, too,' Goodnight said. 'But there's nothing but nothing "back" of that sector.'

'So what idea have you got out of that?'

'This is where a crafty criminal mind like mine comes in,' Goodnight said. 'There are two things a criminal does for profit. One is being a criminal; the other is finding ways to make money without being that much of a criminal or, of course, actually working.'

'Brilliant, Professor. I'll bet I could have figured that out myself.'

'One of the finest ways to sort of avoid getting in too much trouble with the law is the old protection racket,' Goodnight went on, ignoring M'chel. 'Pay me money and I won't kidnap your kid, blow up your store, steal your jewels, whatever. In extreme cases, protection also means a real defense against another, of course weaker, set of goons.

'But mainly it's just a way to keep scared people scared, and you with pocket change.'

'You're theorizing this particular sector's not been hit because—'

'Because just maybe somebody's paying off,' Goodnight said. 'Or more likely a bunch of somebodies.'

'Might be worthwhile paying the area a visit and stirring things up some,' Riss said.

'Might be,' Goodnight agreed. 'It's maybe a couple of ship-days away.'

'What about our claim here?'

'Since it was abandoned once, let's hew to tradition.'

I've been too long out of the service,' Goodnight said. 'I forgot how deadly dull puttering around in-system can be, especially in a hogwallower like the *Busted*.'

'Poor ickle baby,' M'chel crooned. 'Does oo want to be the big-time jewel thief, raffling his way between the stars with a smile on his lips, a song in his heart and a load in his pants?'

'Hah,' Goodnight said. 'Now, how do we go about looking for a claim, so we're real legit like you insist? Can't we just grab an old chunk of rubble like we did before?

'They'll never check.'

'They just might.'

'Awright. But this sounds like work. I say again my last. How do we go about finding a claim?'

'According to my handy-dandy *Basic Handbook of Mining* here onscreen,' Riss said, 'the ores we should be interested in, that'll power the machines of industry, can be discovered, and I quote, "When surrounded by a display of heavier metals, that will give a solidometer reading of 543 or higher. Visually, these ores may be distinguished by a gray to green shading, and striations in shades of gray to black." Endquote.'

'Wonderful,' Goodnight said. 'I'm staring at this goddamned rock floating out there, and the whole thing is black, black, black.

'I'll just fire up the old solidosolidthingie here, which I think is this little screen here . . . it works. Now, I guess it'll range out on this beam here . . . umm.

'We've got a good reading flickering between 200 and 215.'

'Now what? Pootle over to another rock and check that?'

'That's what the book says.'

'Under drive,' Goodnight announced automatically. 'Closing. Braking. Checking. Meter reading 185. Jesus. This mining has all the fascination of watching rocks turn into sand.'

'As soon as we find something that reads right,' Riss said, 'that's exactly what we're going to be doing.'

'I don't care what miners get paid,' Goodnight said. 'It ain't enough.'

Eventually they found a chunk of tumbling rock that read right. But there were no visual confirmations that matched the handbook.

Riss chanced taking a few core samples with a drill which told her she'd been wasting her time.

They moved on.

'I can't believe it,' Goodnight said. 'This one actually reads and looks right on the gauge. Sumbeech: 784. I'm enthralled. So what next?'

The bit of exploded world wasn't more than half a dozen times bigger than their ship.

'We suit up, go on out, and start taking samples. You punch some holes over here, and I'll go around the far side.'

'That sounds uncomfortably like work,' Goodnight said, but started climbing into his suit. Riss followed, and, burdened with tools, left the ship, plugged into an external power source, and floated over to their rock, anchoring it firmly to the ship when they arrived.

Goodnight set to work, drilling out core samples, and

taking them back to the ship. He extruded loading claws to the asteroid, then went back to the rock and, by eye, began chopping out big chunks of mineral. Even he could distinguish the desirable ore from just plain rock.

He was thinking about the pure monotony of this job, and how the drone of the drill came through his gauntlets, up his arms, and into his brain.

It reminded him, but not enough, of some of the electronic music he used to dance to.

He tumbled another chunk of ore into the ship's waiting claws, watched them retract into the hold, started for another, when his com opened.

'Holy shit,' Riss said in a weak voice.

'What's the matter?'

'I think . . . you'd better come over here.'

Goodnight, mind running up wonderful thoughts of Riss having drilled a hole in herself, or some other thrilling accident that happened when people actually started wearing tin cans and going places where there weren't essentials like air and water.

He clipped the drill to the claw as it returned, then kicked free of the asteroid, and, using the suit's low-power jet, went around the rock, wanting to put on full power, knowing he'd kick himself out into orbit, the asteroid's escape velocity being about a meter a year.

Riss was floating just off the rock, motionless.

'Are you all right?'

'I'm fine.' She giggled. 'I think I'm more than fine.'

Goodnight, a little irritated, closed on her.

'So what's the problem?'

'Look.'

He looked.

'Rock,' he identified.

'Yeah,' Riss said, almost religiously. 'Greasy, dark rock.'

'More ore?'

'Not frigging likely,' she said. 'That's diamond.'

'*That?* Where's the glitter? Where's the sparkle?'

'Waiting at the jeweler's, you oaf. You think diamonds come out all nice and shaped and cut and refracting?'

'Hell if I know,' Goodnight said. 'I never had any interest in the goddamned things until they were in a nice setting, or even just cut, in some nice, available box somewhere.'

'This is diamond,' Riss said. 'A pipe. It goes . . . I don't know how deep. Normally a diamond pipe, which happens in the heart of a planet, with heat and pressure, is rock with a bunch of diamonds in it. This . . . at least this what we can see . . . is one great big frigging rock.'

'Come on,' Goodnight said. He reached out, ran his fingers around the cropping. 'You mean from here to here?'

'And who knows how deep,' Riss said, her voice dreamy.

'You mean we're rich?'

'I mean *somebody's* rich. Note that somebody, singular. And in the female gender.'

'How rich?' Goodnight asked.

'I don't know. Let's cut this rock out, and go on back to the ship. I think I need a drink.'

'I still don't believe it,' Chas Goodnight said. The chunk of crystal sat between them on the *Busted*'s chart table. There was a bit of a gleam to it now that it'd been run through an ultrasonic cleaner, but Goodnight wouldn't have bothered to pick it up if he'd tripped over it. It weighed a bit more than half a kilogram.

'So what do we have?' he asked.

Riss hit sensors on a pad, shook her head, tried again. 'According to what I keep coming up with, that makes this rock, uncut, about three thousand carats. Not the biggest diamond that's ever been found, but sure as hell one of the top ten.'

'Yow,' Goodnight said reverently. 'So we don't need Transkootenay's credits. We can tell my brother to sit on his job, and go back to Trimalchio and be rich, rich, rich.'

'What, might I inquire,' Riss asked in a silky voice, 'is this *we* shit? *I'm* the one who found it.'

'But we're partners?'

'You got anything in writing?' she asked. 'Ah, yes. To be rich, rich, rich.

'I remember, back when I was starving on Trimalchio, somebody left a holo on in one of the canalside restaurants, and I flipped through it. It was set on some for-sale service, and there was this island, complete with palace and servants.

'Just right for my declining years.'

'Boy,' Goodnight said. 'Talk about loyalty.'

'And who was going to run out on us back on Puchert if we hadn't booby-trapped his fallback ID?'

'That was different,' Goodnight said. 'Plus you aren't supposed to know about that.'

'Right, different.' Riss patted Goodnight. 'When are you going to realize we know everything, absolutely everything about you?'

Goodnight flushed.

Riss picked up the crystal, juggled it, shook her head.

'You know, everybody in my damned life has been taking advantage of my stupid sense of loyalty. Star Risk is in a noble tradition.

'I guess we better abort for a bit, and run this crystal back to Sheol, and hide it somewhere.

'Maybe with King. I'm not sure how far I trust Freddie.'

'Or with Grok,' Goodnight said. 'He doesn't seem to care much about credits.'

'Maybe,' Riss said. 'This sure is a good backup against having to go back to Desolation Row.'

'After we take it back to the *Boop*,' Goodnight said, 'what'll happen then?'

'I guess,' Riss said slowly, 'we'll go back to playing miner, and working that claim, and eventually nail Murgatroyd. Or he'll nail us.'

'No. I meant to that chunk of diamond.'

'Probably . . . when the time is right . . . we'll fence it to one of your jeweler friends. They'll cut it, work it, and, most likely, hide it somewhere until the time is right.'

'Huh?'

'There's a lot more diamonds out there than show up in Tiffany's,' Riss said. 'Hell, you're the jewel thief. You ought to know that the big diamond guys sit on their rocks to make sure the value stays high.'

'Yeah,' Goodnight said. 'Sorry. My mind's a little fuddled.'

'*Your* mind,' Riss said. 'But before it gets worse, I'll give this damned thing a name. Great big hunkers of diamonds always seem to have names.

'This is going to be the Kinnison.'

'Why that name?'

'Something I read,' Riss said. 'The same romance that gave me Murgatroyd's name. Which seems to be bringing us luck.'

Goodnight didn't reply, but gave her a curious look and went to the ship controls.

'I dreamed,' Grok said dreamily, 'of a ruby the size of a pigeon's egg . . .'

'What?' Goodnight looked at him irritatedly.

'Never mind,' the hulking alien said. 'Now Star Risk

can repay my investment . . . and we can, if we wish, tell Reg Goodnight and Transkootenay to go examine their entrails.'

'Uh, aren't we forgetting something?' King said. 'By rights, this rock is M'chel's.'

'Never mind,' Riss said, a bit tiredly. 'Chas wore me down on the trek back here to Mfir from the asteroids.'

'That is what I most appreciate,' Friedrich said. 'A person whose vision extends beyond dreams of her own wealth.'

'How much is it worth, anyway?' Grok asked.

'I don't know,' Goodnight said. 'It's the biggest gem I've ever seen, outside of holos, and my own larcenous visions. Millions to a museum, I'd think. More to a collector. Still more if we can find a collector who thinks it's hot.'

'Technically, it is,' King said. 'Or at least a part of it belongs to the Foley System, given standard mining grants.'

'I do not think we should advertise our . . . M'chel's, rather . . . acquisition,' Baldur said. 'It now is clear that Murgatroyd is part of the system's shadow government, or at least Mar Trac is.

'Which development suggests what is going on, with all these ships and raiders zooming about, and why someone is willing to compensate them.

'The explanation is quite simple, and I should have thought of it before. Consider: Transkootenay and the miners get run out by Murgatroyd and his raiders. The Foley System will, of course, cancel their agreement with Transkootenay.

'Murgatroyd then surfaces, and requests permission to go mining using some sort of legal, clean cover corporation. That permission is granted by someone in league with them, and with the party out of power.

'That, in turn, funds the next election, which, the Foley System being parliamentarian, should be called for as soon as possible.

'The party on the outside spends money as if they have bottomless pockets, which, in a sense, they would.

'Very handily, then, we have a new party in power, one linked at the neck with Murgatroyd, which would suggest that the Foley System's government, which appears to me to be no more than averagely corrupt, will become as corrupt as . . . as . . .'

'Trimalchio?' King suggested.

'A good comparison,' Baldur said.

'Which brings up another question,' Goodnight said. 'Since we're just passing honest, do we want to try to get in touch with Murgatroyd, and doublecross Transkootenay?'

'Your own brother?' Riss asked, a bit incredulous.

'My brother has a rare ability to land on his feet,' Goodnight said. 'Besides, if that's the option, we can tip him in the wink in time, and make it his idea.'

'That *is* an interesting concept,' Baldur said. 'If we get in bed with Murgatroyd and, say, promise that we shall stumble about ineffectually for a time, until discharged, will Murgatroyd make us an honest deal? I.e., will everyone stay corrupted?'

'No,' King said flatly. 'You're forgetting Cerberus.'

Baldur drooped a little. 'Yes. Yes I am. Most likely, they have already made an arrangement such as I outlined with Murgatroyd for them to come aboard sometime around the election I have posited.

'All that would be accomplished if we did as we are discussing would most likely be the delivery of another bomb.'

'I don't like anything that's been talked about,' Riss said, keeping her voice very even. 'What about the option of skating out of this whole deal with my . . . oh, hell it might as well be our . . . rock, and looking for another gig?'

Grok started to say something, looked closely at Riss.

'You don't like that idea.'

'I don't,' Riss said, and let her building anger show. 'I don't like being run off of something I haven't finished. Especially when there's a few bodies, like L. C. Doe's, that wouldn't stay buried in my mind if we did.'

'You're a damn romantic!' Goodnight said.

'Whatever,' Riss said.

'I don't like that, either,' King said. 'But since I'm an employee, I'll go with the majority.'

'We stay,' Riss said.

Grok thought. 'It might be harder to get a job without having accomplished this one with bells and bugles, might it not?'

'It might,' Baldur conceded. 'I shall vote to stay on the job.'

'I vote the same,' Grok said.

'Aw hell,' Goodnight said. 'You guys *did* pull my ass out of a crack. I'll stick around.'

'Then it's unanimous,' Riss said.

'I suppose so,' Baldur said. 'Which means you and Chas should get back out to working your claim, and going wherever that leads you.'

'Since nobody's got another option . . .' Goodnight said, letting his voice trail off. 'Maybe we can stir things up, plant a bug on whoever and whatever responds, and follow-my-leader back to the baddies.'

'I agree,' Riss said. 'Right now, the only way into the heart of this mess appears to be nailing that damned cruiser. And I'd like to find out where it's based, so we can do more than just stomp one snake.

'It's a pity we can't just send a bullet through this Mar Trac. But that'd mean we have no links at all to Murgatroyd.

'Let's go for the slow, sweaty, and bloody.'

'I also have some things that are worth investigating here on Mfir,' King said.

'In the meantime, where do we stash my rock?' Riss said. 'I certainly don't trust any bank around here. And I don't much like the idea of leaving it here on the *Boop*, in case somebody starts tossing air-to-surface missiles around.'

'Why, in plain sight, of course,' King said. 'We rent a locker at Miner's Rest, wrap the diamond in an old ship-suit, and no one will ever look.'

'All right, then,' von Baldur said. 'Let us go back to war.'

FORTY-NINE

An N-space transmission, coded with one-time-only pad:
   ADVISE ALL PERSONNEL STRRSK TO MOUNT UNDERCOVER OP. NO DATA ON SPECIFIC TARGET BUT OBVIOUS BASE THULE AND HEAVY HITTER. OP S/B REPORTED AND TERMINATED ASAP. SUCCESS WILL BE NEAR LAST STRAW FOR TRANSKOOT. PREPARE ALL UNITS FOR TERMINAL OP AS PLANNED ONCE STRRSK TAKEN OUT.

FIFTY

'Now, if we were good, honest, straightforward people, we'd hie our little butts back out to that stupid rock that's our stupid claim, sweat our balls off to get some rocks so we can then hie our little butts over to this other rock named 47 Alpha, flash said little butts around as big spenders until whoever's running this hyah protection scheme, who's reporting to Murgatroyd, makes himself known, and we then do something terribly intellectual and heroic that'll lead us to Murgatroyd's Home Base, where he slash she sits, curling his slash her mustachios,' Goodnight said. 'Right?'

'I don't believe you managed that in one breath,' Riss said.

'Because my drugs are pure . . .' Goodnight said.

'How-someever,' he continued, 'since we are not repeat not good, honest, nor straightforward, I have a slight alternate on the above plan.'

'Remembering that above plan was yours from the get-go,' M'chel said, 'what brilliances do you propose?'

'A very minor . . . pun intended . . . one,' Goodnight said. 'Which is to the part of the plan wot suggests hard, backbreaking, morally admirable work digging said chunks of ore from our damnable rock.

'Instead, what I've done is go to my loveable little brother, and gotten him to donate six tons of the highest grade ore . . . a good, solid eight hundred-plus on the solidometer.

'No muss, no dirty paws, and off we go to 47 Alpha, and continue the mission.

'Right?'

M'chel thought about it.

'Why not?' she said. 'I'm as bored with breaking up rocks as you are.'

'Four Seven Alpha . . . uh, Advisory,' Goodnight said. 'This is *Busted*. Inbound, arrival time about one-four minutes. Request docking instructions, over.'

It took seven calls before there was a response on the com.

'This is Four Seven Alpha Advisory,' a woman's voice answered. 'Be advised this is an advisory only. We do not, repeat do not, give instructions. Clear to dock where you think it's safe. Over.'

'I think,' Goodnight told M'chel, 'we've definitely wandered beyond the realm of Alliance regulation.'

Forty-seven Alpha, being a temporary, haphazard station, meant only to survive until available mineral resources were played out, was somewhere beyond a mess.

It sprawled across an irregular asteroid shaped like a spread, most-leprous palm, with fingers jutting here and there. Spiked, tied, or cabled to the rock were various buildings, whose sole requirement was that they be fairly airtight.

Hitched to the central rock were mining and ore-carrying ships, some purpose built, more converts, either home or factory built, everything from huge exwarships bought for a credit a ton to passenger ships changing economies, styles, or efficiencies had put out of service to a scattering of former in-system yachts.

Completing the melange was one very strange bulbous ship painted red, green, and yellow, with ornate lettering on either side:

THE WEST BANDORF YACHTING AND DRINKING CLUB

Little 'taxis,' no more than steel or alloy frames with some sort of reaction drive bolted to the rear arced here and there. Few of their builders had bothered to enclose the frame, or pressurize them, and space-suited passengers and freight dangled here and there inside the 'birdcases.'

Goodnight braked the *Busted*, judiciously used steering rockets to stabilize the ship, shut down the drive.

Both he and Riss wore space suits, the helmets beside them.

'Now, let's anchor this turd to something, and go sell some high-grade.'

'Wrong. After we tie this barge up, we find a hotel or whatever these people call a hotel,' Riss said. 'A bath. With real water, and I don't give a damn what it costs. It'll give us a chance to establish a reputation as go-for-broke, spend-it-all, drink-it-up, wild and foolish miners.'

Goodnight glanced down at his armpit.

'That might not be that bad an idea,' he said. 'I have this feeling that if I wasn't used to smelling me, I might think me came out of a slightly used shitter.'

'I wasn't going to say anything,' M'chel said. 'However . . .'

There was a hotel.

Of sorts.

It had been made up of three transports, welded

together, then gutted and rebuilt, with passages going here and there, rooms anywhere from the size of a fresher to big enough to hold a smallish scout ship.

It had no name. The owner/builders had vanished about an E-year earlier, leaving a wizened old miner who only used the name Pelee to run things, with the help of a handful of casual workers and some rebuilt military robots.

It was surprisingly spotless.

Pelee explained that he couldn't stand dirt, which is why he preferred space to being groundside.

'And once you put in proper cycling machines, and have all these machines set up so they shriek when they see dust, it's easy to maintain.'

Room rates were equally eccentric.

Pelee looked them up and down, tugged at a bushy eyebrow, said:

'Looks like you people would hold still for . . . oh, fifty credits a night.'

'A little steep,' Riss said. Poverty stayed in memory.

'Awright,' Pelee said amiably. 'Make it twenty-five. You sleeping together?'

Both shook their heads.

'Kind of a pity,' Pelee said. 'You're both good looking enough.' Then, confirming Goodnight's suspicions, he added, 'Once you get the scum scraped off, anyways.

'Fork over some money, and I'll take you to your rooms.'

They obeyed.

'You, sir, are in 45. You, lady, are in 33. You can leave those ore cases the spitter unloaded outside. Nobody'll steal 'em.'

'You sure?' Riss asked.

'Sure sure,' Pelee said, and suddenly there was a large

blaster in his hand. The muzzle showed extensive wear. Then it vanished.

'Let's hike.'

They went to a lift, went up a level, down a passageway, down a level.

'Here you are,' Pelee said. 'You, sir, are three on down the hall.'

'Uh, what about the room numbers?' Goodnight asked.

'Don't mean a thing. They got numbered when they got finished off.'

'All right,' Riss said. 'Do I get a key?'

'Nope,' Pelee said. 'Had a few, for a while, but people kept losing 'em, or not giving 'em back, and so I just said the hell with it, pardon, lady, and now there's no lock.'

'Naturally, there's no problem with thieves,' Riss said.

'Nope. Heh. Heh.'

'What about somebody wandering into somebody else's bedroom in the middle of the night?' Goodnight asked.

'Happens every now and again,' Pelee admitted. 'Sometimes there's a fight . . . sometimes just a misunderstanding . . . sometimes . . . well, there's been at least two marriages made right here that're still hanging together.'

There was a bath, and M'chel wondered why she'd told Goodnight she'd be ready to go about their business in an hour instead of a week.

She was ignoring her stomach, which was chanting quietly for real food that didn't come out of a pack and more importantly wasn't prepared by her or Goodnight.

The 'hotel' had antigravity generators, but the bath

was still a little strange. The fresher itself had its own grav setting.

The bath proper was a large, clear bubble, with an adjustable collar to fit around the bather's neck and keep her from drowning, plus enough hoses to keep a hydra happy. Riss set the gravity to about a quarter E-normal, 'put on' the bathtub. She set the water temperature, turned on all the jets, and was pounded by spray from every direction.

Obeying the instructions fixed to the wall, she reluctantly turned the spray off after a few seconds, took soap from a zip-locked compartment, and lathered herself well. Shampoo came from another compartment. Then she, a bit hesitantly, considering her touch of claustrophobia, tucked her head inside the bubble and sprayed herself off.

Finally, she put her head back out, touched the sensor for EARTH LILAC bath salts and let the spray fill the bubble up, until she floated in her own private, scented ocean.

She could have turned on the holo, but didn't want to hear another voice, nor had the energy to get out of the bubble and tune the machine.

M'chel Riss just floated until her damnable internal sensor told her it was time to meet Goodnight.

She reluctantly drained the water out, back into the hotel's recycling center, found a towel and, while drying herself, wondered which of her clothes were the least obnoxious to wear long enough to buy new ones.

The clerk in the assay office's eyes bulged a trifle when he read the gauges on the cores Goodnight handed over.

'If it's all like that—'

'It's all like that,' Goodnight said.

The clerk's eyes blinked four times rapidly.

'You want to get paid in?'

'Hard, cold cash,' Riss said. 'Whatever spends easiest around here.'

The clerk half smiled.

'Anything spends, so long as it's not snide. And if it is, there'll be some really unhappy sorts looking you up.

'How much you got in those cases?'

Goodnight told him. The clerk tapped eyes, named a price.

Riss jolted. It was about what she'd made, in five years, as an Alliance Major, with combat and proficiency bonuses.

Goodnight, however, curled a lip.

The clerk considered, named another figure, about a third larger.

'And that's as high as I'll go. More, you'll have to take what you've got all the way to Mfir, and sell them direct to Transkootenay.'

'Too far,' Goodnight said. 'We'll take your deal.'

The clerk opened a safe, and counted out bundles of credits.

'We thank you,' Goodnight said.

'Thank you,' the clerk replied. 'Hope your strike stays rich, and that you'll keep coming back here.'

'Assuming everything and everybody works out,' Goodnight said, 'there's no reason not to.'

As they sealed their suits and cycled out through the business's lock, Riss glanced back, saw the clerk on a com, talking excitedly, and glancing repeatedly after them.

Goodnight whistled.

Riss checked the mirror, shook her head sadly.

'That's really the kind of women you go for?'

'Well . . . yeah. What's the matter with your outfit? I think it's sexy.'

'In a cheap, tawdry sort of way, maybe.'

'So what? We aren't in the Ritz, you know. What do you think of what I'm wearing?' Goodnight demanded. 'I look like a pimp. A cheap pimp.'

M'chel looked at him. He did. He wore tight, too tight, pants in a light green hue, a matching shirt, a dark green half-jacket, and a burgundy neck scarf.

'Yikh,' she said.

What she was wearing suddenly didn't look all that bad, compared to his garb. It was a gown, with a deep vee-neck, in hues of black. It was cut too low, slit too high, and clung far too closely to be suitable for anyone but a call girl or a guest at a beaux arts ball.

Matching thigh boots went under it.

'I can't understand why you don't like my clothes,' the store's manager, a man a meter and a half tall, and two meters wide, worried. 'Most people who come in here wanting duds for celebrating are perfectly satisfied.'

'See?' Goodnight said. 'You at least look expensive.'

'Well . . .'

'Besides, there aren't a lot of choices.'

M'chel looked around the 'store,' once a freight barge. It seemed to sell everything. Along one wall were space suits, along another hung various arcane pieces of mining equipment. Farther back in the cavernous hold were foodstuffs, dry and in bulk, gourmet flash-frozen meals.

Beyond them were appliances and furniture.

Near the front was a big gun cabinet, and to the side clothing.

Hanging from the overhead was a 'taxi,' probably fueled and ready to run.

'I say again my last,' Goodnight said. 'This is not the rue Montaigne.'

'I noticed.'

'So let's pay the man and go get ourselves noticed.'

'I might as well go naked.'

'We really would be noticed then, wouldn't we?' Goodnight said, putting on a monstrous leer.

'Ring it up, my friend.'

'Yes, sir,' the storeman said.

'And answer us one question.'

'Gladly, sir.'

'Where's the most dangerous place to eat?'

Alloy tubing, about five meters in diameter, snaked here and there, so miners didn't have to suit up every time they went somewhere.

The tunnels were thronged with miners, their prey, and those further up the food chain who, in turn, fed off the momentarily flush miners.

Goodnight's eyes were darting about, as if expecting someone to push through the crowd wearing a sign saying I WORK FOR MURGATROYD.

M'chel still feeling claustrophobic, tried to lose the feeling she was moving through the cloaca of a large, metalloid creature, and match Goodnight's cheer.

They found the restaurant/tavern the store owner had recommended. It had a sign out: SOUPY'S, and was the largest structure on 47 Alpha.

Unlike most of the other businesses and buildings, Soupy's wasn't a converted anything. It was a warren of passages, booths, and rooms, jutting off from a central bar where half a dozen bartenders, archaically wearing black trousers, long-sleeved white shirts with black bow ties, bustled about the three-deep bar.

There was a quieter lounge to one side, and Riss saw a dozen women in there, nursing drinks and sharkishly surveying prospective business.

Riss truly hoped none of them saw her as competition.

Goodnight went to a central desk, where an arrogant-
faced maitre d' looked at him, then suddenly smiled.

'Ah. M'sieu . . .'

'Atherton,' Goodnight said. 'Atherton and Smedley.'

Riss covered surprise.

'Of course,' the man said. 'You just arrived on 47
Alpha today, and we wish to welcome you, and hope
your stay is a happy one.'

'I'm sure it will be,' Goodnight said. 'We've got credits out the ka-yahoo that we really need to lose.'

'Ah. Then you'll be interested in our gaming area, in
the next section.'

'Maybe. After dinner.'

They were escorted to a table, and a waiter materialized.

'Soupy's will be proud to buy you two a drink,' the
matire d' said. 'In the hopes of a long, enjoyable associ-
ation.'

'Bourbon Sazarac,' Goodnight said.

'I would like,' Riss said, 'a Flaming Tomorrow.'

The waiter didn't even flicker.

'I shall be right back with your order.'

'A question,' Goodnight started.

'No,' M'chel said. 'Me first. Why Atherton as your
cover name? Don't you think anybody remembers the
cave?'

'I don't care if they do,' Chas said carelessly. 'I'm a bit
tired of slinking about in the shadows, and wouldn't mind
having some nice, clear-cut enemies to take a shot at.'

'I don't know,' M'chel said. 'Seems to me like setting
yourself up before you know the game rules.'

'Maybe,' Goodnight said. 'But there's no point in
second guessing, is there?'

'Second question, then,' Riss asked. 'Why in the name of whatever, am I going to have to drag around the name of Smedley? Stupid sounding at best.'

Goodnight laughed.

'Basic harassment, that was. I've been too good a boy to you for too long.'

The drinks arrived, Riss's in a tall goblet that tucked in at the lip.

The waiter touched a match, a real wooden match to the mixture, and fire shot toward the ceiling.

'Great Leaping Zot,' Goodnight exclaimed. 'What's in that?'

'Various liqueurs,' the waiter said. 'It has an . . . interesting taste.'

Riss slid her hand across the top, and the flames went out. She lifted the goblet, drank, set it back on the table, and smiled.

'M'dam clearly is familiar with her drink,' the waiter said, impressed. He took menus from the back of his belt, handed them over.

'I shall return in a few moments.'

'What's so special about . . .' Goodnight picked up Riss's drink, took a taste, opened his mouth, panted wordlessly two or three times.

'It sends signals, doesn't it?' Riss asked.

'It . . . does . . . such as my lungs . . . and gut would really like it . . . if I could breathe . . . sometime this century,' Goodnight said laboriously.

Riss wanted something large and rare, with moving being an acceptable addition. She sent back the first steak with a sneer for being rubber carpet, dove into the second, making small satisfied sounds as she did.

Goodnight, who preferred slices of a spiced fowl loaf, watched her eat.

'Like a bester,' he said.

Riss nodded.

'When I get on solid . . . well, semisolid land, I want some kind of reward for my cleancuttedness.'

'I don't believe that's a word.'

'It is now,' she said.

They ate on, contentedly, making idle chat.

Goodnight told her that, while he was waiting for her to get ready to go out, he had gone through a few of the hotel's rooms.

'Just in case,' Riss asked, 'you happened to spot someone with a great big pearl necklace? Or just for old time's sake?'

'Probably the latter,' Goodnight said, and went on to describe some of the rooms. It seemed someone, possibly the previous owners, had romance in their soul.

'They went berserk with casting 'plas and what they could scrounge,' he said. 'There's everything from what, I think, is supposed to be an Earth medieval princess's chambers to a cave to a room with leather walls and straps that I decided not to think about.'

He shook his head.

'And here I was the lad who grew up thinking all men are created moral. I tell you, M'chel, dreams die hard.'

Riss realized Chas, when he wasn't trying to be the universal lothario, could be quite charming.

They finished with a real chocolate mousse, and Riss was considering a cheese plate when the waiter put down a white plate with a handwritten card on it:

I would appreciate a moment of your time when you finish dining, if you would not mind the imposition.

Soupy Schmid

Goodnight grinned at the waiter.

'We wouldn't mind at all. Would you direct us?'

It took no imagination to pick Schmid out of the crowd in the gaming room. He sat on an oversize lookout's chair, about a meter above the heads of the crowd, surveying what Riss was sure he thought was his kingdom in an appropriately regal manner.

Schmid was a big man, bigger even than Goodnight, with a barrel chest, and thick, straight black hair he wore long. He would have been in his fifties, and his face was lined, cruel.

His neck had a wide scar, where someone had almost succeeded in cutting his head off.

He saw them approach, came down easily from the chair.

'Mr. Atherton . . . Miss Smedley . . . my table is over here.'

It was in a corner, and had a decanter and three crystal glasses on it.

Schmid took the chair with its back against the wall indicated the others with a wave.

'I'm more comfortable not having to worry about someone coming up behind me,' he explained and, without asking any preference, poured the glasses half full.

Neither Riss nor Goodnight argued.

'Word travels fast,' Schmid said. 'The story is that you're most fortunate in your workings.'

'Thanks,' Goodnight said, tasting the drink to find, a bit to his surprise, that it was a very sweet, very potent fruit brandy, not at all to his liking. But he sipped, set the glass back down.

'Thank you for choosing to patronize Soupy's,' Schmid said. 'I assume your meal . . . which, of course, I choose to put on my tab . . . was satisfactory?'

'It was,' Riss said.

'Are you a gambler, either of you?'

'Not generally on tables,' Riss said. 'Punching holes in rocks is enough of a chance for me.'

'I'm not quite as definite about that as my partner,' Goodnight said. 'But I'm no more than indifferent to games of chance.'

'I wish I could share your control,' Schmid said. 'Unfortunately, the whiffle of cards or the rattle of dice is like a mating call to a wild animal.

'Which is why I'm very grateful that Soupy's, as prosperous as it is, isn't my main source of income.'

'And that is?' Riss asked.

'I am, primarily, an insurance agent. I particularly specialize in high risk policies.'

'Such as?' Goodnight asked.

'My most successful field is in the mining area, insuring against accidents and even acts of God, if anyone today still believes in Him.'

'You mean, like earthquakes?' Riss said.

'No, of course not. I mean such things as unfortunate industrial accidents, which your field is most prone to, and particularly against these damnable raiders who've made life such a grief here in the belt.'

'You mean you can guarantee a claim won't be hit by those bastards?' Goodnight put heavy disbelief in his voice.

'Be as skeptical as you will,' Schmid said. 'But it is a fact, which you're welcome to verify tomorrow at my office, that none of the claims or miners I've written policies on have been hit by these highgraders.

'The percentage of success is far greater than any interpretation of chance could allow.'

'How are your policies set?' Riss asked.

'I'm a very just, very fair man,' Schmid said. 'I

predicate the cost of my policies on the income of the insured miner.'

'So someone with a rich strike pays more than someone who's just shoveling sand?' Goodnight asked.

'It's only fair.'

'And in just these few minutes, I've truly grown to respect you, Mr. Schmid, for your truth, honesty, and fairness,' Goodnight said, standing, and, with a bit of ceremony, pulling the stopper from the decanter and upending it across Schmid's head.

'You bastard!' Schmid growled, and his hand went under the table.

Goodnight reached into his rear waistband, and came out with a small blaster.

'If your hand comes out with anything but fingers, Schmid, you are one dead gangster.'

Schmid moved carefully back from the table, empty hands spread, palm up.

'After this contretemps,' Goodnight said, 'I certainly couldn't expect you to still pay for dinner.'

He reached with his free hand into a pocket, took out a sheaf of credits, and put them on the table.

'Good night, Mr. Schmid.'

He and Riss made their way through the gambling room, now hushed, and out of the restaurant.

'That's what I like about you,' Riss said. 'Always the first with the subtle move.'

'Yeah,' Goodnight said. 'So now we know who's running the protection racket and that Schmid is sure as hell in bed with Murgatroyd, which'll make our Freddie happy as soon as we report the evening to him.

'Now all we have to do is wait for them to come out in the open, survive the encounter, and run the trail back to Murgatroyd and that frigging cruiser.'

'Survive the encounter. You say that with such non-chalance. Like it's a mere frip of a frippery,' Riss said.

'Yeah,' Goodnight said again. 'I worry about gang-sters like I worry about whether my hair's parted right.

'Hey, M'chel. Did I pronounce "contretemps" right?'

FIFTY-ONE

'And what seems to be the problem, Mr. von Baldur? Is there some problem with the ships? Or has that unlucky transport . . . the one you named the *Boop-Boop-A-Doop*, brought ill fortune?' Winlund, the used warship salesperson asked, concern evident.

Von Baldur wondered, cynically, if her bosses hadn't gotten around to paying her commission yet, dismissed the thought as unworthy.

'None of that,' he reassured her. 'The only problem, and it is very slight, is getting the paperwork straightened out with Transkootenay Mining.'

'That's strange,' Winlund said. 'Even though they haven't done business with us lately, we certainly did in the past, as I told you, and everything was most amicable.'

'That puzzles me, too,' von Baldur said. 'Would it be too much trouble for you to look up a couple of invoices previous to ours, and see who the authorizing person was? Perhaps we are going to . . . or, I should say, trying to go through, the wrong bureaucrat.'

'It's irregular, of course,' Winlund said. 'But there's no reason I can't help you. Hold on.'

Her screen blanked. Von Baldur turned to another keyboard, and continued bringing Star Risk's logbook up to date.

That should have been Jasmine King's job, but she was busy in another part of the ship, chasing something or other around the bowels of Glace.

Von Baldur's screen reopened.

'Here we have it,' Winlund said. 'Yes. The authorization . . . several of them . . . came from Mfir. From a Reg Goodnight. Terrible handwriting the man has.'

Von Baldur had kept his face blank, calm.

'Very good.'

'Do you want me to transmit a copy?'

'No,' he said. 'I do not think so. And I certainly wish to thank you for your help. Oh. One further question. Might I ask what Goodnight was buying?'

Winlund looked off screen.

'It must have been part of the security requirement,' she said. 'This one at least was for ten of the old N'yar ships. We offered them quite a deal, since they're somewhat obsolescent.'

'No wonder they liked your idea of buying those Pyrrhus-class ships from me.'

'Of course,' von Baldur said. 'One final question, and this one has little to do with Transkootenay. Have you heard of anyone buying a large ship, one of the Sensei-class cruisers that used to be standard Alliance issue?'

Winlund considered, shook her head.

'I haven't, sir. And I think I would've, since that's a fairly large chunk of iron, and would be noticed out here on the fringe.'

'Yes,' von Baldur said. 'Yes, it would, would it not?' He thanked her again, and broke the connection.

'Oh what a tangled web we do interlink indeed,' he said thoughtfully, as Grok came into the wardroom.

He carried a printout, and was gently growling to himself.

'We have trouble,' he said. 'Or, rather, M'chel and Chas have trouble.

'One of my mechanized sweeps picked this up about four E-hours ago. It appeared to come from somewhere beyond the asteroids, possibly a ship, possibly from one of the ice giants' moons. It wasn't long enough to get a positive direction.

'The transmission is in a code I broke some time ago, one the raiders were using just before we got here. I thought it might give us a lead to their current codes, but without luck.

'Their current codes are very current; this one is a simple scramble. Fairly simple, anyway. It uses one-time pads, which is good, but commercially available one-time pads, which is most sloppy.'

'So what is it, man?' von Baldur asked.

Grok stared at him.

'Man? Did you drink your lunch?'

'Sorry. No insult intended,' von Baldur said. 'What does it say?'

Grok handed it across. 'The x's are, of course, symbols I'm not able to translate as yet, and the words in parentheses are my probably correct extrapolations. I don't have the sending station decoded yet, and there was no closing.'

Now von Baldur gave Grok a glare as good as the one he got.

'Sorry,' Grok said. 'I became too used to explaining the basics to admirals and their like and it's become a habit.'

'Lose the habit,' von Baldur growled, and looked at the printout:

XXXX XXXX PROBABLE ID TWO
INQUIRED. NOT FOOLS BUT STRRSK ON
PREVIOUSLY WARNED UNDERCOVER OP.

XXXX (NEED) MORE THAN A LESSON.
STAY CLEAR OF THEM. TERMINATION
XXXX ON WAY. PROVIDE COVER AND
SUPPORT.

'That's all I have so far,' Grok said.

'That is enough,' von Baldur said. 'Have you alerted Goodnight and Riss?'

'I attempted to message them, but their ship is not replying. Nor is any recorder active. We've had no com from them since their first report from 47 Alpha.'

'Wonderful,' von Baldur muttered. 'And they are about—?'

'About four E-days distant.'

'Not good at all,' von Baldur said. 'Just like professionals under deep cover. Or idiots on a spree. This is something we need to establish an SOP for, when all this is over.

'Where is Spada?'

'On standby.'

'Get him on the way with three . . . no, four . . . P-boats. Tell him to chance jumping closer to the belt than he would normally. Tell him . . . oh, hell. I shall contact him myself.'

FIFTY-TWO

'Boy, have I miscalled this one,' Chas Goodnight grumbled. 'We go out and spit in ol' Soupy's soup, and what happens? I expected contract killers, bombs, mobs, confrontations. What do I get?'

'Rest and relaxation,' M'chel said, from where she was curled up on Goodnight's couch, halfway through A Treatise on Fifth-Dimensional Math, or a Position Paper on the Possibility of Time Travel as an Interdimensional Reality.

'Time enough for relaxation when you're dead,' Goodnight said.

'Poor choice of words.'

'Bah,' Goodnight said. 'Put on your dancing shoes, girl. Let's go stir things up some.'

'So,' Redon Spada mused, looking from screen to screen, 'assuming that Murgatroyd's boys are here, which is something we'd best not accept as an absolute certainty, how in hell do we know where to look, or even if we've got cause to panic?'

'I think we can take going into panic as a fairly dead cert,' his weapons officer, Lopez, said. 'Look.'

Nestled to a mooring, next to two archaic and abandoned-looking converted minekillers, was a very sleek, very dangerous-looking runabout.

'Nice, unobtrusive little yacht, that. Somebody told me once that the only reason there's crooks in jail is because the cops are even stupider,' Lopez said.

'Why, you little anarchic son of a bitch,' Spada said. 'Are you trying to hint that putter down there isn't exactly what a miner uses to visit his claim?'

'Not anarchic,' the officer said. 'Realistic.'

'What next?'

'Park this pig,' Lopez said, 'or better yet, turn it over to the engineer, and you and me go looking for our bosses in a bit of a hurry is my suggestion.'

'I guess so,' Spada said. 'I guess we can start with that hotel they said they were at, and work outward. Can't be more than five or six thousand people on 47 Alpha.

'*Damn*, but sometimes I wish I knew more about sol-diering and spying and such instead of just being a ship driver.'

He caught himself.

'No. Second is going to that hotel. First is we set that cute little ship down there to sing to us.'

There were three men. Schmid considered them, and hid a shiver. He'd killed, of course. But it had generally been in a fight, or at any rate in the heat of passion.

These three had cold, dead eyes, and Schmid knew it didn't matter at all, if you were in their way, whether it was easier to say 'excuse me,' or just pull a trigger.

The three ran and reran the standard security vids of M'chel and Chas as they'd entered Soupy's three 'nights' earlier.

'Got them?' the leader said.

The other two nodded.

'Do we take them at their hotel?' one asked.

'Probably easiest,' the third said.

There was a hurried rap at the door to Schmid's office. His maitre d' came in.

'Those two . . . the ones who were here three nights ago,' the man said breathlessly. 'They're back.'

'What was I saying about easiest?' one of the killers said.

'You don't mean you're going to take them here?' Schmid asked, incredulously.

The trio's leader thought.

'Why not? Nobody'll ever think you had someone chilled in your own place. Don't worry, Mr. Schmid. We'll try not to leave blood on your tablecloth . . . or murder any of your cash customers.'

'Now,' M'chel said. 'What can we order that isn't easily poisoned? You've noticed, I imagine, all those little heads peeping out of the kitchen to look at us.'

'Any of them Soupy's?'

'Not that I saw.'

'Hmm. Tonight I'll have steak,' Goodnight said. 'Two of them. Blood raw, to put me in the mood.'

'You think something's going to happen?'

'I hope so. If not here . . . maybe you'll let me hold your hand later.'

'That could only lead to something promiscuous,' M'chel said. 'Like dancing.'

'Oh brother. Maybe I'll get drunk.'

'No, you won't. I'm going to have the spiced pork, with a big platter of noodles.'

'What about a cocktail?'

'Cold tea.'

'Do we at least get a glass of wine with dinner?' Goodnight asked.

'We do. One with our salad, one with the main course.'

'Damn, but you're profligate,' Goodnight said.

'We're going to move to that table that just cleared, two levels above the targets,' the assassin leader told his partners. 'We'll start shooting when I signal.

'Take the bester out first. He's the most dangerous.'

Spada and his weapons officer, both with blasters ready under the jackets over their arms, came into Soupy's, eyes scanning the crowd.

'That goddamned old fart at the hotel had better have been right,' Lopez grumbled.

'Don't worry about it,' Spada said. 'If they're not here, we'll grab a bite and then – hey! There they are!'

He waved.

Riss saw them from her seat in the booth on an upper level. She waved back, and the two fliers pushed their way through the crowd up the ramp toward them.

'Who the hell are *they*?' one of the killers asked.

'Who cares?' the leader said. 'That changes the odds. Take these two now, those other two if they get in the way, then out the way we planned.'

Blasters came out of hidden holsters, and the leader stood, aiming, gun in a two-hand grip, down at Goodnight, about fifteen meters away.

'Hey!' the weapons officer said. 'Look at those bastards up there!'

'Goodnight! Get down!' Spada shouted.

The waiter approached Riss's and Goodnight's table.

'Would either of you care for a cocktail before—'

The leader of the killers fired. The blast caught the

waiter as he moved between the trio and Goodnight.

The man gasped, hurled his tray high in the air, fell.

Riss spun out of her seat, gun coming up. She shot, hit the second killer in the head, blowing the top of his skull off.

Spada and Lopez were running up the ramp. The weapons officer aimed, shot, and hit a little old lady in mid-scream in her back.

A second later, he was hit by a bolt from the third killer, slumped.

'Screw this!' the third killer said, diving to the floor in a roll, coming up, firing three rounds at random.

A very fat man in the middle of his soup course grunted, put his face down in the plate liquidly.

The killers' leader went after his teammate, running back the way they'd entered, toward the kitchen.

Spada fired, blew a gilt statue off its stand, swore.

Goodnight was out of the booth, hand touching the switch at the angle of his jaw, and the world slowed, and sound went down the spectrum, and he was a moving blur.

Gun out, he ran after the two killers as they went through the swinging doors into the kitchen.

A chef turned from basting her roast.

'Here now! What's this non—'

The lead killer shot her in the stomach before she could finish her complaint, ran toward a service door at the rear.

A blur that was Chas Goodnight hurtled through the door, snapped a shot after the running killer that missed and spanged off the tile floor, blew a hanging rack of pots to clatter across the room.

There were screams, shouts, and Riss and Spada came into the kitchen behind Goodnight, who was going after the pair of assassins.

Spada braced against an oven, swore at its heat, jerked away as he fired.

The blast took an enormous roast, just being seasoned by a sous-chef, and blood and red wine sprayed across the kitchen.

The third killer stopped, halfway through the door, aimed carefully, and Goodnight shot him in the throat.

Chas pelted after the leader, jumped over the third killer's body, ran out into a corridor. Two dozen meters away, the leader ran into a lifter, and the door slid closed behind him.

Goodnight, still in bester, went downstairs, slammed into a kitchen helper carrying a case of fruit up, sent him spinning, the fruit bouncing down the stairs with Chas.

He paused at the lift door, heard the platform inside hum on down, went after it.

Goodnight went down two more flights, but the lifter was faster than he was.

The door was just sliding closed as he reached the bottom of the stairs, and a nearby sliding door crashed shut.

Blaster bolts slammed against the door on the other side, and it buckled and jammed.

Goodnight punched the open button, and machinery whined, but nothing happened.

He shot the door off its hinges, came into a huge loading dock, with three small ships parked in it.

One of the three ships' airlocks banged closed, and the ship lifted on antigrav, reversed into the lock entrance. It started cycling, and then the ship was out, into space beyond.

Goodnight touched his cheek, came out of bester.

'Goddamnit, goddamnit, goddamnit, and I didn't get a chance to put one of Grok's bugs on his frigging ship!'

'I did,' Spada said calmly behind him. 'Before we came looking for you two.'

He and Riss were panting hard. 'And I've got three ships out there to track it.'

Adrenaline was burning down in Goodnight. He only managed a nod.

'But I still lost Lopez,' Spada went on. 'And I want somebody's ass for that.'

'There's a whole restaurant upstairs to work out on.'

'Let's go.'

They went back up the stairs, through the kitchen, and into the dining room.

'Everybody out!' Goodnight shouted, firing a bolt into the ceiling. 'This place is for the wrecking yard!'

He switched the blaster to full automatic, chattered a burst across the ceiling. Light fixtures exploded, and chemical extinguishers sprayed.

The screams were getting louder again.

A service door opened, and Soupy Schmid came out. His face was purple in rage, and he was bubbling obscenities.

He carried a heavy Alliance blast rifle in his hands, lifted it, just as Riss shot him in the chest, and Spada put another bolt into him as he folded to the deck.

'Good,' Goodnight approved. He spotted a wine rack, and sent rounds into that, grinning as he saw old-fashioned glass shatter and wine spray.

Spada saw two men with guns come through a door, didn't bother asking before he killed one.

Riss got his partner.

Goodnight had a tight grin on his face.

'I think we'd best be going,' he said, then spotted a large steak on the carpet that'd been knocked from a serving platter.

He grabbed and looked at it.

'Not *too* dusty,' he said, took an enormous bite.

'Let's get out of town before the sheriff shows up,' he managed through a very full mouth.

FIFTY-THREE

'The fox appears to be running out of dens,' Friedrich von Baldur said, trying to keep from gleefully rubbing his hands together.

'It appears that way,' Grok said. He pointed to a screen.

'The fleeing killer made one jump away from the asteroids, which Spada was able to track. Then a second jump, which emerged out here near this ice giant . . . Ice Four, it's known as.

'The pilot was too clever to send out a call for help, possibly being aware of what was done to his confrères earlier.

'He homed very steadily on the fifth satellite, and landed on it. Spada was close enough to pinpoint its landing site, didn't get any closer.

'He's on return here . . . ETA tomorrow sometime with Riss and Goodnight.'

'Very good,' von Baldur said. 'I think it is now about time to put together an expeditionary force, or at any rate a good strafing expedition, find and destroy that damned cruiser, and then we should be in the endgame.'

'Maybe,' Jasmine King said, coming in from one of the computer compartments.

'Maybe?' von Baldur asked.

'I've gotten interested in things that are missing, missing in a way that's very convenient for Murgatroyd,' she said.

'The Foley government still hasn't provided us with the location of those abandoned research bases. I'm starting to wonder if we ever will be, or if one of Murgatroyd's crew on Glace hasn't arranged to have those records purged.'

'That is all right,' von Baldur said, refusing to shed his cheeriness. 'We can do a reccie and see what we have got before hitting them.'

'We have worse problems,' King went on.

'After M'chel found her rock, I started wondering about what other precious metals had been found and how Transkootenay is handling them.

'There was a miner named Dmitri Herndon that the late L. C. Doe told me about. He supposedly found significant traces leading toward another diamond pipe before he was killed by raiders.

'His claim records were destroyed when Murgatroyd's raiders blew up the Transkootenay claims office.

'But there is no civilized or even semicivilized system of government I can think of that doesn't keep records in at least duplicate.

'So I did a little searching by com, and sure enough, on Glace, there is a central office that records all, repeat all mineral claims in the Foley System.

'I approached them, and asked.

'I think that office is manned entirely by musty old farts,' King went on. 'Because none of them had noticed there are no claims from the asteroid belt that have been filed with them for the past five years.'

'What?' von Baldur's cheerful mood was gone.

'Yes. Such claims would have been required to have been filed for the miners by Transkootenay Mining, or in

the name of Transkootenay if the miners were contract
workers or had sold their claim.

'Nothing, nothing, nothing.

'I did a little checking here in Sheol, and found it curious that Transkootenay has never reopened its claims
office after the old one was destroyed. And no one seems
to know where those claims have been filed.'

'Son of a bitch,' von Baldur said. 'Two sons of bitches,
in fact.

'I think I am a dunderbrain. In fact, I am sure of it.

'First there's the contradiction that Reg Goodnight
says Transkootenay didn't do business with our Miss
Winlund and her company. Contradicted by Miss
Winlund, verified by paperwork in her possession.

'Second is that Tan Whitley, who is Minister of
Offworld Development, wants to cancel the contract
with Transkootenay. Is she one of Murgatroyd's agents?

'With no claims filed on the asteroid belt, once
Transkootenay's contract is voided, those poor damned
miners won't even be able to take anyone to court, without any records.'

'Third,' Grok broke in, 'if I may interrupt, is my
curiosity on how those killers twigged . . . I think that's
a word . . . to Chas and M'chel's recent wanderings out to
the asteroids to investigate that area where no raiders had
struck.

'You may recall that Chas was very proud of having
gotten some high-grade ore to use as part of his cover,
rather than having to do the physical work of hacking
out the rock himself.

'Said high-grade ore was procured from . . .'

'From Reg Goodnight,' King said. 'His brother.'

'But why in all of Loki's hells did Reg Goodnight give
us the contract in the first place? Oh,' von Baldur said.
'We showed up, having rescued his brother. Which

would make it very simple for Mr. Goodnight to choose a small, new, possibly inept company for security, assuming that we would screw up, rather than picking an established firm.

'The worst he could be accused of, in the event of a collapse, would be being soft-hearted. Enough to get him fired, but not prosecuted.

'The question mark is Cerberus. I do not know if they're waiting in the wings, or if they're already linked with Cerberus or what. Nowotny looked puzzled when I mentioned Mar Trac's name, but that may have been playacting.

'Reg was betraying Transkootenay for what reason?' King asked.

Von Baldur shook his head.

'Once again, I do not know. But I rather imagine Reg might tell us if we, say, plugged his great toe into an electric socket for a while.'

'Why don't you com him,' Grok said. 'And let's set a meeting.'

'Not a bad idea,' von Baldur said. 'Even if he will not confess, we can surely find a way to keep him incommunicado until we take out that cruiser and a good helping of the raiders.'

He went to a com, touched a sensor.

A man's face appeared.

'Good day, Mr. von Baldur.'

'Good afternoon, Mikael,' von Baldur said. 'May I speak to Reg?'

'Afraid not, sir,' the secretary said. 'Mr. Goodnight left yesterday on an extended inspection of our holdings.'

'Did he say where he would be going, specifically?'

'He didn't, sir. He told me he wanted to surprise and shake up some of the people out there.'

'What escort did he take?'

'None, sir. Said he didn't need it.'

Von Baldur's smile was very fixed.

'If he happens to check in, please ask him to contact me. It is quite important.'

He blanked the screen.

'What a *convenient* trip,' he said.

'If it's not genuine,' Grok said, 'we must wonder what triggered the alarm.'

'Who knows?' King said. 'Maybe some of those duddy old clerks weren't as stupid as I thought. Maybe one of them was on the payroll. Or maybe someone reported me digging around here, looking for recent claims.

'I think we'd best assume the worst, and that Goodnight has been alerted,' Grok said. 'As for why he engaged in this conspiracy, Goodnight might well have decided to sell out Transkootenay. A very good reason might be to league himself with Murgatroyd and those politicians.

'I'm sure they'd pay a great deal more for the painless delivery of an entire asteroid belt full of minerals, a great many already pinpointed by the already-filed claims, than whatever Transkootenay is paying him now.

'In any event, we must move swiftly, if we wish to end this matter. Murgatroyd may well decide to go for broke, as you people have it, and mount some sort of offensive.

'Also, Goodnight and Murgatroyd may be able to force motion on Glace, and somehow cancel the Transkootenay and therefore our contracts, which would leave us with a hatful of knowledge, and a pocketful of nothing.'

'I must also bring up another unpleasant possibility,' Grok said. 'Is there any possibility that our Chas has become partners in deceit with his brother?'

Baldur thought, made a face. 'I am not sure.'

'I am,' King said. 'I thought about that, ran probabilities on Chas being a double, and willingly put himself in the danger he has put himself into, and that we have witnesses as to its reality.

'There can be too many wheels within wheels.'

Baldur relaxed.

'I am delighted to be able to take our brilliant analyst's word for things.'

'It *has* to be Reg,' Chas Goodnight said grimly.

He paced back and forth across the wardroom of the *Boop*.

'He told me he was getting fed up with the way Transkootenay ran things, that you weren't allowed any mistakes at all before your head would be on the block. Maybe he wasn't quite the company darling I thought he was.

'And he did say he was getting burnt out.'

Goodnight grinned twistedly. 'Or maybe he's just got the same streak of crookedness I do.

'But I don't *think* I'm sleazy enough to put my brother's head in a noose, the way he's done me, more than once now.'

He went to a porthole of the *Boop*, looked out at the yard beyond.

'I think I want to take care of that recon out on Moon Five, and I agree we've got to move very, very fast,' he said.

'Well, you would be a natural,' von Baldur said cautiously. 'But you must be somewhat shocked, and—'

'Don't worry about it,' Goodnight said. 'I need some work to get my mind off . . . off things.'

'You'll need a teammate,' Riss said.

'I can do it by myself.'

'Don't be ridiculous.'

'And I would hardly encumber a ship, and need some exercise,' Grok said.

Goodnight hesitated, then nodded.

'All right, then. Let's go stir up the ants' nest.'

FIFTY-FOUR

Moon Five was a desolate chunk of rock, spinning slowly about 200,000 kilometers from its parent. It was irregular, pocked with craters, and lined with jagged canyons.

The transponder Spada had planted on the assassin's speedster had narrowed the raiders' base to a square, ten kilometers on a side, before the snitch's power pak evidently died.

Unfortunately, it seemed those ten klicks were the ruggedest part of the moon.

'About the best that could be said about having to live on one of these boulders,' Spada said, looking up through the ship's greenhouse at the overhanging bulk of Ice Four, 'is you'd get some *great* sunsets.'

'Not for me,' Goodnight said. 'I'd keep thinking that big goddamned planet up there was gonna fall on me. Sunset-schmundset.'

Riss realized with a bit of a start that was the closest thing to a joke Chas had made since they left Mfir.

Spada's P-boat, and one other, were parked on another of Ice Four's moons that they'd used to mask their approach to Five.

The other patrol boats had slipped away from Mfir one or two at a time, so Murgatroyd's assumed spies wouldn't think Star Risk had either gone into panic mode or, worse yet, had anything resembling a plan, and were patrolling the belt and waiting for orders.

Spada had dropped a communications satellite half a million miles distant from the planet, and coms went, via tight beam, to and from that. There was little likelihood of Murgatroyd being aware of the sparse, coded messages that flashed back and forth between the *Boop-Boop-A-Doop* and Spada.

Grok had brought more than his looming presence — there was about a kiloton of various electronics packed in and around the three crewmen, three Star Risk operatives sardine-packed on the patrol boat.

Goodnight and Riss waited while Grok, growling happily, started running checks. It took about an E-day.

'Murgatroyd isn't an utter fool,' Grok said.

'No one ever assumed that,' Riss said.

'He does have some perimeter warning,' Grok said. 'Fortunately . . . for us . . . it's a pair of orbital satellites, which they're flying no more than ten kilometers above the surface, almost within gravitational pull.'

'Why fortunate?' Goodnight asked.

'I've been very gently querying them, on several frequencies,' Grok said. 'They're not very good guardians, I'm afraid. I'll tentatively identify them as HRNY slash Seven or Eight, ex-Alliance, of course.

'The Alliance obsoleted them because they're very easy to spoof.'

'Or else,' Riss said, amused, 'because of the unfortunate acronym.'

'What?' Grok asked.

'Never mind,' Riss said. 'So you can fry them?'

'I'd never do something like that,' Grok said. 'An absence of signal would be almost as bad as if they twigged . . . I *do* like that word . . . us.

'No. What I've done is blanket their signal so that no

matter what we do, the receiving station will get nothing
but a *nothing . . . nothing . . . nothing* signal.

'So we can proceed with the next stage of the operation,' Grok said. 'Narrowing down the location of
their base so we won't have to hike up hill and down
dale.

'What a puzzling phrase that is. As far as I know, Dale
is an archaic name. Why would anyone want . . . ?'

Grok trailed off, and went back to his breadboarding.

Two hours later, a message came in from Mfir. Riss fed
it through the decoder.

P-BOATS REPORT FOUR RAIDERS IN BELT.
NO ATTACKS MOUNTED. WE ARE
TRACKING. IT APPEARS RAIDER SHIPS
ARE RECONNING EXTANT TRANSKOOT
PROCESSING PLANTS, BUT TAKING NO
ACTION. WHETHER CONCERTED ATTACK
PLANNED OR SOMETHING ELSE
UNKNOWN. DO NOT LIKE
DEVELOPMENTS. TAKING APPROPRIATE
MEASURES. VON BALDUR.

'And what the hell are appropriate measures?' Goodnight
wondered.

'Damfino,' Riss said. 'Guess Freddie'll tell us when it
suits him.'

Later that 'day,' Grok launched his toy, a modified,
warhead-less missile.

Spada's new weapons officer, a woman named
Nkrumah, flew the bird to Five at low drive, made a
high pass for an aerial projection of the square to be
searched, then brought it in close to the moon's surface
on the far side of the square.

The control room of the P-boat was very quiet, and no

one spoke except in whispers, as if Murgatroyd could somehow hear them.

Nkrumah shook her head as the missile made one pass, then banked, came back across the square, its sensors covering about two hundred meters on each sweep.

Then, on the third, she grinned.

'I have a nice little infrared indicator here, and here. Does that give you anything?'

'I'll put a map onscreen,' Grok said. 'Helpful indeed. An IR leak here and here, right where the map indicates a canyon, suddenly no canyon, then another canyon beginning.

'It might suggest that a base was put in that canyon, and masked, probably for insulating practicalities.

'I would think this is an area worthy of our investigations.'

He turned to Spada.

'You may insert us any time. I'd suggest a nice, low approach from the other side, the same as the missile made, then, keeping below any radar horizon if they've got secondary warnings set, and set down here, behind this mountain.'

'Thank you for your valued insights, Dr. Grookonomonslf,' Spada said sarcastically. 'I, of course, am at your beck and call.'

The patrol boat touched down gently, pumice swirling behind its drive, then settled.

The port opened, and Riss, Goodnight, and Grok waddled out. The ET was even more grotesque than normal in the huge space suit he'd been sausage-stuffed into.

Goodnight waved back at the ship, then led off, through the rubbled nightmare.

Goodnight and Riss, used to space-suited trundling,

still were tired, needing a breather inside of an hour. Grok was in marginally better shape, due only to his size.

They found a niche, and Riss ran leads from her suit to connectors on the other two. She waited until the panting in her headphones died, then keyed a chin mike.

'We keep pushing until we're on the canyon.' It wasn't quite an order.

'Right,' Goodnight said.

'Then what?' Riss asked.

'Then we figure out if they've sealed that base off and pressurized it. Easier for me to look innocent if everybody's wearing a suit until they get into a compartment.'

'Go back one. What's this "me"?' Riss asked suspiciously.

'Me,' Goodnight said confidently. 'Just me. I want you on the outside, ready to come in if I holler, and Grok as a standby.'

'That's a little close in for a recon,' Riss said.

'Just what they'll be thinking. Which'll keep there from being any nasty surprises,' Chas said. 'I hope.'

Riss considered, decided not to say anything at the moment.

'Let's hike,' Goodnight said. 'We want to hit them when they're still in this holding pattern it looks like they're in, trying to figure out what to do next.'

They drank water from their hydration systems, went on.

They were about two kilometers from the canyon when Goodnight, still on point, felt vibration under his feet. He motioned to the others and they found cover behind boulders.

In the perpetual twilight from the overhead loom of Ice Four, they saw three of the N'yar ships used by the raiders spurt up into the sky, and vanish.

Goodnight held out perplexed arms to the other two, and they continued.

They spotted proof of the base inside of a kilometer. Heavy stand plates had been anchored in the moon's surface. Alloy girders stretched out over the canyon, and a dome was formed with layers of plas. At one end, the dome's girders were mounted on rails, and hydraulics opened the 'hatch' to allow ships to enter and leave.

Riss nodded in appreciation of the builders' cleverness.

Grok spotted a nearby crater, pointed to it.

They crouched inside, plugged in their connectors.

'Over there looked like an inspection hatch.' Goodnight pointed. 'I'll go in it, and get a look around.'

'What happens if you get in trouble?' Grok asked.

'I'll start hollering on the watch frequency,' Goodnight said. 'Then I'll go bester, and get my ass out, sprinkling grenades as I go.

'I'd appreciate it if you'd be just beyond that hatchway, and devastate anyone who comes after me.'

'That's about as thin a plan as I've ever heard,' Riss said.

'Yeah, well you got anything better?' Goodnight asked.

Riss shook her head. 'Other than going on back to the patrol ship, call for Freddie, and bring in the clowns with bombs, hoping the cruiser's inside.

'Inside, and not lurking on the outside, ready for a counterambush,' she added.

'I'll only be an hour or so,' he said, unplugged, and went toward the hatch. Even in a bulky suit he still moved gracefully, Riss thought.

She waited until Goodnight knelt by the hatch, found a way to open it, went into the dome.

'I think our Chas is playing games.'

'This is certainly as slapdash an operation as I've ever known,' Grok agreed.

'I think all he's got on his mind is finding his brother and getting revenge.'

'Not good.'

'No,' Riss agreed. 'I'm going down after him. You want to follow me just inside and shoot the shit out of anyone who thinks hostile thoughts about either one of us?'

'I can manage that,' Grok said.

They went to the hatch, which was big enough for a lifter.

The two went through.

Below them spread the raiders' base, a huge cavern, lit in the dimness by glaring floods along the girders.

In the center of the cave was the cruiser, N'yar raiding ships, and other spacecraft.

The walls of the cavern had been cut out into caves, sealed, and made into compartments. Large double-plas windows faced out.

On the floor of the cave, and on walkways, suited figures moved about.

One of them was Goodnight.

He melded well into the bustle. Some of the suits were Alliance issue, more civilian or even alien in manufacture.

No one took notice of Goodnight, nor the heavy pack he wore carrying various munitions.

He was not the only armed man, with his holstered blaster and slung, heavy blaster.

Goodnight found a nook, scanned the floor below, spotted the small ship his brother used for his transport.

He wasn't aware of it, but his face drew back into a humorless, skull-like grin.

He went down spidery iron stairs toward the floor.

M'chel tapped Grok's helmet, put hers against his.

'There he is. I'm going on down.'

'I do not think this is wise,' Grok said. 'We were only supposed to recon the area.'

'No one said anything about wisdom.'

'True,' Grok said. 'And it *would* be refreshing to see a few bodies bounce, would it not?'

Goodnight reached the floor, went to the transport. It was empty, lock yawning.

He thought a minute, saw a man pushing what looked to be a generator cart toward him. Goodnight went to the mechanic, stalking as imperiously as a man wearing a suit that doubled his size in all directions could stalk.

He held out his com plug. The mechanic looked up at the dome roof tiredly, almost certainly thinking here's one more goddamned boss with weird ideas, plugged it in.

'What's *your* grief?'

'Who belongs to that ship?' Goodnight asked.

'Some muckety, came in a few days ago.'

'Well, we've got to move it all the way to the back, clear the way for some incomings.'

'How come nobody told me?' the man complained. 'All I was told was to plug into the damned thing, and figure out why it's got a hiccup in the antigravs.'

'I don't care about that,' Goodnight said. 'Where can I find the pilot? *I'm* sure not going to maneuver some bucket around, 'specially if its antigravs don't work.'

'Hell, if I know,' the man said. 'Go ask the muckety.' He snickered. 'If you've got the balls to bother him. All of the clout is upstairs, yoinking around with meetings and that. I guess we're getting pretty close to ending this whole thing, which is fine with me.

'Next contract, I find one that'll let me scratch my

balls when I want and not spend so much time in this stinking tin can.'

'Where do I find your muckety?'

'Prob'ly up there. Somewhere on the command floor.' The man pointed vaguely.

'You got a name?'

'Nope,' the man said, pulling his com plug out and turning away.

Goodnight didn't think it was wise to ask further – a raider should be expected to be somewhat familiar with his base. He nodded, unplugged, and started back toward the stairs. Halfway there, he saw a lifter, went to it.

Another suited figure came up beside him, handed him a com plug.

Irritated, he took it.

'What?'

'You look like you need company,' Riss said.

Goodnight jumped a little.

'Goddamnit, I told you—'

'Nobody tolds nobody nothin' around here, Chas. Remember? Come to think about it, I outrank you anyway.'

'You can get killed doing something dumb like this.'

'And you can't?'

Goodnight felt his icy mood defrost a little, and smiled.

'Anybody ever told you you're a damned fool?'

'Frequently. Anybody ever told you you're worse?'

They went into the lifter. As it took them up to the top, Goodnight told her what the mechanic had said.

'So what's your plan?'

'I'm going after Reg.'

'About what I thought,' Riss said.

The lift door opened, and they walked out, toward a

lock. There were portholes into the compartments inside, a huge suite of offices.

Goodnight saw expensively dressed men and women, carpeting, desks that could have been made out of real wood.

There were two armed men outside the lock, sitting behind a table.

One stood, holding up a hand.

Riss and Goodnight stopped.

The man tapped his chest, where there was a plas badge clipped on, held out his hand for ID.

Riss smiled, shot him.

His partner's mouth dropped, and he reached for his holstered blaster. M'chel cut him down before Goodnight had his gun up.

Chas smiled, bowed her toward the lock.

Riss smiled back, and entered, Goodnight behind her.

The lock door closed, air hissed, and Goodnight turned on his outside mike.

'How do you want to hit them?'

Riss frowned, as if she couldn't hear, opened the faceplate of her suit.

Chas Goodnight opened his as well.

'What's the matter with—'

Riss hit him, quite hard on the forehead, with the heel of her palm. Goodnight's head banged against the inside of his helmet, and he collapsed.

'Poor bastard,' Riss said. 'But nobody should have to live with what you're thinking about doing.'

She dragged him to a corner of the lock.

'Now, you just lie there, like a good little casualty for a few seconds. I'll be right back, as soon as I finish my own shift at being a prime fool.'

She closed her faceplate, opened the lock's inner door, taking a pair of grenades from her backpack.

The reception area belonged on another world, one with a sun and air. There were a pair of men, and a woman, waiting to be summoned, trying to look casual on very modern office furniture.

A receptionist looked up, smiled.

'You wish?' came through Riss's outside com system.

Riss didn't answer, but thumbed the first grenade, rolled it into the reception area, then the second.

The second, a blast grenade, detonated, and men and women screamed. Then the first, a gas grenade, exploded.

Smoke spread through the room, and M'chel saw people holding their throats, staggering, dropping.

Riss forgot about them, ran down the hall toward the inner suite.

A man came out of an office, looking bewildered, saw M'chel and her gun, reached for a tiny gun in a shoulder harness.

Riss shot him, rolled another grenade into his office, went on into a central meeting area.

There was a large double door, real wood. Riss shot it down.

Inside was a conference room with a long table, and three or four men and women, intent on papers, screens glowing around them. They turned at the blasts, and one came to his feet.

Riss recognized none of them.

Except Reg Goodnight.

For an instant M'chel wished real life was a romance, and she could have a second to tell Goodnight he was finally paying some past-due debts.

But it wasn't, and she blew his head off, then threw two grenades her thoroughly conditioned fingers told her were fragmentation into the room, and was headed back toward the lock, spraying bolts as she went.

She was chanting as she ran — 'What an idiot, what an idiot, what an idiot.'

Alarms dinned.

M'chel reached the lock, hit the cycle button. Chas had stumbled to his feet, and was retching.

'Close it up, soldier,' she ordered. 'And don't puke in your suit.'

He nodded, numbly.

Riss snapped her faceplate shut.

The lock hissed the last of the air out, and the noise of the alarms went away.

Riss saw suited men, carrying blast rifles, coming up the steps toward them, and shot the first three, ducked as a bolt ricocheted off the steel beside her.

Somehow Chas, staggering, semiconscious, had his blaster up, was shooting, not accurately, but close enough to drive the guards to cover.

Other blaster bolts were spitting down, from above her, and she saw the enormous Grok, kneeling and firing systematically into the compartments in the wall across the canyon.

He suddenly stopped and, moving faster than anyone as big as he was should be able, ran along the top walkway, sliding out of his pack as he did.

Riss couldn't figure what he was doing, didn't have time to wonder as she pushed Goodnight up steps, toward the same level Grok was on.

Grok was about one hundred meters away from her, fumbling with his pack.

Riss suddenly realized what he was doing.

A hundred meters below him was the huge cruiser. There was a ramp, and an open lock into the control cabin just below Grok.

Grok now had the pack whirling like an ancient sling. He let it go.

It sailed far out, hit one of the cruiser's nose stabilizers, bounced onto the ramp, and then the grenade Grok had activated went off, setting off the other explosives in the pack.

Flame balled, rolled into the lock, and Riss saw fire spurt out.

Grok was running back toward her, and had Goodnight by one arm.

None of the raiders were paying any attention to the three as they scrambled up the last ramp, intent on their own catastrophe.

Smoke was boiling up from the great ship below as the three pushed through the hatch onto the moon's surface.

M'chel wanted to collapse, but there was no time.

Smoke was leaking through the plas covers.

It took us two tries, but I think we finally got the bastard, she thought.

They staggered about two hundred meters, and Riss saw a nice, safe, deep crater. They piled into it, crouched against the rock, feeling vibrations shake them as explosions went off in the base.

Then the ground shook, as if an earthquake had struck, and a sheet of flame gouted up, ripping away the plas, a man-made volcano as the cruiser exploded, hell rolling through the raiders' base.

The three found their feet, looked at each other.

Nobody reached for a com plug.

There weren't any words just then.

They turned away, back toward the mountain, where Spada waited.

FIFTY-FIVE

Grok, shaking his head, came out of one of the *Boop*'s recreation rooms.

'There is such a thing as irony.'

'Oh?' Goodnight said, where he sat nursing a very large brandy and a purple-bruised forehead.

'The news 'cast from Glace,' Grok said. 'It was announced by the government today that the asteroid mining contract let to Transkootenay Mining has been canceled, due to inadequate performance.'

Then it hit him.

'That means we do not get paid, either!'

'Now, that's irony,' Riss said. 'Although I'm not laughing at the moment.'

'True irony,' Grok agreed. 'Not to mention that we'll never know who Murgatroyd was, or if we got all of them.'

'Probably not,' Riss said. 'I doubt if that Mar Trac was on Moon Five. Nor whoever introduced this legislation.

'All we got were the operational sorts.'

'Like my brother,' Goodnight said, with a strange expression. 'And most of the throat-cutters. But even some of them, those that were offworld, got a running start.

'If Reg had hung in place, stonewalling everybody

with some kind of logical story for a couple of weeks, instead of cutting and running, he'd be in the catbird's seat right now.'

'It doesn't look like this is a nice, neat ending,' Riss agreed.

'All that time, wasted, lost,' Goodnight mourned. 'Shit, shit, shit. Where's King and Freddie? I want off this world, out of this system, so I can go feel sorry for myself.'

Riss, not wanting to bring up Reg, glanced out the port.

'Here they come. Let's give them the bad news and scarper.'

But von Baldur seemed undisturbed, and King's glowing smile didn't diminish when they got the word.

'All right,' Riss said. 'Either of you two bird-eating cats can explain why you aren't sprinkling ashes on your heads.'

'First, this,' von Baldur said, holding up a large parcel. He took a huge bottle of champagne out of it.

'I didn't know they had methuselahs this far in the outback,' Chas said. 'Let alone full of nice earth Taitinger champagne.'

'Open, pour, and I shall explain our unconcern about what the Foley System Government chooses to do,' von Baldur said.

'I got a little curious a few weeks ago,' King said, before the cork came out of the bottle.

'I went looking for diamonds. Diamonds, precious metals, and such, wondering what Transkootenay did with them.'

She nodded to Riss.

'Obviously your Kinnison rock sparked my interest.

'Imagine my surprise when we had a chat with a couple of staff mineralogists, and found Transkootenay was holding these precious metals right here on Mfir. I don't know under what pretext, and if they'd always been doing that, or if this was something Mr. Goodnight started recently. But Glace didn't have them, nor had they been shipped on to Transkootenay's headquarters.

'Possibly Goodnight was keeping them as a departure bonus, or for emergency expenses. Not that it matters.

'Anyway, Friedrich and I went looking for these preciouses, and found them in a large vault in a downtown bank.

'I "just happened" to have paperwork with me suggesting that we were the authorized representatives of Transkootenay Mining, and were here to expedite transshipment of said precious minerals to its proper owner.'

She pointed out a porthole.

'Those two armored lifters dripping with security guards coming in at the gate are taking care of the scutwork transferring all that lovely, lovely wealth into the *Boop-Boop-A-Doop*'s holds right now.'

'I shall be *dipped*,' Chas Goodnight said. 'So we're not broke.'

'We're not broke,' King agreed.

'But what if somebody comes looking?' M'chel Riss asked.

'Those *damnable* raiders, stealing everything around!' von Baldur said.

'The thing I don't know,' Riss said, 'is what the hell's Cerberus's position was . . . is . . . in all of this.'

'An excellent question,' Baldur said. 'It is apparent they weren't in league with Murgatroyd. Fairly apparent, anyway, since we didn't find any other tracks other than that chat Nowotny had. I shall discount the bomb, which might have been intended just to frighten us a bit. I guess they were just sniffing around the fringes, looking for a profit.'

'I'd just as soon figure they were trying to kill us with that bomb,' King said. 'And if you hadn't been the sneaky sort, we would have been all over the walls.'

'It'll give me motivation the next time we run into the shitheels.'

'Fine with me,' Riss said. 'There's nothing wrong with having a good enemy to dream about.'

Goodnight, still a bit concussed, moving carefully, flipped the cork off with his thumbs, let champagne boil up for an instant, then started filling the glasses.

'So there are happy endings, after all,' M'chel said dreamily.

'Of course there are,' Baldur said comfortingly.

'I never doubted it for a minute,' Jasmine King said.

Chas Goodnight raised his glass.

'To crime!'

The four members of Star Risk, Ltd., drank deeply.

THE STAR RISK SERIES

Chris Bunch

If you've got the cash, they'll take the risk.

STAR RISK

M'chel Riss spent years of her life in the Alliance Marines, only to be assigned to a desolate outpost. Then she came to the attention of Star Risk, Ltd. A mercenary outfit struggling for recognition, Star Risk has the required ragtag bunch of misfits. But why do they take on such a multitude of insane missions, with so many odds stacked against them? Money, fame, glory . . . but mostly the money.

THE SCOUNDREL WORLDS

Skyball is popular, challenging, and violent. In other words, the greatest sport in the universe – and the mercenary team of Star Risk, Ltd. has been hired to keep it galaxy-friendly. Two opposing worlds are neck and neck, and lately the game's been a real killer . . .

THE DOUBLECROSS PROGRAM

The Star Risk, Ltd. team find themselves in the middle of a strange assignment: a staged bank robbery that involves putting the money back. But the job takes an even stranger turn when they get caught up in a full-fledged war over an addictive new consumer product.

THE DOG FROM HELL

While escorting a group of privileged and wild girls from a finishing school on Earth to one of the luxury worlds, the Star Risk Ltd. team crosses paths with the much feared Cerebus Systems – and they have just put Star Risk, Ltd. at the top of their enemies list.

SHADOW WARRIOR

Chris Bunch

The complete Joshua Wolfe trilogy in one explosive
volume from the master of military SF.

The Great War is over. The last pockets of resistance long
eliminated. For many, the alien Al'ar are now little more
than a memory. But there is one man who cannot forget:
Joshua Wolfe. Friend, prisoner, then betrayer and
executioner of the Al'ar.

To humans he is a hero, a legend. To the aliens he is the
Shadow Warrior, master of the arts of killing. And his
story has only just begun.

TRADING IN DANGER

Elizabeth Moon

Ky Vatta is a highly promising military cadet with a great future ahead of her, until an apparently insignificant act of kindness makes her the focus of the Academy's wrath. She is forced to resign, her dreams shattered.

For the child of a rich trading family, this should mean disgrace on a grand scale. And yet, to her surprise, Ky is offered the captaincy of a ship headed for scrap with its final cargo.

Her orders are absolutely clear, but Ky quickly sees the potential profit in altering the parameters of the journey. Because, whatever the risks, it's in her blood to trade — even if the currency is extreme danger.

THE RISEN EMPIRE

Scott Westerfeld

The undead Emperor has ruled the Eighty Worlds for sixteen hundred years. His is the power to grant immortality to those he deems worthy, creating an elite class known as the Risen. Along with his sister, the eternally young Child Empress, his power within the empire has been absolute. Until now.

The Empire's great enemies, the Rix, hold the Child Empress hostage. Charged with her rescue is Captain Laurent Zai. But when Imperial politics are involved the stakes are unimaginably high, and Zai may yet find the Rix the least of his problems. On the homeworld, Zai's lover, Senator Nara Oxham, must prosecute the war against the Rix while holding the inhuman impulses of the Risen councillors in check. If she fails at either task, millions will die.

And at the centre of everything is the Emperor's great lie: a revelation so shattering that he is willing to sanction the death of entire worlds to keep it secret . . .

FOR THE LATEST NEWS AND THE HOTTEST EXCLUSIVES ON ALL
YOUR FAVOURITE SF AND FANTASY STARS, SIGN UP FOR:

ORBIT'S <u>FREE</u> MONTHLY E-ZINE

PACKED WITH

BREAKING NEWS
THE LATEST REVIEWS
EXCLUSIVE INTERVIEWS
STUNNING EXTRACTS
SPECIAL OFFERS
BRILLIANT COMPETITIONS

**AND A GALAXY OF
NEW AND ESTABLISHED SFF STARS!**

TO GET A DELICIOUS SLICE OF SFF IN <u>YOUR</u> INBOX EVERY MONTH, SEND YOUR
DETAILS BY EMAIL TO: <u>ORBIT.UK@TWBG.CO.UK</u> OR VISIT:

WWW.ORBITBOOKS.CO.UK
THE HOME OF SFF ONLINE